HOW THE GARCÍA GIRLS
LOST THEIR ACCENTS

HOW THE GARCÍA GIRLS LOST THEIR ACCENTS

JULIA ALVAREZ

BLOOMSBURY

First published in 1991 by Algonquin Books of Chapel Hill, USA
and Thomas Allen & Sons, Canada
This paperback edition published by Bloomsbury 2004

Some of these stories have appeared, in slightly different versions, in *The
Caribbean Writer*, *The Greensboro Review*, *Third Woman*, *The Syracuse
Scholar*, *Outlooks and Insights* (St Martin's Press 1983), *Unholy Alliances*
(Cleis Press 1989), *The Writer's Craft* (Scott, Foresman Co, 1986, 1989),
Heresies, the new renaissance, An American Christmas (Peachtree 1989), *MSS*

Bloomsbury Publishing Plc, 38 Soho Square, London W1D 3HB

A CIP catalogue record for this book is available from the British Library

ISBN 0 7475 7265 8

10 9 8 7 6 5 4 3 2 1

All paper used by Bloomsbury Publishing is a natural, recyclable product
made from wood grown in well-managed forests. The manufacturing
processes conform to the environmental regulations of the country of origin

Printed in Great Britain by Clays Ltd, St Ives plc

www.bloomsbury.com/juliaalvarez

∎∎∎

*For Bob Pack
and, of course,
the sisters*

∎∎∎

Contents

▼▲▼▲▼IIII▼▲▼▲▼▲▼▲▼▲▼▲▼▲▼▲▼▲▼▲▼▲▼▲▼▲▼▲▼▲▼

■■■

Special thanks to
Judy Yarnall
Shannon Ravenel
Susan Bergholz
Judy Liskin-Gasparro

▼▲▼■■■▼▲▼

The National Endowment for the Arts
Research Board at the University of Illinois
Ingram Merrill Foundation
Altos de Chavon

▼▲▼■■■▼▲▼

Bill
compañero
through all these pages

■■■

How the García Girls Lost Their Accents

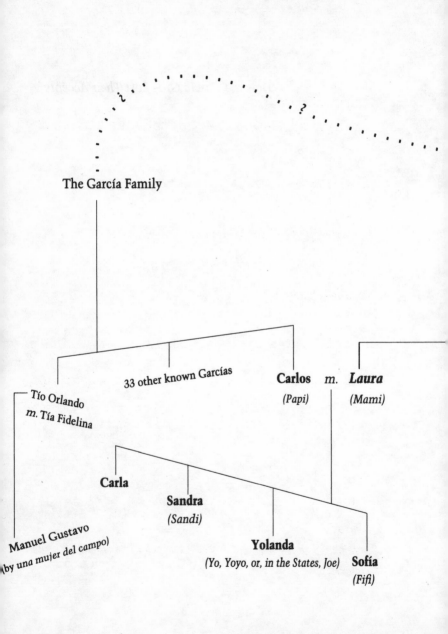

¿ ?

The García Family

33 other known Garcías

Carlos *m.* *Laura*
(Papi)   *(Mami)*

Tío Orlando
m. Tía Fidelina

Manuel Gustavo
(by una mujer del campo)

Carla

Sandra
(Sandi)

Yolanda
(Yo, Yoyo, or, in the States, Joe)

Sofía
(Fifi)

The Conquistadores

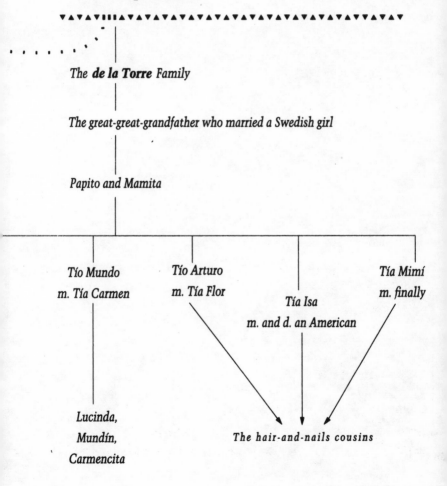

The **de la Torre** *Family*

The great-great-grandfather who married a Swedish girl

Papito and Mamita

Tío Mundo
m. Tía Carmen

Tío Arturo
m. Tía Flor

Tía Isa
m. and d. an American

Tía Mimí
m. finally

Lucinda,
Mundín,
Carmencita

The hair-and-nails cousins

I

▼▲▼▲▼▐▐▐▼▲▼▲▼▲▼▲▼▲▼▲▼▲▼▲▼▲▼▲▼▲▼▲▼▲▼▲▼

1989–1972

Antojos

▼▲▼▲▼▲▼▲▼▲▼▲▼▲▼▲▼▲▼▲▼▲▼▲▼▲▼▲▼III▼▲▼▲▼

Yolanda

T he old aunts lounge in the white wicker armchairs, flipping open their fans, snapping them shut. Except that more of them are dressed in the greys and blacks of widowhood, the aunts seem little changed since five years ago when Yolanda was last on the Island.

Sitting among the aunts in the less comfortable dining chairs, the cousins are flashes of color in turquoise jumpsuits and tight jersey dresses.

The cake is on its own table, the little cousins clustered around it, arguing over who will get what slice. When their squabbles reach a certain mother-annoying level, they are called away by their nursemaids, who sit on stools at the far end of the patio, a phalanx of starched white uniforms.

Before anyone has turned to greet her in the entryway, Yolanda sees herself as they will, shabby in a black cotton skirt and jersey top, sandals on her feet, her wild black hair held back with a hairband. Like a missionary, her cousins will say,

3

like one of those Peace Corps girls who have let themselves go so as to do dubious good in the world.

A maid peeks out of the pantry into the hall. She is a skinny brown woman in the black uniform of the kitchen help. Her head is covered with tiny braids coiled into rounds and pinned down with bobby pins. "Doña Carmen," she calls to Yolanda's hostess aunt, "there are no matches. Justo went to Doña Lucinda's to get some."

"*Por Dios*, Iluminada," Tía Carmen scolds, "you've had all day."

The maid stares down at the interlaced hands she holds before her, a gesture that Yolanda remembers seeing illustrated in a book for Renaissance actors. These clasped hands were on a page of classic gestures. *The gesture of pleading*, the caption had read. Held against the breast, next to the heart, the same interlaced hands were those of *a lover who pleadeth for mercy from his beloved*.

The gathering spots Yolanda. Her cousin Lucinda leads a song of greeting with an off-key chorus of little cousins. "Here she comes, Miss America!" Yolanda clasps her brow and groans melodramatically as expected. The chorus labors through the first phrase and then rushes forward with hugs, kisses, and—from a couple of the boys—fake karate kicks.

"You look terrible," Lucinda says. "Too thin, and the hair needs a cut. Nothing personal." She is the cousin who has never minced her words. In her designer pantsuit and frosted, blown-out hair, Lucinda looks like a Dominican magazine model, a look that has always made Yolanda think of call girls.

"Light the candles, light the candles!" the little cousins say, taking up a chant.

Tía Carmen lifts her open hands to heaven, a gesture she no doubt picked up from one of her priest friends. "The girl forgot the matches."

"The help! Every day worse," Tía Flor confides to Yolanda, flashing her famous smile. The cousins refer to their Tía Flor as "the politician." She is capable of that smile no matter the circumstances. Once, the story goes, during who-knows-which revolution, a radical young uncle and his wife showed up at Tía Flor's in the middle of the night wanting asylum. Tía Flor greeted them at the door with the smile and "How delightful of you to stop by!"

"Let me tell you about the latest at *my* house," Tía Flor goes on. "The chauffeur was driving me to my novena yesterday. Suddenly the car jerks forward and dies, right there on the street. I'm alarmed, you know, the way things are, a big car stalled in the middle of the university *barrio*. I say, *César, what can it be?* He scratches his head. *I don't know, Doña Flor.* A nice man stops to help, checks it all—and says, *Why, señora, you're out of gas.* Out of gas! Can you imagine?" Tía Flor shakes her head at Yolanda. "A chauffeur who can't keep a car in gasoline! Welcome home to your little Island!" Grinning, she flips open her fan. Beautiful wild birds unfold their silver wings.

At a proprietary yank from one of the little cousins, Yolanda lets herself be led to the cake table, festive with a lacy white tablecloth and starched party napkins. She dumb-shows surprise at the cake in the shape of the Island. "Mami thought of it," Lucinda's little girl explains, beaming.

"We're going to light candles all over," another little cousin adds. Her face has a ghostly resemblance to one of Yolanda's generation. This one has to be Carmencita's daughter.

"Not all over," an older brother says, correcting her. "The candles are just for the big cities."

"All over!" Carmencita's reincarnation insists. "Right, Mami, all over?" She addresses a woman whose aging face is less familiar to Yolanda than the child's facsimile.

"Carmencita!" Yolanda cries out. "I wasn't recognizing you before."

"Older, not wiser." Carmencita's quip in English is the product of her two or three years away in boarding school in the States. Only the boys stay for college. Carmencita continues in Spanish: "We thought we'd welcome you back with an Island cake!"

"Five candles," Lucinda counts. "One for each year you've been away!"

"Five major cities," the little know-it-all cousin calls out.

"No!" his sister contradicts. Their mother bends down to negotiate.

Yolanda and her cousins and aunts sit down to await the matches. The late sun sifts through the bougainvillea trained to climb the walls of the patio, to thread across the trellis roof, to pour down magenta and purple blossoms. Tía Carmen's patio is the gathering place for the compound. She is the widow of the head of the clan and so hers is the largest house. Through well-tended gardens beyond her patio, narrow stone paths diverge. After cake and *cafecitos*, the cousins will disperse down these paths to their several compound houses. There they will supervise their cooks in preparing supper for the husbands, who will troop home after Happy Hour. Once a male cousin bragged that this pre-dinner hour should be called Whore Hour. He was not reluctant to explain to Yolanda that this is the hour during which a Dominican male of a certain class stops in on his mistress on his way home to his wife.

"Five years," Tía Carmen says, sighing. "We're going to have to really spoil her this time"—Tía cocks her head to imply collaboration with the other aunts and cousins—"so she doesn't stay away so long again."

"It's not good," Tía Flor says. "You four girls get lost up there." Smiling, she indicates the sky with her chin.

"So how are *you four girls?*" Lucinda asks, a wink in her eyes. Back in their adolescent days during summer visits, the four girls used to shock their Island cousins with stories of their escapades in the States.

In halting Spanish, Yolanda reports on her sisters. When she reverts to English, she is scolded, "*¡En español!*" The more she practices, the sooner she'll be back into her native tongue, the aunts insist. Yes, and when she returns to the States, she'll find herself suddenly going blank over some word in English or, like her mother, mixing up some common phrase. This time, however, Yolanda is not so sure she'll be going back. But that is a secret.

"Tell us now exactly what you want to do while you're here," says Gabriela, the beautiful young wife of Mundín, the prince of the family. With the pale skin and dramatic dark eyes of a romantic heroine, Gabriela's face reminds Yolanda of the lover's clutch of hands over the breast. But, Gabriela herself is refreshingly straightforward. "If you don't have plans, believe me, you'll end up with a lot of invitations you can't turn down."

"Any little *antojo*, you must tell us!" Tía Carmen agrees.

"What's an *antojo?*" Yolanda asks.

See! Her aunts are right. After so many years away, she is losing her Spanish.

"Actually it's not an easy word to explain." Tía Carmen exchanges a quizzical look with the other aunts. How to put it? "An *antojo* is like a craving for something you have to eat."

Gabriela blows out her cheeks. "Calories."

An *antojo*, one of the older aunts continues, is a very old Spanish word "from before your United States was even thought of," she adds tartly. "In fact, in the countryside, you'll still find some *campesinos* using the word in the old sense. Altagracia!" she calls to one of the maids sitting at the other end of the patio. A tiny, old woman, her hair pulled back tightly in a white bun, approaches the group of women. She is asked to tell Yolanda what an *antojo* is. She puts her brown hands away in her uniform pockets.

"*U'té que sabe*," Altagracia says in a small voice. You're the one to know.

"Come now, Altagracia," her mistress scolds.

The maid obeys. "In my *campo* we say a person has an *antojo* when they are taken over by *un santo* who wants something."

Altagracia backs away, and when not recalled, turns and heads back to her stool.

"I'll tell you what my *santo* wants after five years," Yolanda says. "I can't wait to eat some guavas. Maybe I can pick some when I go north in a few days."

"By yourself?" Tía Carmen shakes her head at the mere thought.

"This is not the States," Tía Flor says, with a knowing smile. "A woman just doesn't travel alone in this country. Especially these days."

"She'll be fine." Gabriela speaks with calm authority. "Mundín will be gone if you want to borrow one of our cars."

"Gabi!" Lucinda rolls her eyes. "Have you lost your mind? A Volvo in the interior with the way things are!"

Gabriela holds up her hands. "All right! All right! There's also the Datsun."

"I don't want to put anyone out," Yolanda says. She has sat back quietly, hoping she has learned, at last, to let the mighty wave of tradition roll on through her life and break on some other female shore. She plans to bob up again after the many *don'ts* to do what she wants. From the corner of her eye she sees Iluminada enter with a box of matches on a small silver tray. "I'll take a bus."

"A bus!" The whole group bursts out laughing. The little cousins, come forward to join the laughter, eager to be a part of the adult merriment. "Yolanda, *mi amor*, you *have* been gone long," Lucinda teases. "Can't you see it!?" She laughs. "Yoyo climbing into an old *camioneta* with all the *campesinos* and their fighting cocks and their goats and their pigs!"

Giggles and head shakings.

"I can take care of myself," Yolanda reassures them. "But what's this other trouble you keep mentioning?"

"Don't listen to them." Gabriela waves her hand as if scaring off an annoying fly. Her fingers are long and tapered; her wedding and engagement rings have been welded together into one thick band. "It's easier this way," she once explained, handing the ring over to Yolanda to try on.

"There *have* been some incidents lately," Tía Carmen says in a quiet voice that does not brook contradiction. She, after all, is the reigning head of the family.

Almost as if to prove her point, a private guard, his weapons clicking, passes by on the side of the patio open to the back gardens. He wears an army-type khaki uniform, a gun swung over his shoulder. A tall wall has surrounded the compound for as far back as Yolanda can remember, a wall she believed as a child was there to keep the sea back in case during a hurricane it rose up to the hillside the family houses were built on.

"Things *are* looking ugly." Tía Flor again smiles brightly. In the Renaissance book of acting, this grimace of a smile might be captioned, *The lady is caught in a smile she cannot escape.* "There's talk, you know, of guerrillas in the mountains."

Gabriela crinkles her nose. "Mundín says that talk is only talk."

Iluminada has now crept forward to the edge of the circle to offer the matches to her mistress. In the fading light of the patio, Yolanda cannot make out the expression on the dark face.

Tía Carmen rises to approach the cake. She begins lighting

candles and laying the spent matches on the tray Iluminada holds out to her. One light for Santo Domingo, one for Santiago, one for Puerto Plata. The children plead to be allowed to light the remaining cities, but no, Tía Carmen tells them, they may blow out the candles and, of course, eat the cake. Lighting is grownup business. Once the candles are all ablaze, the cousins and aunts and children gather around and sing a rousing *"Bienvenida a ti,"* to the tune of "Happy Birthday."

Yolanda gazes at the cake. Below her blazes the route she has worked out on the map for herself, north of the city through the mountains to the coast. As the singing draws to a close, the cousins urge her to make a wish. She leans forward and shuts her eyes. There is so much she wants, it is hard to single out one wish. There have been too many stops on the road of the last twenty-nine years since her family left this island behind. She and her sisters have led such turbulent lives—so many husbands, homes, jobs, wrong turns among them. But look at her cousins, women with households and authority in their voices. Let this turn out to be my home, Yolanda wishes. She pictures the maids in their quiet, mysterious cluster at the end of the patio, Altagracia with her hands in her lap.

By the time she opens her eyes, ready, a half dozen little substitute puffs have blown out all the candles. There is a burst of clapping. Small arguments erupt over dividing the cake's cities: Lucinda's two boys both want Santiago since they went gliding there last weekend; Lucinda's girl and Carmencita's girl both insist on the capital because that's where they were born, but one agrees to cede the capital if she can have La Romana, where the family has a beach house. But, of course, La Romana has already been spoken for by Tía Flor's little goddaughter, who suffers from asthma and shouldn't be contradicted. Lucinda, whose voice is hoarse with disciplining the rowdy crew, hands Yolanda the knife. "It's your cake, Yoyo. You decide."

The road up through the foothills is just wide enough for two small cars, and so at each curve, as she has been instructed, Yolanda slows and taps her horn. Just past one bad curve, a small shrine has been erected, La Virgen surrounded by three concrete crosses recently whitewashed.

She pulls the Datsun over and enjoys her first solitary moment since her arrival. Every compound outing has been hosted by one gracious aunt or another, presenting the landscape as if it were a floor show mounted for her niece's appreciation.

All around her are the foothills, a dark enormous green, the sky more a brightness than a color. A breeze blows through the palms below, rustling their branches, so they whisper like voices. Here and there a braid of smoke rises up from a hillside—a *campesino* and his family living out their solitary life. This is what she has been missing all these years without really knowing that she has been missing it. Standing here in the quiet, she believes she has never felt at home in the States, never.

When she first hears it, she thinks it is her own motor she has forgotten to turn off, but the sound grows into a pained roar, as if the engine were falling apart. Yolanda makes out an undertow of men's voices. Quickly, she gets into the car, locks the door, and pulls back onto the road, hugging her right side.

A bus comes lurching around the curve, obscuring her view.

Belching exhaust, the driver saluting or warning with a series of blasts on his horn, it is an old army bus, the official name brushed over with paint that doesn't quite match. The passengers see her only at the last moment, and all up and down her side of the bus, men poke out of the windows, hooting and yelling, holding out bottles and beckoning to her. She speeds up and leaves them behind, the quiet, well-oiled Datsun climbing easily up the snaky highway.

The radio is all static—like the sound of the crunching metal of a car; the faint, blurry voice on the airwaves her own, trapped inside a wreck, calling for help. In English or Spanish? she wonders. That poet she met at Lucinda's party the night before argued that no matter how much of it one lost, in the midst of some profound emotion, one would revert to one's mother tongue. He put Yolanda through a series of situations. What language, he asked, looking pointedly into her eyes, did she love in?

The hills begin to plane out into a high plateau, and the road widens. Left and right, roadside stands begin appearing. Yolanda keeps an eye out for guavas. Piled high on wooden stands are fruits Yolanda hasn't seen in years: pinkish-yellow mangoes, and tamarind pods oozing their rich sap, and small cashew fruits strung on a rope to keep them from bruising each other. Strips of meat, buzzing with flies, hang from the windows of butcher stalls. It is hard to believe the poverty the radio commentators keep talking about. There seems to be plenty here to eat—except for guavas.

The fruit stands behind her now, Yolanda approaches a compound very like her family's in the capital. A high concrete wall continues for about a quarter of a mile. A guard rises to his post beyond an iron grillwork gate. He seems—glimpsed through the flowering bars—a man locked in a strangely gorgeous prison. Beyond him up the shady driveway is a three-story country house, a wide verandah all the way around it. Parked at the door is a chocolate brown Mercedes. Perhaps the owners have come up to their country home to avoid the troubles in the capital. They are probably relatives. The dozen rich families have intermarried so many times that family trees are tangles of roots. In fact, her aunts have given her a list of names of uncles and aunts and cousins she might call on along her way. By each name is a capsule description of what Yolanda might remember of that relative: *the one with the kidney bean swimming pool, the fat one, the one who was an ambassador.* Before she even left the compound, Yolanda put the list away in the glove compartment. She is going to be just fine on her own.

A small village spreads out before her—ALTAMIRA, say the rippling letters on the corrugated tin roof of the first house. A little cluster of houses on either side of the road, Altamira is just the place to stretch her legs before what she has heard is a steep and slightly (her aunts warned "very") dangerous descent to the coast. Yolanda pulls up at a cantina, its thatched roof held up by several posts, its floor poured cement, and in its very center, a lone picnic table over which a swarm of flies hover.

Tacked to one of the central posts is a yellowing poster for Palmolive soap. A creamy, blond woman luxuriates under a refreshing shower, her head thrown back in seeming ecstasy, her mouth opened in a wordless cry.

"*¡Buenas!*" Yolanda calls out.

An old woman emerges from a shack behind the cantina, buttoning up a torn housedress. She is followed closely by a little boy, who keeps ducking behind her whenever Yolanda smiles at him. Asking his name drives him further into the folds of the old woman's skirt.

"You must excuse him, doña," the woman apologizes. "He's not used to being among people." People with money who drive through Altamira to the beach resorts on the north coast, she means. "Your name," the old woman repeats, as if Yolanda hasn't asked him in Spanish. The little boy mumbles at the ground. "Speak up!" the old woman scolds, but her voice betrays pride when she speaks up for him. "This little know-nothing is José Duarte, Sánchez y Mella."

Yolanda laughs. A lot of names for such a little boy—the surnames of the country's three liberators!

"Can I serve the doña in any way?" the old woman asks. "*¡Un refresco? ¿Una Coca Cola?*" By the pride in her voice, Yolanda understands the old woman wants to treat her to the best on her menu.

"I'll tell you what I would like." Yolanda gives the tree line beyond the old woman's shack a glance. "Are there any guavas around?"

The old woman's face scrunches up. "*¿Guayabas?*" she murmurs, and thinks to herself a second. "Why, they grow all around, doña. But I can't say as I've seen any lately."

"With your permission—" José Duarte has joined a group

of little boys who have come out of nowhere and are milling around the car, boasting how many automobiles they have ridden in. At Yolanda's mention of guavas, he springs forward, pointing across the road towards the summit of the western hills. "I know where there's a whole grove of ripe ones." Behind him, his little companions nod.

"Go on, then!" His grandmother stamps her foot as if she were scatting an animal. "Get the doña some."

A few boys dash across the road and disappear up a steep path on the hillside, but before José can follow, Yolanda calls him back. She wants to go along too. The little boy looks towards his grandmother, unsure of what to think. The old woman shakes her head. The doña will get hot, her nice clothes will get all dirty. José will bring the doña as many guavas as she is wanting.

"But they taste so much better when you've picked them yourself." Yolanda hears the edge in her voice. The old woman has turned into the long arm of her family.

The few boys who have stayed behind with José have again congregated around the car. Each one claims to be guarding it for the doña. It occurs to Yolanda that there is a way to make this a treat all the way around. "What do you say we take the car?" The little boys cheer.

Now that is not a bad idea, the old woman agrees. If the doña insists on going, she can take that dirt road up ahead and then cross over onto the road that is paved all the way to the coffee barns. The old woman points south in the direction of the big house. Many workers take that shortcut to work.

They pile into the car, half a dozen little boys in the back, and José as co-pilot in the passenger seat beside Yolanda. They turn onto a bumpy road off the highway, which grows bumpier and bumpier as it climbs up into wilder, more desolate country. Branches scrape the sides and pebbles pelt the underside of the car. Yolanda wants to turn back, but there is no room. Finally, with a great snapping of twigs and thrashing of branches across the windshield, as if the countryside is loath to release them, the car bursts forth onto smooth pavement and the light of day. On either side of the road are groves of guava trees. The boys who have gone ahead on foot are already pulling down branches and shaking loose a rain of guavas.

Yolanda eats several right on the spot, relishing the slightly bumpy feel of the skin in her hand, devouring the crunchy, sweet white meat. The boys watch her.

The group scatters to harvest the guavas. Yolanda and José, partners, wander far from the path that cuts through the grove. Soon they are bent almost double to avoid getting entangled in the thick canopy of branches overhead. Each addition to Yolanda's beach basket causes a spill from the stash already piled high above the brim.

The way back seems much longer than the way there. Yolanda begins to worry that they are lost, and then, the way worry sprouts worry, it strikes her that they haven't heard or seen the other boys in quite a while. The latticework of branches reveals glimmers of a fading sky. The image of the guard in his elaborate flowering prison flashes through her head. The rustling leaves of the guava trees echo the warnings of her old aunts: you will get lost, you will get kidnapped, you will get raped, you will get killed.

Just ahead, the thicket of guava branches clears, and there is the footpath, and beyond, the gratifying sight of the car still on the side of the road. It is a pleasure to stand upright again. José rests his burden on the ground and straightens his back to full measure. Yolanda looks up at the sky. The sun is low on the western horizon.

"The others must have gone to gather kindling," José observes.

Yolanda glances at her watch—it is past six o'clock. At this rate, she will never make the north coast by nightfall. She hurries José back to the car, where they find a heap of guavas the other boys left behind on the shoulder of the road. Enough guavas to appease even the greediest Island *santo* for life!

They pack the trunk quickly, and climb in, but the car has not gone a foot before it lurches forward with a horrible hobble. Yolanda closes her eyes and lays her head down on the wheel, then glances over at José. His eyes are searching the inside of the car for a clue as to what could have happened. This child won't know how to change a flat tire either.

Soon the sun will set and night will fall swiftly, no lingering dusk as in the States. She explains to José that they have a flat tire and must go back down the road to the big house. Whoever tends to the brown Mercedes will surely know how to change a tire.

"With your permission," José offers. The doña can just wait in the car, and he will be back in no time with someone from the Miranda place.

Miranda, Miranda. . . . Yolanda leans over and gets her aunt's list out of the glove compartment, and sure enough, there they are. *Tía Marina y tío Alejandro Miranda—Altos de Altamira.*

A note elaborates that Tío Alejandro was the one *who used to own English saddle horses and taught you four girls to ride.* "All right," she says to the boy. "I'll tell you what." She points to her watch. "If you're back by the time this hand is over here, I'll give you"—she holds up one finger—"a dollar." The boy's mouth falls open. In no time, he has shot out of his side of the car and is headed at a run toward the Miranda place. Yolanda climbs out as well and walks down a pace, until the boy has disappeared in one of the turnings of the road.

From the footpath that cuts through the grove on the opposite side of the road, she hears the sound of branches being thrust aside, twigs snapping underfoot. Two men, one short and dark, and the other slender and light-skinned, emerge. They wear ragged work clothes stained with patches of sweat; their faces are drawn. Machetes hang from their belts.

The men's faces snap awake at the sight of her. Then they look beyond her at the car. The darker man speaks first. "Yours?"

"Is there some problem?" he speaks up again. The taller one is looking her up and down with interest. They are now both in front of her on the road, blocking any escape. Both—she has sized them up as well—are strong and quite capable of catching her if she makes a run for it. Not that she can move, for her legs seem suddenly to have been hammered into the ground beneath her. She considers explaining that she is just out for a drive before dinner at the big house, so that these men will think someone knows where she is, someone will come looking for her if they try to carry her off. But her tongue feels as if it has been stuffed in her mouth like a rag to keep her quiet.

The two men exchange a look—it seems to Yolanda—of collusion.

Then the shorter, darker one speaks up again. "Señorita, are you all right?" He peers at her. He is a short man, no taller than Yolanda, but he gives the impression of being quite large, for he is broad and solid, like something not yet completely carved out of a piece of wood. His companion is slim and tall and of a rich honey-brown color that matches his honey-brown eyes. Anywhere else, Yolanda would find him extremely attractive, but here on a lonely road, with the sky growing darker by seconds, his good looks seem dangerous, a lure to catch her off her guard.

"Can we help you?" the shorter man repeats.

The handsome one smiles knowingly. Two long, deep dimples appear like gashes on either side of his mouth. "*Americana*," he says to the darker man, pointing to the car. "*No comprende.*"

The darker man narrows his eyes and studies Yolanda a moment. "*¿Americana?*" he asks her, as if not quite sure what to make of her.

She has been too frightened to carry out any strategy, but now a road is opening before her. She clasps her hands on her chest—she can feel her pounding heart—and nods. Then, as if the admission itself loosens her tongue, she begins to speak, English, a few words, of apology at first, then a great flood of explanation: how it happens that she is on a back road by herself, her craving for guavas, having never learned to change a flat. The two men stare at her, uncomprehending, rendered docile by her gibberish. Only when she mentions the name Miranda do their eyes light up with respect. She is saved!

Yolanda makes the motions of pumping. The darker man looks at his companion, who shrugs, baffled as well. Yolanda waves for them to follow her. And as if after dragging up roots, she has finally managed to yank them free of the soil they have clung to, she finds she can move her own feet toward the car.

The small group stands staring at the sagging tire a moment, the two men kicking at it as if punishing it for having failed the señorita. They squat by the passenger's side, conversing in low tones. Yolanda leads the men to the rear of the car, where they lift the spare out of its sunken nest—then set to work fitting the interlocking pieces of the jack, unpacking the tools from the deeper hollows of the trunk. They lay their machetes down on the side of the road, out of the way. Above them, the sky is purple with twilight. The sun breaks on the hilltops, spilling its crimson yolk.

Once the flat has been replaced with the spare, the two men lift the deflated tire into the trunk and put away the tools. They hand Yolanda her keys.

"I'd like to give you something," she begins, but the English words are hollow on her tongue. She rummages in her purse and draws out a sheaf of bills, rolls them up and offers them to the men.

The shorter man holds up his hand. Yolanda can see where he has scraped his hand on the pavement and blood has dried dark streaks on his palm. *"No, no, señorita. Nuestro placer."*

Yolanda turns to the taller one. "Please," she says, urging the bills on him. But he too looks down at the ground—Iluminada's gesture, José's gesture. Quickly, she stuffs the bills in his pocket.

The two men pick up their machetes and raise them to their shoulders like soldiers their guns. The tall man motions towards the big house. "*Directo,* Mirandas." He enunciates the words carefully. Yolanda looks in the direction of his hand. In the faint light of what is left of day, she can barely make out the road ahead. It is as if the guava grove has grown into the road and woven its matt of branches tightly in all directions.

She reaches for each man's hand to shake. The shorter man holds his back at first, as if not wanting to dirty her hand, but finally, after wiping it on the side of his pants, he gives it to Yolanda. The skin feels rough and dry like the bark of trees.

Yolanda climbs into the car while the two men wait a moment on the shoulder to see if the tire will hold. She eases out onto the pavement and makes her way slowly down the road. When she looks for them in her rearview mirror, they have disappeared into the darkness of the guava grove.

Ahead, her lights catch the figure of a small boy. Yolanda leans over and opens the door for him. The overhead light comes on; the boy's face is working back tears. He is cradling an arm. "The *guardia* hit me. He said I was telling stories. No *dominicana* with a car would be out at this hour getting *guayabas.*"

"Don't you worry, José." Yolanda pats the boy. She can feel the bony shoulder through the thin fabric of his shirt. "You can still have your dollar. You did your part."

But his shame seems to obscure any pleasure he might feel

in her offer. Yolanda tries to distract him by asking what he will buy with his money, what he most craves, thinking that on a subsequent visit, she might bring him his own little *antojo*. But José Duarte, Sánchez y Mella says nothing, except a mumbled *gracias* when she lets him off at the cantina with several more than his promised dollar.

In the glow of the headlights, Yolanda makes out the figure of the old woman in the black square of her doorway, waving goodbye. And above the picnic table on a near post, the Palmolive woman's skin gleams a rich white; her head is still thrown back, her mouth still opened as if she is calling someone over a great distance.

The Kiss

▼▲▼▲▼▲▼▲▼▲▼▲▼▲▼▲▼▲▼▲▼▲▼▲▼▲▼▲▼▲▼▲▼▲▼III▼▲▼▲▼

Sofía

Even after they'd been married and had their own families and often couldn't make it for other occasions, the four daughters always came home for their father's birthday. They would gather together, without husbands, would-be husbands, or bring-home work. For this too was part of the tradition: the daughters came home alone. The apartment was too small for everyone, the father argued. Surely their husbands could spare them for one overnight?

The husbands would just as soon have not gone to their in-laws, but they felt annoyed at the father's strutting. "When's he going to realize you've grown up? You sleep with us!"

"He's almost seventy, for God's sake!" the daughters said, defending the father. They were passionate women, but their devotions were like roots; they were sunk into the past towards the old man.

So for one night every November the daughters turned back into their father's girls. In the cramped living room, surrounded by the dark oversized furniture from the old house they grew up in, they were children again in a smaller, simpler version of the world. There was the prodigal scene at the door. The father opened his arms wide and welcomed them in his broken English: "This is your home, and never you should forget it." Inside, the mother fussed at them—their sloppy clothes; their long, loose hair; their looking tired, too skinny, too made up, and so on.

After a few glasses of wine, the father started in on what should be done if he did not live to see his next birthday. "Come on, Papi," his daughters coaxed him, as if it were a modesty of his, to perish, and they had to talk him into staying alive. After his cake and candles, the father distributed bulky envelopes that felt as if they were padded, and they were, no less than several hundreds in bills, tens and twenties and fives, all arranged to face the same way, the top one signed with the father's name, branding them his. Why not checks? the daughters would wonder later, gossiping together in the bedroom, counting their money to make sure the father wasn't playing favorites. Was there some illegality that the father stashed such sums away? Was he—none of the daughters really believed this, but to contemplate it was a wonderful little explosion in their heads— was he maybe dealing drugs or doing abortions in his office?

At the table there was always the pretense of trying to give the envelopes back. "No, no, Papi, it's *your* birthday, after all."

The father told them there was plenty more where that had come from. The revolution in the old country had failed. Most of his comrades had been killed or bought off. He had escaped to this country. And now it was every man for himself, so what he made was for his girls. The father never gave his daughters money when their husbands were around. "They might receive the wrong idea," the father once said, and although none of the daughters knew specifically what the father meant, they all understood what he was saying to them: Don't bring the men home for my birthday.

But this year, for his seventieth birthday, the youngest daughter, Sofía, wanted the celebration at her house. Her son had been born that summer, and she did not want to be traveling in November with a four-month-old and her little girl. And yet, she, of all the daughters, did not want to be the absent one because for the first time since she'd run off with her husband six years ago, she and her father were on speaking terms. In fact, the old man had been out to see her—or really to see his grandson—twice. It was a big deal that Sofía had had a son. He was the first male born into the family in two generations. In fact, the baby was to be named for the grandfather—Carlos— and his middle name was to be Sofía's maiden name, and so, what the old man had never hoped for with his "harem of four girls," as he liked to joke, his own name was to be kept going in this new country!

During his two visits, the grandfather had stood guard by the crib all day, speaking to little Carlos. "Charles the Fifth; Charles Dickens; Prince Charles." He enumerated the names of famous Charleses in order to stir up genetic ambition in the boy. "Charlemagne," he cooed at him also, for the baby was large and big-boned with blond fuzz on his pale pink skin, and blue eyes just like his German father's. All the grandfather's Caribbean fondness for a male heir and for fair Nordic looks had surfaced. There was now good blood in the family against a future bad choice by one of its women.

"You can be president, you were born here," the grandfather crooned. "You can go to the moon, maybe even to Mars by the time you are of my age."

His macho babytalk brought back Sofía's old antagonism towards her father. How obnoxious for him to go on and on like that while beside him stood his little granddaughter, wide-eyed and sad at all the things her baby brother, no bigger than one of her dolls, was going to be able to do just because he was a boy. "Make him stop, please," Sofía asked her husband. Otto was considered the jolly, good-natured one among the brothers-in-law. "The camp counselor," his sisters-in-law teased. Otto approached the grandfather. Both men looked fondly down at the new Viking.

"You can be as great a man as your father," the grandfather said. This was the first compliment the father-in-law had ever paid any son-in-law in the family. There was no way Otto was going to mess with the old man now. "He is a good boy, is he not, Papi?" Otto's German accent thickened with affection. He clapped his hand on his father-in-law's shoulders. They were friends now.

But though the father had made up with his son-in-law, there was still a strain with his own daughter. When he had come to visit, she embraced him at the door, but he stiffened and politely shrugged her off. "Let me put down these heavy bags, Sofía." He had never called her by her family pet name, Fifi, even when she lived at home. He had always had problems with his maverick youngest, and her running off hadn't helped. "I don't want loose women in my family," he had cautioned all his daughters. Warnings were delivered communally, for even though there was usually the offending daughter of the moment, every woman's character could use extra scolding.

His daughters had had to put up with this kind of attitude in an unsympathetic era. They grew up in the late sixties. Those were the days when wearing jeans and hoop earrings, smoking a little dope, and sleeping with their classmates were considered political acts against the military-industrial complex. But standing up to their father was a different matter altogether. Even as grown women, they lowered their voices in their father's earshot when alluding to their bodies' pleasure. Professional women, too, all three of them, with degrees on the wall!

Sofía was the one without the degrees. She had always gone her own way, though she downplayed her choices, calling them accidents. Among the four sisters, she was considered the plain one, with her tall, big-boned body and large-featured face. And yet, she was the one with "non-stop boyfriends," her sisters joked, not without wonder and a little envy. They admired her and were always asking her advice about men. The third daughter had shared a room with Sofía growing up. She liked to watch her sister move about their room, getting ready for bed, brushing and arranging her hair in a clip before easing herself under the sheets as if someone were waiting for her there. In the dark, Fifi gave off a fresh, wholesome smell of clean flesh. It gave solace to the third daughter, who was always so tentative and terrified and had such troubles with men. Her sister's breathing in the dark room was like having a powerful, tamed animal at the foot of her bed ready to protect her.

The youngest daughter had been the first to leave home. She had dropped out of college, in love. She had taken a job as a secretary and was living at home because her father had threatened to disown her if she moved out on her own. On her vacation she went to Colombia because her current boyfriend was going, and since she couldn't spend an overnight with him in New York, she had to travel thousands of miles to sleep with him. In Bogotá, they discovered that once they could enjoy the forbidden fruit, they lost their appetite. They broke up. She met a tourist on the street, some guy from Germany, just like that. The woman had not been without a boyfriend for more than a few days of her adult life. They fell in love.

On her way home, she tossed her diaphragm in the first bin at Kennedy Airport. She was taking no chances. But the father could tell. For months, he kept an eye out. First chance he got, he went through her drawers "looking for my nail clippers," and there he found her packet of love letters. The German man's small, correct handwriting mentioned unmentionable things—bed conversations were recreated on the thin blue sheets of aerogramme letters.

"What is the meaning of this?" The father shook the letters in her face. They had been sitting around the table, the four sisters, gabbing, and the father had come in, beating the packet against his leg like a whip, the satin hair ribbon unraveling where he had untied it, and then wrapped it round and round in a mad effort to contain his youngest daughter's misbehavior.

"Give me those!" she cried, lunging at him.

The father raised his hand with the letters above both their heads like the Statue of Liberty with her freedom torch, but he had forgotten this was the daughter who was as tall as he was. She clawed his arm down and clutched the letters to herself as if they were her babe he'd plucked from her breast. It seemed a biological rather than a romantic fury.

After his initial shock, the father regained his own fury. "Has he deflowered you? That's what I want to know. Have you gone behind the palm trees? Are you dragging my good name through the dirt, that is what I would like to know!" The father was screaming crazily in the youngest daughter's face, question after question, not giving the daughter a chance to answer. His face grew red with fury, but hers was more terrible in its impassivity, a pale ivory moon, pulling and pulling at the tide of his anger, until it seemed he might drown in his own outpouring of fury.

Her worried sisters stood up, one at each arm, coaxing him like nurses, another touching the small of his back as if he were a feverish boy. "Come on, Papi, simmer down now. Take it easy. Let's talk. We're a family, after all."

"Are you a whore?" the father interrogated his daughter. There was spit on the daughter's cheeks from the closeness of his mouth to her face.

"It's none of your fucking business!" she said in a low, ugly-sounding voice like the snarl of an animal who could hurt him. "You have no right, no right at all, to go through my stuff or read my mail!" Tears spurted out of her eyes, her nostrils flared.

The father's mouth opened in a little zero of shock. Quietly, Sofía drew herself up and left the room. Usually, in her growing-up tantrums, this daughter would storm out of the house and come back hours later, placated, the sweetness in her nature reasserted, bearing silly gifts for everyone in the family, refrigerator magnets, little stuffed hairballs with roll-around eyeballs.

But this time they could hear her upstairs, opening and closing her drawers, moving back and forth from the bed to the closet. Downstairs, the father prowled up and down the length of the rooms, his three daughters caging him while the other great power in the house, tidily—as if she had all the time in the world—buttoned and folded all her clothes, packed all her bags, and left the house forever. She got herself to Germany somehow and got the man to marry her. To throw in the face of the father who was so ambitious for presidents and geniuses in the family, the German nobody turned out to be a world-class chemist. But the daughter's was not a petty nature. What did she care what Otto did for a living when she had shown up at his door and offered herself to him.

"I can love you as much as anybody else," she said. "If you can do the same for me, let's get married."

"Come on in and let's talk," Otto had said, or so the story went.

"Yes or no," Sofía answered. Just like that on a snowy night someone at his door and a cold draft coming in. "I couldn't let her freeze," Otto boasted later.

"Like hell you couldn't!" Sofía planted a large hand on his shoulder, and anyone could see how it must be between them in the darkness of their love-making. On their honeymoon, they traveled to Greece, and Sofía sent her mother and father and sisters postcards like any newlywed. "We're having a great time. Wish you were here."

But the father kept to his revenge. For months no one could mention the daughter's name in his presence, though he kept calling them all "Sofía" and quickly correcting himself. When the daughter's baby girl was born, his wife put her foot down. Let him carry his grudge to the grave, *she* was going out to Michigan (where Otto had relocated) to see her first grandchild!

Last minute, the father relented and went along, but he might as well have stayed away. He was grim and silent the whole visit, no matter how hard Sofía and her sisters tried to engage him in conversation. Banishment was better than this cold shoulder. But Sofía tried again. On the old man's next birthday, she appeared at the apartment with her little girl. "Surprise!" There was a reconciliation of sorts. The father first tried to shake hands with her. Thwarted, he then embraced her stiffly before taking the baby in his arms under the watchful eye of his wife. Every year after that, the daughter came for her father's birthday, and in the way of women, soothed and stitched and patched over the hurt feelings. But there it was under the social fabric, the raw wound. The father refused to set foot in his daughter's house. They rarely spoke; the father said public things to her in the same tone of voice he used with his sons-in-law.

But now his seventieth birthday was coming up, and he had agreed to have the celebration at Sofía's house. The christening for little Carlos was scheduled for the morning, so the big event would be Papi Carlos's party that night. It was a coup for the youngest daughter to have gathered the scattered family in the Midwest for a weekend. But the real coup was how Sofía had managed to have the husbands included this year. The husbands are coming, the husbands are coming, the sisters joked. Sofía passed the compliment off on little Carlos. The boy had opened the door for the other men in the family.

But the coup the youngest daughter most wanted was to reconcile with her father in a big way. She would throw the old man a party he wouldn't forget. For weeks she planned what they would eat, where they would all sleep, the entertainment. She kept calling up her sisters with every little thing to see what they thought. Mostly, they agreed with her: a band, paper hats, balloons, buttons that broadcast THE WORLD'S GREATEST DAD. Everything overdone and silly and devoted the way they knew the father would like it. Sofía briefly considered a belly dancer or a girl who'd pop out of a cake. But the third daughter, who had become a feminist in the wake of her divorce, said she considered such locker-room entertainments offensive. A band with music was what she'd pitch in on; her married sisters could split it three ways if they wanted to be sexists. With great patience, Sofía created a weekend that would offend no one. They were going to have a good time in her house for the old man's seventieth, if it killed her!

The night of the party, the family ate an early dinner before the band and the guests arrived. Each daughter toasted both Carloses. The sons-in-law called big Carlos, "Papi." Little Carlos, looking very much like a little girl in his long, white christening gown, bawled the whole time, and his poor mother had not a moment's peace between serving the dinner she'd prepared for the family and giving him his. The phone kept ring-ing, relatives from the old country calling with congratulations for the old man. The toasts the daughters had prepared kept getting interrupted. Even so, their father's eyes glazed with tears more than once as the four girls went through their paces.

He looked old tonight, every single one of his seventy years was showing. Perhaps it was that too much wine had darkened his complexion, and his white hair and brows and mustache stood out unnaturally white. He perked up a little for his gifts, though, gadgets and books and desk trophies from his daughters, and cards with long notes penned inside "to the best, dearest Papi in the world," each one of which the old man wanted to read out loud. "No you don't, Papi, they're private!" his daughters chimed in, crowding around him, wanting to spare each other the embarrassment of having their gushing made public. His wife gave him a gold watch. The third daughter teased that that's how companies retired their employees, but when her mother made angry eyes at her, she stopped. Then there were the men gifts—belts and credit card wallets from the sons-in-law.

"Things I really need." The father was gracious. He stacked up the gift cards and put them away in his pocket to pore over later. The sons-in-law all knew that the father was watching them, jealously, for signs of indifference or self-interest. As for his girls, even after their toasts were given, the gifts opened, and the father had borne them out of the way with the help of his little granddaughter, even then, the daughters felt that there was something else he had been waiting for which they had not yet given him.

But there was still plenty of party left to make sure he got whatever it was he needed for the long, lonely year ahead. The band arrived, three middle-aged men, each with a silver wave slicked back with too much hair cream. DANNY AND HIS BOYS set up a placard with their name against the fireplace. There was one on an accordion, another on a fiddle, and a third was miscellaneous on maracas and triangle and drums when needed. They played movie themes, polkas, anything familiar you could hum along to; the corny songs were all dedicated to "Poppy" or "his lovely lady." The father liked the band. "Nice choice," he congratulated Otto. The youngest daughter's temper flared easily with all she'd had to drink and eat. She narrowed her eyes at her smiling husband and put a hand on her hip. As if Otto had lifted a finger during her long months of planning!

The guests began to arrive, many with tales of how they'd gotten lost on the way; the suburbs were dark and intricate like mazes with their courts and cul-de-sacs. Otto's unmarried colleagues looked around the room, trying to single out the recently divorced sister they'd heard so much about. But there was no one as beautiful and funny and talented as Sofía had boasted the third oldest would be. Most of these friends were half in love with Sofía anyway, and it was she they sought out in the crowded room.

There was a big chocolate cake in the shape of a heart set out on the long buffet with seventy-one candles—one for good luck. The granddaughter and her aunts had counted them and planted them diagonally across the heart, joke candles that wouldn't blow out. Later, they burned a flaming arrow that would not quit. The bar was next to the heart and by midnight when the band broke out again with "Happy Birthday, Poppy," everyone had had too much to eat and drink.

They'd been playing party games on and off all night. The band obliged with musical chairs, but after two of the dining room chairs were broken, they left off playing. The third daughter, especially, had gotten out of hand, making musical chairs of every man's lap. The father sat without speaking. He gazed upon the scene disapprovingly.

In fact, the older the evening got, the more withdrawn the father had become. Surrounded by his daughters and their husbands and fancy, intelligent, high-talking friends, he seemed to be realizing that he was just an old man sitting in their houses, eating up their roast lamb, impinging upon their lives. The daughters could almost hear his thoughts inside their own heads. He, who had paid to straighten their teeth and smooth the accent out of their English in expensive schools, he was nothing to them now. Everyone in this room would survive him, even the silly men in the band who seemed like boys—imagine making a living out of playing birthday songs! How could they ever earn enough money to give their daughters pretty clothes and send them to Europe during the summers so they wouldn't get bored? Where were the world's men anymore? Every last one of his sons-in-law was a kid; he could see that clearly. Even Otto, the famous scientist, was a schoolboy with a pencil, doing his long division. The new son-in-law he even felt sorry for—he could see this husband would give out on his strong-willed second daughter. Already she had him giving her backrubs and going for cigarettes in the middle of the night. But he needn't worry about his girls. Or his wife, for that matter. There she sat, pretty and slim as a girl, smiling coyly at everyone when a song was dedicated to her. Eight, maybe nine, months he gave her of widowhood, and then she'd find someone to grow old with on his life insurance.

The third daughter thought of a party game to draw her father out. She took one of the baby's soft receiving blankets, blindfolded her father, and led him to a chair at the center of the room. The women clapped. The men sat down. The father pretended he didn't understand what all his daughters were up to. "How does one play this game, Mami?"

"You're on your own, Dad," the mother said, laughing. She was the only one in the family who called him by his American name.

"Are you ready, Papi?" the oldest asked.

"I am perfect ready," he replied in his heavy accent.

"Okay, now, guess who this is," the oldest said. She always took charge. This is how they worked things among the daughters.

The father nodded, his eyebrows shot up. He held on to his chair, excited, a little scared, like a boy about to be asked a hard question he knows the answer to.

The oldest daughter motioned to the third daughter, who tiptoed into the circle the women had made around the old man. She gave him a daughterly peck on the cheek.

"Who was that, Papi?" the oldest asked.

He was giggling with pleasure and could not get the words out at first. He had had too much to drink. "That was Mami," he said in a coy little voice.

"No! Wrong!" all the women cried out.

"Carla?" he guessed the oldest. He was going down the line. "Wrong!" More shouts.

"Sandi? Yoyo?"

"You guessed it," his third oldest said.

The women clapped; some bent over in hilarious laughter. Everyone had had too much to drink. And the old man was having his good time too.

"Okay, here's another coming at you." The eldest took up the game again. She put her index finger to her lips, gave everyone a meaningful glance, quietly circled the old man, and kissed him from behind on top of his head. Then she tiptoed back to where she had been standing when she had first spoken. "Who was that, Papi?" she asked, extra innocent.

"Mami?" His voice rode up, exposed and vulnerable. Then it sank back into its certainties. "That was Mami."

"Count me out," his wife said from the couch where she'd finally given in to exhaustion.

The father never guessed any of the other women in the room. That would have been disrespectful. Besides, their strange-sounding American names were hard to remember and difficult to pronounce. Still he got the benefit of their kisses under cover of his daughters. Down the line, the father went each time: "Carla?" "Sandi?" "Yoyo?" Sometimes, he altered the order, put the third daughter first or the oldest one second.

Sofía had been in the bedroom, tending to her son, who was wild with all the noise in the house tonight. She came back into the living room, buttoning her dress front, and happened upon the game. "Ooh." She rolled her eyes. "It's getting raunchy in here, ha!" She worked her hips in a mock rotation, and the men all laughed. She thrust her girlfriends into the circle and whispered to her little girl to plant the next kiss on her grandfather's nose. The women all pecked and puckered at the old man's face. The second daughter sat briefly on his lap and clucked him under the chin. Every time the father took a wrong guess, the youngest daughter laughed loudly. But soon, she noticed that he never guessed her name. After all her hard work, she was not to be included in his daughter count. Damn him! She'd take her turn and make him know it was her!

Quickly, she swooped into the circle and gave the old man a wet, open-mouthed kiss in his ear. She ran her tongue in the whorls of his ear and nibbled the tip. Then she moved back.

"Oh la la," the oldest said, laughing. "Who was that, Papi?"

The old man did not answer. The smile that had played on his lips throughout the game was gone. He sat up, alert. There was a long pause; everyone leaned forward, waiting for the father to begin with his usual, "Mami?"

But the father did not guess his wife's name. He tore at his blindfold as if it were a contagious body whose disease he might catch. The receiving blanket fell in a soft heap beside his chair. His face had darkened with shame at having his pleasure aroused in public by one of his daughters. He looked from one to the other. His gaze faltered. On the face of his youngest was the brilliant, impassive look he remembered from when she had snatched her love letters out of his hands.

"That's enough of that," he commanded in a low, furious voice. And sure enough, his party was over.

The Four Girls

▼▲▼▲▼▲▼▲▼▲▼▲▼▲▼▲▼▲▼▲▼▲▼▲▼▲▼▲▼▲▼▲▼III▼▲▼▲▼

Carla, Yolanda, Sandra, Sofía

The mother still calls them *the four girls* even though the youngest is twenty-six and the oldest will be thirty-one next month. She has always called them *the four girls* for as long as they can remember, and the oldest remembers all the way back to the day the fourth girl was born. Before that, the mother must have called them *the three girls*, and before that *the two girls*, but not even the oldest, who was once the only girl, remembers the mother calling them anything but *the four girls*.

The mother dressed them all alike in diminishing-sized, different color versions of what she wore, so that the husband sometimes joked, calling them *the five girls*. No one really knew if he was secretly displeased in his heart of hearts that he had never had a son, for the father always bragged, "Good bulls sire cows," and the mother patted his arm, and the four girls tumbled and skipped and giggled and raced by in yellow and baby blue and pastel pink and white, and strangers counted them, "One, two, three, four girls! No sons?"

40

"No," the mother said, apologetically. "Just the four girls."

Each of the four girls had the same party dress, school clothes, underwear, toothbrush, bedspread, nightgown, plastic cup, towel, brush and comb set as the other three, but the first girl brushed in yellow, the second one boarded the school bus in blue, the third one slept in pink, and the baby did everything she pleased in white. As the baby grew older, she cast an envying look at pink. The mother tried to convince the third daughter that white was the best color, and the little one wanted pink because she was a baby and didn't know any better, but the third girl was clever and would not be persuaded. She had always believed that she had gotten the best deal since pink was the color for girls. "You girls are going to drive me crazy!" the mother said, but the girls had gotten used to the mother's rhetorical threats.

The mother had devised the color code to save time. With four girls so close in age, she couldn't indulge identities and hunt down a red cowboy shirt when the third daughter turned tomboy or a Mexican peasant blouse when the oldest discovered her Hispanic roots. As women, the four girls criticized the mother's efficiency. The little one claimed that the whole color system smacked of an assembly-line mentality. The eldest, a child psychologist, admonished the mother in an autobiographical paper, "I Was There Too," by saying that the color system had weakened the four girls' identity differentiation abilities and made them forever unclear about personality boundaries. The eldest also intimated that the mother was a mild anal retentive personality.

The mother did not understand all that psychology talk, but

she knew when she was being criticized. The next time the four girls were all together, she took the opportunity of crying a little and saying that she had done the best she could by the four girls. All four girls praised the good job the mother had done in raising four girls so close in age, and they poured more wine into the mother's glass and into the father's glass, and the father patted the mother's arm and said thickly, "Good cows breed cows," and the mother told the story she liked to tell about the oldest, Carla.

For although the mother confused their names or called them all by the generic pet name, "Cuquita," and switched their birthdates and their careers, and sometimes forgot which husband or boyfriend went with which daughter, she had a favorite story she liked to tell about each one as a way of celebrating that daughter on special occasions. The last time she told the story she liked to tell about the eldest was when Carla got married. The mother, tipsy on champagne, seized the mike during the band's break and recounted the story of the red sneakers to the wedding guests. After her good cry at the dinner table, the mother repeated the story. Carla, of course, knew the story well, and had analyzed it for unresolved childhood issues with her analyst husband. But she never tired of hearing it because it was her story, and whenever the mother told it, Carla knew she was the favorite of the moment.

"You know, of course, the story of the red sneakers?" the mother asked the table in general.

"Oh no," the second daughter groaned. "Not again."

Carla glared at her. "Listen to that negativity." She nodded at her husband as if to confirm something they had talked about.

"Listen to that jargon," the second one countered, rolling her eyes.

"Listen to my story." The mother sipped from her wine glass and set it down a little too heavily. Wine spilled on her hand. She looked up at the ceiling as if she had moved back in time to when they were living on the Island. Those downpours! Leaks, leaks—no roof could keep them out during rainy season. "You all know that when we were first married, we were really really poor?" The father nodded, he remembered. "And your sister"—the stories were always told as if the daughter in question were not present—"your sister wanted some new sneakers. She drove me crazy, night and day, she wanted sneakers, she wanted sneakers. Anyhow, we couldn't afford to make any ends, no less start in with sneakers! If you girls only knew what we went through in those days. Words can't describe it. Four—no, three of you, back then—three girls, and no money coming in."

"Well," the father interrupted. "I was working."

"Your father was working." The mother frowned. Once she got started on a story, she did not acknowledge interruptions. "But that measly little paycheck barely covered the rent." The father frowned. "And my father," the mother confided, "was helping us out—"

"It was only a loan," the father explained to his son-in-law. "Paid every penny back."

"It was only a loan," the mother continued. "Anyhow—the point is to make the story short—we did not have money for one little frill like sneakers. Well, she drove me crazy, night and day, I want sneakers, I want sneakers." The mother was a good mimic, and everybody laughed and sipped their wine. Carla's husband rubbed the back of her neck in slow, arousing circles.

"But the good Lord always provides." Although she was not particularly religious, the mother liked to make her plots providential. "It just so happened that a very nice lady who lived down the block with a little girl who was a little older than Carla and much bigger—"

"Much bigger." The father blew out his cheeks and made a monkey face to show how much bigger.

"This little girl's grandmother had sent her some sneakers for her birthday from New York, not knowing she had gotten so much bigger, and the little sneakers wouldn't fit her."

The father kept his cheeks puffed out because the third oldest burst into giggles every time she looked over at him. She never held her liquor well.

The mother waited for her to control herself and gave the father a sobering stare. "So the nice lady offers me the sneakers because she knows how much that Carla has been pestering me that she wants some. And you know what?" The table waited for the mother to enjoy answering her own question. "They were just her size. Always provides," the mother said, nodding.

"But Señorita Miss Carla could not be bothered with white sneakers. She wanted red sneakers, she wanted red sneakers." The mother rolled her eyes the same way that the second daughter had rolled her eyes at her older sister. "Can you believe it?"

"Uh-huh," the second daughter said. "I can believe it."

"Hostile, aren't we?" Carla said. Her husband whispered something in her ear. They laughed.

"Let me finish," the mother said, sensing dissension.

The youngest got up and poured everyone some more wine. The third oldest turned her glass, stem up, and giggled without much enthusiasm when the father puffed out his cheeks again for her benefit. Her own cheeks had gone pale; her lids drooped over her eyes; she held her head up in her hand. But the mother was too absorbed in her story to scold the elbow off the table.

"I told your sister, *It's white sneakers or no sneakers!* And she had some temper, that Carla. She threw them across the room and yelled, *Red sneakers, red sneakers.*"

The four girls shifted in their chairs, anxious to get to the end of the story. Carla's husband fondled her shoulder as if it were a breast.

The mother hurried her story. "So your father, who spoiled you all rotten"—the father grinned from his place at the head of the table—"comes and rescues the sneakers and, behind my back, whispers to Carlita that she's going to have red sneakers just like she wants them. I find them, the both of them on the floor in the bathroom with my nail polish painting those sneakers red!"

"To Mami," the father said sheepishly, lifting his glass in a toast. "And to the red sneakers," he added.

The room rang with laughter. The daughters raised their glasses. "To the red sneakers."

"That's classic," the analyst said, winking at his wife.

"Red sneakers at that." Carla shook her head, stressing the word *red*.

"Jesus!" the second oldest groaned.

"Always provides," the mother added.

"Red sneakers," the father said, trying to get one more laugh from the table. But everyone was tired, and the third oldest said she was afraid she was going to throw up.

Yolanda, the third of the four girls, became a schoolteacher but not on purpose. For years after graduate school, she wrote down *poet* under profession in questionnaires and income tax forms, and later amended it to *writer*-slash-*teacher*. Finally, acknowledging that she had not written much of anything in years, she announced to her family that she was not a poet anymore.

Secretly, the mother was disappointed because she had always meant for her Yo to be the famous one. The story she told about her third daughter no longer had the charm of a prophetic ending: "And, of course, she became a poet." But the mother tried to convince her daughter that it was better to be a happy nobody than a sad somebody. Yolanda, who was still as clever as when the mother had tried to persuade her that white was a better color than pink, was not convinced.

The mother used to go to all the poetry readings her daughter gave in town and sit in the front row applauding each poem and giving standing ovations. Yolanda was so embarrassed that she tried to keep her readings a secret from her mother, but somehow the mother always found out about them and appeared, first row, center. Even when she behaved herself, the mother threw her daughter off just by her presence. Yolanda often read poems addressed to lovers, sonnets set in bedrooms, and she knew her mother did not believe in sex for girls. But the mother seemed not to notice the subject of the poems, or if she did, to ascribe the love scenes to her Yoyo's great imagination.

"That one has always had a great imagination," the mother confided to whoever sat next to her. At a recent reading the daughter gave after her long silence, the mother's neighbor was the daughter's lover. The mother did not know that the handsome, greying professor at her side knew her daughter at all; she thought he was just someone interested in her poetry. "Of all the four girls," the mother told the lover, "that Yo has always loved poetry."

"That's her nickname, Yo, Yoyo," the mother explained. "She complains she wants her name, but you have to take shortcuts when there's four of them. Four girls, imagine!"

"Really?" the lover said, although Yolanda had already filled him in on her family and her bastardized name—Yo, Joe, Yoyo. He knew better than to take shortcuts. Jo-laahn-dah, she had drilled him. Supposedly, the parents were heavy-duty Old World, but the four daughters sounded pretty wild for all that. There had been several divorces among them, including Yolanda's. The oldest, a child psychologist, had married the analyst she'd been seeing when her first marriage broke up, something of the sort. The second one was doing a lot of drugs to keep her weight down. The youngest had just gone off with a German man when they discovered she was pregnant.

"But that Yo," the mother continued, pointing to her daughter where she sat with the other readers waiting for the sound system to work properly so the program could begin, "that Yo has always had a great imagination." The buzz of talk was punctuated now and then by a crackling, amplified "testing" spoken too close to the microphone. Yolanda watched the absorbed conversation of her mother and lover with growing uneasiness.

"Yes, Yoyo has always loved poetry. Why, I remember the time we went on a trip to New York. She couldn't have been more than three." The mother was warming to her story. The lover noticed that the mother's eyes were those that looked at him softly at night from the daughter's face.

"Testing," a voice exploded into the room.

The mother looked up, thinking the poetry reading had begun. The lover waved the voice away. He wanted to hear the story.

"We went up to New York, Lolo and I. He had a convention there, and we decided to make a vacation of it. We hadn't had a vacation since the first baby was born. We were very poor." The mother lowered her voice. "Words can't describe how poor we were. But we were starting to see better days."

"Really?" the lover said. He had fixed on that word as one that gave the appropriate amount of encouragement but did not interrupt the flow of the mother's story.

"We left the girls back home, but that one"—the mother pointed again to the daughter, who widened her eyes at her lover—"that one was losing all her hair. We took her with us so she could see a specialist. Turned out to be just nerves."

The lover knew Yolanda would not have wanted him to know about this indelicacy of her body. She did not even like to pluck her eyebrows in his presence. An immediate bathrobe after her bath. Lights out when they made love. Other times, she carried on about the Great Mother and the holiness of the body and sexual energy being eternal delight. Sometimes, he complained he felt caught between the woman's libber and the Catholic señorita. "You sound like my ex," she accused him.

"We got on this crowded bus one afternoon." The mother

shook her head remembering how crowded the bus had been. "I couldn't begin to tell you how crowded it was. It was more sardines in a can than you could shake sticks at."

"Really?"

"You don't believe me?" the mother accused him. The lover nodded his head to show he was convinced. "But let me tell you, that bus was so crowded, Lolo and I got our wires totally mixed up. I was sure Lolo had her, and Lolo was sure she was with me. Anyhow, to make it a short story, we got off at our stop, and we looked at each other. *Where's Yo?* we asked at the same time. Meanwhile, that bus was roaring away from us.

"Well, I'll tell you, we broke into a run like two crazy people! It was rush hour. Everyone was turning around to look at us like we were running from the police or something." The mother's voice was breathless remembering that run. The lover waited for her to catch up with the bus in her memory.

"Testing?" a garbled voice asked without much conviction.

"After about two blocks, we flagged the driver down and climbed aboard. And you won't believe what we found?"

The lover knew better than to take a guess.

"We found that one surrounded by a crowd like Jesus and the elders."

"Really?" The lover smiled, admiring the daughter from a distance. Yolanda was one of the more popular instructors at the college where he chaired the Comp Lit Department.

"She hadn't even realized we were gone. She had a circle of people around her, listening to her reciting a poem! As a matter of fact, it was a poem I'd taught her. Maybe you've heard of it? It's by that guy who wrote that poem about the blackbird."

"Stevens?" the lover guessed.

The mother cocked her head. "I'm not sure. Anyhow," she continued, "imagine! Three years old and already drawing crowds. Of course, she became a poet."

"You don't mean Poe, do you? Edgar Allan Poe?"

"Yes, that's him! That's him!" the mother cried out. "The poem was about a princess who lived by the sea or something. Let's see." She began to recite:

Many many years ago, something . . . something,
In a . . . something by the sea . . .
A princess there lived whom you may remember
By the name of Annabel Lee. . .

The mother looked up and realized that the hushed audience was staring at her. She blushed. The lover chuckled and squeezed her arm. At the podium, the poet had been introduced and was waiting for the white-haired woman in the first row to finish talking. "For Clive," Yolanda said, introducing her first poem, " 'Bedroom Sestina.' " Clive smiled sheepishly at the mother, who smiled proudly at her daughter.

The mother does not tell a favorite story about Sandra anymore. She says she would like to forget the past, but it is really only a small part of the recent past she would like to forget. However, the mother knows people listen to absolute statements, so she says in a tired voice, "I want to forget the past."

The last story the mother told about her second oldest was not in celebration but in explanation to Dr. Tandlemann, senior staff psychiatrist at Mount Hope. The mother explained why she and her husband were committing their daughter to a private mental hospital.

"It started with that crazy diet," the mother began. She folded and refolded her Kleenex into smaller and smaller squares. Dr. Tandlemann watched her and took notes. The father sat by the window quietly and followed the movements of a gardener, who was mowing first one, then another, darkening swath across the lawn.

"Can you imagine starving herself to death?" The mother pinched little bits off her Kleenex. "No wonder she went crazy."

"She's had a breakdown." Dr. Tandlemann looked at the father. "Your daughter is not clinically crazy."

"What does that mean, clinically crazy?" The mother scowled. "I don't understand all that psychology talk."

"It means that," Dr. Tandlemann began, looking down at his folder to check the name, "it means that Sandra is not psychotic or schizophrenic, she's just had a small breakdown."

"A small breakdown," the father murmured to himself. In the middle of a row, the gardener stopped, machine roaring. He spat and shrugged his shoulder across his lips, wiping his mouth, then he continued his progress across the lawn. Grass bits spewed into a white sack ballooning behind the motor. The father felt he should say something pleasant. "Nice place you got here, beautiful grounds."

"*Ay*, Lolo," the mother said sadly. She made a fist of what was left of her Kleenex.

Dr. Tandlemann waited for a moment in case the husband wanted to respond to his wife. Then he asked the mother, "You say it started with that diet she went on?"

"It started with that crazy diet," the mother said again as if she had just found her place in a book she had been reading. "Sandi wanted to look like those twiggy models. She was a looker, that one, and I guess it went to her head. There are four girls, you know."

Dr. Tandlemann wrote down *four girls* although the father had already told him this when he asked, "No sons?" Out loud, he noted, noncommittally, "Four girls."

The mother hesitated, then glanced over at her husband as if unsure how much they should disclose to this stranger. "We've had trouble with all of them—" She rolled her eyes to indicate the kind of trouble she meant.

"You mean other daughters have also had breakdowns?"

"Bad men is what they've had!" The mother scowled at the doctor as if he were one of her ex sons-in-law. "Anyhow, that makes sense, heartbreak, breakdown. This is different, this is crazy." The doctor's hand lifted in protest. But the mother ignored the gesture and went on with her story.

"The others aren't bad looking, don't get me wrong. But Sandi, Sandi got the fine looks, blue eyes, peaches and ice cream skin, everything going for her!" The mother spread her arms in all directions to show how pretty and pale and blue-eyed the girl was. Bits of her Kleenex fell to the floor, and she picked off the specks from the carpet. "My great-grandfather married a Swedish girl, you know? So the family has light-colored blood, and that Sandi got it all. But imagine, spirit of contradiction, she wanted to be darker complected like her sisters."

"That's understandable," Dr. Tandlemann said.

"It's crazy, that's what it is," the mother said angrily. "Anyhow, this diet took over. When her sister got married, Sandi wouldn't even taste the wedding cake, taste!"

"Did they get along?" Dr. Tandlemann glanced up; his hand had a life of its own and kept writing.

"Who?" The mother blinked in disapproval. The man asked too many questions.

"The siblings," Dr. Tandlemann said. "Were they close? Was there a lot of rivalry between them?"

"Siblings?" The mother frowned at all this crazy psychology talk. "They're sisters," she said by way of explanation.

"Sometimes they fought," the father added. Although he was looking out the window, he did not miss a word the doctor and his wife were saying.

"Sometimes they fought," the mother raced on. She wanted to get to the end of this story. "So Sandi kept losing weight. At first, she looked good. She had let herself get a little plump, and with her fine bones Sandi can't carry extra weight. So losing a few pounds was okay. Then, she went away to a graduate program, so we didn't see her for awhile. Every time we talked to her over the phone, her voice seemed further and further away. And it wasn't because it was long distance either. I can't explain it," the mother said. "A mother just knows.

"So one day we get this call. The dean. She says she doesn't want to alarm us, but could we come down immediately. Our daughter is in the hospital, too weak to do anything. All she does is read."

The father was timing the gardener's treks across the rolling lawns. When the man did not stop to spit or wipe his forehead, each row took him approximately two minutes.

The mother tried to open the Kleenex in her lap, but it was too ragged to spread out. "We took the next plane, and when we got there, I didn't recognize my own daughter." The mother held up her little finger. "Sandi was a toothpick. And that's not the least of it, she wouldn't put a book down, read, read, read. That's all she did."

At the window the father's view of the lawn was blurring.

The mother looked over at her husband and wondered what he was thinking about. "She had lists and lists of books to read. We found them in her journal. After she finished one, she crossed it off the list. Finally, she told us why she couldn't stop reading. She didn't have much time left. She had to read all the great works of man because soon"—the mother got up her courage to say it—"soon she wouldn't be human."

In the ensuing silence the mother heard the drone of a distant lawnmower.

"She told us that she was being turned out of the human race. She was becoming a monkey." The mother's voice broke. "A monkey, my baby!

"Already the other organs inside her body were a monkey's. Only her brain was left, and she could feel it going."

Dr. Tandlemann stopped writing. He weighed his pen in his hand. "I understood you committed her only because of the weight loss. This is news to me."

"Small breakdown," the father murmured quietly so Dr. Tandlemann wouldn't hear him.

The mother was in control of her voice again. "If she read all the great books, maybe she'd remember something important from having been human. So she read and read. But she was afraid she'd go before she got to some of the big thinkers."

"Freud," the doctor said, listing names on his pad. "Darwin, Nietsche, Erikson."

"Dante," the father mused. "Homer, Cervantes, Calderón de la Barca."

"I told her to stop reading and start eating. I told her those books were driving her crazy. I made her everything she liked: rice and beans, lasagna, chicken à la king. I made her favorite red snapper with tomato sauce. She said she didn't want to eat animals. In her own time, she said, she would be that chicken. She would be that red snapper. Evolution had reached its peak and was going backwards. Something like that." The mother waved the very idea away. "It was crazy talk, I tell you.

"One morning, I go in her room to wake her up, and I find her lying in bed and looking up at her hands." The mother held up her hands and re-enacted the scene. "I call her name, Sandi!, and she keeps turning her hands, this way, that, and staring at them. I scream at her to answer me, and she doesn't even look at me. Nothing. And she's making these awful sounds like she's a zoo." The mother clucked and grunted to show the doctor what the animals had sounded like.

Suddenly, the father leaned forward. He had caught sight of something important.

"And my Sandi holds up her hands to me," the mother continued. She turned her hands towards Dr. Tandlemann and then towards her husband, whose face was pressed up to the window. "And she screams, *Monkey hands, monkey hands.*"

The father shot up from his chair. Outside, a fair, willowy girl and a heavy-set woman in white were walking across the lawn. The woman was pointing out the flowers and the leaves of the bushes in order to cajole the girl forward towards the building. At one end of the lawn, the gardener wiped his forehead, turned the mower around and began a new row. A dark wake spread behind him. The girl looked up, wildly searching the empty sky for the airplane she was hearing. The nurse followed her distracted movements with alarm. Finally, the girl saw a man coming at her with a roaring animal on a leash, its baglike stomach swelling up as it devoured the grasses between them. The girl screamed and broke into a panicked run towards the building where her father, whom she could not see, stood at the window, waving.

At the hospital, the mother leans on the glass with one hand and taps with the other. She makes a monkey face. The cradle has been turned towards her, but the tiny, wrinkled baby is not looking at the grandmother. Instead the baby's eyes roll about as if she hasn't quite figured out how to work them yet. Her lips pucker and stretch, pucker and stretch. The grandmother is sure the baby is smiling at her.

"Look at that," the grandmother says to the young man at her side, who is looking at the baby in the neighboring cradle.

The young man looks at the stranger's baby.

"She's smiling already," the grandmother brags.

The young man nods and smiles.

"Yours is asleep," the grandmother says in a slightly critical voice.

"Babies sleep a lot," the young man explains.

"Some do," the grandmother says. "I had four girls, and they never slept."

"Four girls, no boys?"

The mother shakes her head. "I guess it's in the blood. This one is a girl too. Aren't you, Cuquita?" the grandmother asks her granddaughter.

The young man smiles at his daughter. "Mine is a girl too."

The grandmother congratulates him. "Good bulls sire cows, you know."

"Huh?"

"It's a saying my husband used to tell me after I had one of the girls. *Good bulls sire cows.* I remember the night Fifi was born." The grandmother looks down at her granddaughter and explains, "Your mother."

The young man studies his baby daughter as he listens to the old woman's story.

"That girl gave me more trouble getting born than any of the others. And the funny thing was she was the last and smallest of the four. Twenty-four hours in labor." The grandmother's eyebrows lift for punctuation.

The young man whistles. "Twenty-four hours is a long labor for a small fourth child. Any complications?"

The mother studies the young man a moment. Is he a doctor, she wonders, to know so much about babies?

"Twenty-four hours . . ." The young man is shaking his head, musing. "Ours lasted only three and a half."

The grandmother stares up at the young man. *Ours!* Men! Now they're going to claim having the babies too.

"But I'll tell you, that Fifi, we didn't name her wrong! Sofía, that's her real name. My daughter, the poet, says Sofía was the goddess in charge of wisdom long ago. We Catholics don't believe in that stuff. But still, she's the smart one, all right. And I don't mean books either! I mean smart." The grandmother taps her temple, and then repeats the gesture on the glass. "Smart, smart," the grandmother tells the baby. She shakes her head, musing to herself. "That Fifi, she might look like she's headed for trouble, but it always turns out to be her luck.

"That night she was finally born, her father came in, and I knew he was a little disappointed, especially after such a long wait. And I said, *I can't help it, Lolo, they come out girls*, and all he said was, *Good bulls sire cows*, like it was a credit to him. He was almost falling over with exhaustion. So I sent him home to bed."

The young man yawns and laughs.

"He was so dead tired, he didn't hear the burglars when they broke in. They stole us blind. They even stole my shoes and my under—" The grandmother remembers it is indelicate to say so. "Every last article of clothing," she adds coyly.

The young man pretends to be alarmed.

"But this is what I mean about luck—they caught the burglars, and we got every last stitch back." The grandmother taps the glass. "Cuquita," she coos at the baby.

"Lucky," she says to the young man. "That Fifi has always been the lucky one. Not to mention her luck with"—the grandmother lowers her voice—"with Otto."

The young man looks over his shoulder. Otto? Who would name a poor kid Otto?

"Imagine," the grandmother continues. "Fifi drops out of college and goes off on a church trip to Perú, chaperoned, of course, otherwise we wouldn't have let her go. We don't believe in all this freedom." The grandmother frowns as she looks out over the nursery. Beyond the glass, between the slender white bars of their cribs, half a dozen babies are fast asleep.

"Anyhow she meets this German man Otto in a Peruvian market, who can't speak a word of Spanish but is trying to buy a poncho. She bargains for him, and he gets his poncho for practically nothing. Well, just like that, they fell for each other, corresponded, and here they are, parents! Tell me that isn't lucky?"

"That's lucky," the young man says.

"And you're going to be a lucky one too, aren't you?" The grandmother clucks at her granddaughter, then confides to the young man, "She's going to look just like an angel, pink and blond."

"You never can tell when they're this young," the father says, smiling at his daughter.

"I can," the grandmother claims. "I had four of them."

"Mami picks up like these really gorgeous men," Sandi laughs. She is sitting cross-legged on Fifi's living room floor. The new mother sits in Otto's recliner, the baby asleep on her shoulder. Carla is sprawled on the sofa. At her feet, Yolanda is knitting furiously at a tiny blanket, pink and baby blue and pastel yellow squares with a white border. It is early morning. The family has gathered at Fifi's house for Christmas, which falls a week after the baby's birth. Husbands and grandparents are still asleep in the bedrooms. The four girls lounge in their nightgowns and tell each other the true story of how their lives are going.

Sandi explains that she and the mother were in the waiting room, and the mother disappeared. "I find her at the nursery window talking to this piece of beefcake—"

"That's offensive," Yolanda says. "Just call him a man."

"Lay off me, will you?" Sandi is close to tears. Since her release from Mt. Hope a month ago, she cries so easily she has to carry Kleenex with her anti-depressants in her purse. She looks around the room for her bag. "Miz Poet is so goddamn sensitive to language."

"I don't write poetry anymore," Yolanda says in a wounded voice.

"Goddamn it, you guys," Carla says, refereeing this one. "It's Christmas."

The new mother turns to the second oldest sister and runs her fingers through her hair. This is the first time the family has gathered together in a year, and she wants them all to get along. She changes the subject. "That was really nice of you to come see me at the hospital. I know how you just love hospitals," she adds.

Sandi looks down at the rug and picks at it. "I just want to forget the past, you know?"

"That's understandable," Carla says.

Yolanda lays aside the baby blanket. She has the same scowl on her face her sister wore a moment ago, a family sign of approaching tears. "I'm sorry," she says to Sandi. "It's been the worst week."

Sandi touches her hand. She looks at her other sisters. Clive, they all know, has gone back to his wife again. "He's such a turd. How many times has he done this now, Yo?"

"Yolanda," Carla corrects her. "She wants to be called Yolanda now."

"What do you mean, *wants to be called Yolanda now?* That's my name, you know?"

"Why are you so angry?" Carla's calmness is professional.

Yolanda rolls her eyes. "Spare me the nickel and dime therapy, thank you."

Trouble brewing again, Fifi changes the subject. She touches the evolving blanket. "It's really beautiful. And the poem you wrote the baby made me cry."

"So you *are* writing!" Carla says. "I know, I know, you don't want to hear about it." Carla makes a peace offering of compliments. "You're so good, Yolanda, really. I've saved all your poems. Every time I read something in a magazine, I think, God, Yo's so much better than this! Give yourself credit. You're so hard on yourself."

Yolanda keeps her mouth shut. She is working on a thought about her bossy older sister: Carla has a tendency to lace all her compliments with calls to self-improvement. *Give yourself credit, Believe in yourself, Be good to yourself.* Somehow this makes her praise sound like their mother's old "constructive" criticism.

Carla turns to Sandi. "Mami says you're seeing someone." The eldest weighs her words carefully. "Is it true?"

"What of it?" Sandi looks up defensively, and then, realizing her sister means a man, not a therapist, she adds, "He's a nice guy, but, I don't know—" She shrugs. "He was in at the same time I was."

What was *he* in for? hangs in the air—a question that none of her sisters would dare ask.

"So, tell us about this cute guy at the nursery," Fifi pleads. Each time her sisters seem on the verge of loaded talk, the new mother changes the subject to her favorite topic, her newborn daughter. Every little detail of the baby's being—what she eats, what she poops—seems an evolutionary leap. Surely, not all newborns smile at their mothers? "You met this guy at the nursery?"

"Me?" Sandi laughs. "You mean Mami. She picks this guy up and invites him for lunch at the hospital coffee shop."

"Mami is so fresh," Yolanda says. She notices she has made a mistake and begins unraveling a lopsided yellow row.

Fifi pats her baby's back. "And she complains about us!"

"So we all have lunch together," Sandi continues, "and Mami can't shut up about how God brought you and Otto together from opposite ends of the earth in Perú."

"God?" Carla screws up her face.

"Perú?" Fifi's face mirrors her sister's scowl. "I've never been to Perú. We met in Colombia."

"In Mami's version of the story, you met in Perú," Sandi says. "And you fell in love at first sight."

"And made love the first night," Carla teases. The four girls laugh. "Except that part isn't in Mami's version."

"I've heard so many versions of that story," Sandi says, "I don't know which one is true anymore."

"Neither do I," Fifi says, laughing. "Otto says we probably

met in a New Jersey Greyhound Station, but we've heard all these exciting stories about how we met in Brazil or Colombia or Perú that we got to believing them."

"So was it the first night?" Yolanda asks, her needles poised midair.

"I heard the first night," Carla says.

Sandi narrows her eyes. "I heard it was a week or so after you guys met."

The baby burps. The four girls look at each other and laugh. "Actually"—Fifi calculates by lifting her fingers one by one from the baby's back, then patting them down—"it was the fourth night. But I knew the minute I saw him."

"That you loved him?" Yolanda asks. Fifi nods. Since Clive left, Yolanda is addicted to love stories with happy endings, as if there were a stitch she missed, a mistake she made way back when she fell in love with her first man, and if only she could find it, maybe she could undo it, unravel John, Brad, Steven, Rudy, and start over.

In the pause before someone picks up the thread of conversation, they all listen to the baby's soft breathing.

"Anyhow, Mami tells this guy about your long correspondence." Sandi helps Yolanda wind the unraveled yarn into a ball, stopping now and then to enjoy her story of the mother. *"For months and months after they met in Perú, they were separated, months and months."* Sandi rolls her eyes like her mother. She is a remarkably good mimic. Her three sisters laugh. *"Otto was doing his research in Germany, but he wrote to her every day."*

"Every day!" Fifi laughs. "I wish it had been every day. Sometimes I had to wait weeks between letters."

"But then," Yolanda says in the ominous voice of a radio melodrama, "then Papi found the letters."

"Mami didn't mention the letters," Sandi says. "The story was short and sweet: *He wrote to her every day. Then she went to see him last Christmas, then he proposed, and they married this spring, and here they are, parents!*"

"One, two, three, four," Carla says, beginning a countdown.

Fifi grins. "Stop it," she says. "The baby was born exactly nine months and ten days after the wedding."

"Thank God for the ten days," Carla says.

"I like Mami's version of the story," Fifi laughs. "So she didn't bring up the letters?"

Sandi shakes her head. "Maybe she forgot. You know how she keeps saying she wants to forget the past."

"Mami remembers everything," Carla disagrees.

"Well, Papi had no business going through my personal mail." Fifi's voice grows testy. The baby stirs on her shoulder. "He claims he was looking for his nailclippers, or something. In my drawers, right?"

Yolanda mimics their father opening an envelope. Her eyes widen in burlesque horror. She clutches her throat. She even puts on a Count Dracula accent to make the moment more dramatic. She is not a good mimic. "*What does this man mean, 'Have you gotten your period yet?'*"

Sandi choruses: "*What business is it of Otto's if you've gotten your period or no?*"

The baby begins to cry. "Oh honey, it's just a story." Fifi rocks her.

"*We disown you!*" Sandi mimics their father. "*You have dis-*

graced the family name. Out of this house!"

"*Out of our sight!*" Yolanda points to the door. Sandi ducks the flailing needles. A ball of white yarn rolls across the floor. The two sisters bend over, trying to contain their hilarity.

"You guys are really getting into this." Fifi stands to walk her wailing baby to sleep. "Nothing like a story to take the sting out of things," she adds cooly. "It's not like things are any better between us, you know."

Her three sisters lift their eyebrows at each other. Their father has not uttered a word since he arrived two days ago. He still has not forgiven Fifi for "going behind the palm trees." When they were younger, the sisters used to joke that they would likelier be virgins than find a palm tree in their neck of the woods.

"It's hard, I know." As the therapist in the family, Carla likes to be the one who understands. "But really, give yourself credit. You've won them over, Fifi, you have. Mami's eating out of your hand with this baby, and Papi's going to come around in time, you'll see. Look, he came, didn't he?"

"You mean, Mami dragged him here." Fifi looks down fondly at her baby and recovers her good mood. "Well, the baby is beautiful and well, and that's what counts."

Beautiful and well, Yolanda muses, that's what she had wanted with Clive, all things beautiful and well, instead of their obsessive, consuming passion that left her—each time Clive left her—exhausted and distraught. "I don't understand why he does it," she tells her sisters out loud.

"Old world stuff," Carla says. "You know he got a heavier dose than Mami."

Sandi looks at Yolanda; she understood whom Yolanda

meant. She tries to lighten her sister's dark mood. "Look, if beefcake's not your thing, there's a lot of fish out there," she says. "I just wish that cute guy hadn't been married."

"What cute guy?" Carla asks her.

"What guy?" the mother asks. She is standing at the entrance to the living room, buttoning down a multicolored, flowered houserobe. It is a habit of hers from their childhood to buy rainbow clothes for herself so none of the girls can accuse her of playing favorites.

"The guy you picked up at the hospital," Sandi teases.

"What do you mean, *picked up!* He was a nice young man, and it just so happens that he had a baby daughter born the same time as my little Cuquita." The mother puts out her arms. "Come here, Cuca," she croons, taking the baby from Fifi's hands. She clucks into the blanket.

Sandi shakes her head. "God! You sound like a goddamn zoo."

"Your language," the mother scolds absently, and then, as if the words were an endearment, she coos them at her granddaughter, "your language."

The men trail in slowly for breakfast. First, the father, who nods grimly at all the well-wishing. He is followed by Otto, who wishes everyone a merry Christmas. With his white-gold eyebrows and whiskers and beard, and plump, good-natured, reddish face, Otto looks very much like a young Santa Claus. The analyst shuffles in last. "Look at all those women," he whistles.

The mother is walking her granddaughter up and down the length of the room.

"Just look at them." Otto grins. "A vision! What the three kings saw!"

"Four girls," the father murmurs.

"Five," the analyst corrects, winking at the mother.

"Six," the mother corrects him, nodding towards the bundle in her arms. "Six of us," she says to the baby. "And I was sure of it! Why, a week before you were born, I had the strangest dream. We were all living on a farm, and a bull . . ."

The room is hushed with sleepiness. Everyone listens to the mother.

Joe

▼▲▼▲▼▲▼▲▼▲▼▲▼▲▼▲▼▲▼▲▼▲▼▲▼▲▼▲▼▲▼▲▼III▼▲▼▲▼

Yolanda

Yolanda, nicknamed *Yo* in Spanish, misunderstood *Joe* in English, doubled and pronounced like the toy, *Yoyo* —or when forced to select from a rack of personalized key chains, *Joey*—stands at the third-story window watching a man walk across the lawn with a tennis racket. He touches the border of the shrubbery with the rim of his racket and sets one or two wild irises nodding.

"Don't," Yo mumbles to herself at the window, outlining her hairline with a contemplative index finger. It is her secret pride: Her hair grows to a point on her forehead, arches up, semicircling her face, a perfect heart. "Don't disturb the flowers, Doc." She wags her finger at his thumb-sized back.

The man stops. He throws an imaginary ball in the air and serves it to the horizon. The horizon misses. He walks on towards it and the tennis courts.

He is dressed in white shorts and a white shirt, an outfit which makes him look like a boy . . . a good boy . . . the only

68

son of monied, unloving tycoons. Both of them are tycoons, Yo posits. Daddy Coon is a Fruit of the Loom tycoon. The band on her underwear squeezes gently.

Mama Coon is—Yo looks around the room—*scarf, mirror, soap, umbrella*—an umbrella tycoon. A dark cloud rolls lazily towards her in the sky. The ghost of the tennis ball is coming to haunt the man. Yo smiles, appreciating her charms.

An umbrella tycoon will never do. One more turn around the room: *typewriter, red satchel*—nice sound to that. But he isn't a red satchel tycoon. A breeze blows the white curtains in on either side of her, two ghostly arms embracing her. A room tycoon. . . .

The world is sweetly new and just created. The first man walks in the garden on his way to a tennis date. Yo stands at the third-story window and kisses her fingers and blows him the kiss. "Kiss, kiss," she hisses from the window. She wishes: Let him rip off his white shirt, push back the two halves of his chest like Superman prying open a door and let the first woman out.

Eve is lovely, a valentine hairline, white gossamer panties.

"In the beginning," Yo begins, inspired by perspective. Four floors down, her doctor, shrunk to child size, sits on the lawn. "In the beginning, Doc, I loved John."

She recognizes the unmistakable signs of a flashback: a woman at a window, a woman with a past, with memory and desire and wreckage in her heart. She will let herself have them today. She can't help herself anyway.

In the beginning, we were in love. Yo smiles. That was a good beginning. He came to my door. I opened it. My eyes asked, *Would you like to come in out of the rest of the world?* He answered, *Thank you very much, just what I had on the tip of my tongue.*

It was at the beginning of time, and a river ran outside Yo's window, bordered by cypresses, willows, great sweating ferns, thick stalks and palms. Huge creatures of the imagination scuttled across the muddy bottom of the river. At night as the lovers lay in bed and connected the stars into rams and crabs and twins, they heard the barks and howls of the happy mating beasts.

"I love you," John said, rejoicing, tricked by the barks and the howls.

But Yolanda was afraid. Once they got started on words, there was no telling what they could say.

"I love you," John repeated, so she would follow suit.

Yolanda kissed each eye closed, hoping that would do.

"Do you love me, Joe? Do you?" he pleaded. He wanted words back; nothing else would do.

Yo complied. "I love you too."

"I'll always love you!" he said, splurging. "Marry me, marry me."

A beast howled from the river. The ram galloped away from the sky, startled by human sound.

"One." John bowed Yolanda's thumb towards him. "Two." He folded up the index finger. "Three." He kissed the nail.

"All you need is love," the radio wailed, as if it were hungry.

"Four," she joined in, bending her fourth finger. "Five," they chimed in unison.

His hand met hers, palm to palm, as if they were sharing a prayer.

"Love," the song snarled, starved. "Love . . . love . . ."

"John, John, you're a pond!" Yolanda teased, straddling him by Merritt Pond.

John was lying on his back; he had just said that when you look up at the sky, you realize nothing that you ever do really matters.

"John's a hon, lying by the pond, having lots of fun," Yolanda punned, nuzzling the hollow of his shoulder.

He stroked her back. "And you're a little squirrel! You know that?"

Yolanda sat up. "Squirrel doesn't rhyme," she explained. "The point's to rhyme with my name."

"Joe-lan-dah?" He quibbled, "What rhymes with Joe-lan-dah?"

"So use Joe. *Doe, roe, buffalo,*" she rhymed. "Okay, now, you try it." She spoke in the voice she had learned from her mother when she wanted a second helping of the good things in life.

"My dear Joe," John began, but put on the spot, he was blocked for a rhyme. He hemmed, he hawed, he guffawed. Finally, he blahhed: "My dear, sweet little squirrel, you mean more to me than all the gold in the world." He grinned at his inadvertent rhyme.

Yo sat up again. "C minus!" She rolled away from him onto the grass. "Where'd you learn to talk Hallmark?"

Hurt, John stood and brushed off his pants as if the grass spears were little annoying bits of Yo. "Not everyone can be as goddam poetic as you!"

She nibbled all up his leg in playful apology.

John pulled her up by the shoulders. "Squirrel." He forgave her.

She winced. Anything but a squirrel. Her shoulders felt furry. "Can I be something else?"

"Sure!" He swept his hand across the earth as if he owned it all: "What do you want to be?"

She turned away from him and scanned the horizon: *trees, rocks, lake, grass, weeds, flowers, birds, sky. . . .*

His hand came from behind her; it owned her shoulder.

"Sky," she tried. Then, the saying of it made it right: "Sky, I want to be the sky."

"That's not allowed." He turned her around to face him. His eyes, she noticed for the first time, were the same shade of blue as the sky. "Your own rules: you've got to rhyme with your name."

"*I*"—she pointed to herself—"rhymes with the *sky!*"

"But not with *Joe!*" John wagged his finger at her. His eyes softened with desire. He placed his mouth over her mouth and ohhed her lips open.

"*Yo* rhymes with *cielo* in Spanish." Yo's words fell into the dark, mute cavern of John's mouth. *Cielo, cielo,* the word echoed. And Yo was running, like the mad, into the safety of her first tongue, where the proudly monolingual John could not catch her, even if he tried.

▮▮▮

"What you need is a goddam shrink!" John's words threw themselves off the tip of his tongue like suicides.

She said what if she did, he didn't have to call them *shrinks*.

"Shrink," he said. "Shrink, shrink."

She said that just because they were different, that was no reason to make her feel crazy for being her own person. He was just as crazy as she was if push came to shove. My God! she thought. I'm starting to talk like him! Push comes to shove! She laughed, still half in love with him. "Okay, okay," she conceded. "We're both crazy. So, let's both go see a shrink." She winced, taking on his language only to convince him.

He shoved her peacemaking hand away. She was the one who was crazy, remember? No way he was going to go be shrunk.

She kissed him in silent persuasion, but she could tell he wasn't convinced.

"I love you. Isn't that enough?" he resisted. "I love you more than it's good for me."

"See! You're the one who's crazy!" she teased.

Already she had begun to mistrust him.

Because his pencils were always sharpened, his clothes always folded before lovemaking. Because he put his knife between the tines of his fork between mouthfuls of the dishes she made that were always just this side of not tasting like they were supposed to—the lasagna like fried eggs, the pudding like frosting. Because he accused her of eating her own head by thinking so much about what people said. Because he believed in the Real World, more than words, more than he believed in her.

But this time it was because he made for-and-against lists before doing anything, and she had discovered the *for-and-against-slash-Joe-slash-wife* list. Number one *for* was *intelligent*; number one *against* was *too much for her own good*. Number two *for* was *exciting*; number two *against* was *crazy*, question mark.

"What does this mean?" She met him at the door with the sheet of his calculations in her hand.

"What's that, Violet?" He had named her Violet after *shrinking* violet when she had started seeing Dr. Payne. John balked the first time Yo told him the doctor's name and fees. "A pain in the bloody pocket all right!" His name became a joke between them. But secretly for luck, Yo called Payne, Doc.

"What the hell you have to make a list of the pros and cons of marrying me for?" Yo followed John into their bedroom, where he began to undress.

"Come on, Violet—"

"Stop violeting me! I hate it when you do that."

"Roses are red, violets are blue," he recited, instead of counting to ten so as not to have two lost tempers in one room.

"You really had to *decide* you loved me?" She read the pro and then the con list out loud, shaking her head as she did so, ducking whenever John grabbed for his list. "Looks to me like the cons have it. Why'd you marry me?"

"My way is to make lists. I could say the same thing to you about words—"

"Words?" She swatted him with his paper. "Words? Wasn't I the one always saying, *Don't say it. Don't say it!* I was the one who tried to keep words out of it."

"I made a list because I was confused. Yes, me, confused!"

John reached for her arm, more as a test of her temper than a touch of desire. She could tell the difference and pushed the hand away.

"Ah, come on, Joe," he said, his voice softening; he folded his tie ruler-size; he dressed the chair-back with his jacket.

She said *no* as sweetly as if it were *yes*. "Nooooh," the word opening her mouth, soft and ripe and ready for him to bite into it.

"Come on, sweetie, tell us what's for supper?" he coaxed. He took her hands and led her towards him.

"Sugared spaghetti with glazed meatballs and honeydew spinach. Sweetie," she taunted, tugging away in play.

He drew her towards him, in play, and pressed his lips on her lips.

Her lips tightened. She set her teeth, top on bottom row, a calcium fortress.

He pulled her forward. She opened her mouth to yell, *No, no!* He pried his tongue between her lips, pushing her words back in her throat.

She swallowed them: *No, no.*

They beat against her stomach: *No, no.* They pecked at her ribs: *No, no.*

"No!" she cried.

"It's just a kiss, Joe. A kiss, for Christ's sake!" John shook her. "Control yourself!"

"Nooooooo!" she screamed, pushing him off everything she knew.

He let her go.

∎∎∎

John and Yo were lying in bed with the lights off because it was too hot to have them on or to be afoot. John's hand slipped down to her hips, beating a beat.

"It's too hot," Yo said, silencing it.

He tried to humor her, playing on a new nickname. "Not tonight, Josephine?" He turned on his side to face her and outlined her features in the dark. He traced the heart line from her chin to her forehead and down again. He kissed her chin to seal the valentine. "Beautiful. Do you know your face is a perfect heart?" He discovered this every time he wanted to make love to her.

The valentine was too hot. "I'm sweating," it moaned. "Don't."

The hand wouldn't listen. The middle finger traced a heart on her lips. The pinkie shaped a heart on the fleshiness above her right breast.

"Please, John!" His fingertips felt like rolling beads of sweat.

"John, please," he echoed. He printed J-o-h-n on her right breast with a sticky finger as if he were branding her his.

"John! It's too hot." She appealed to his common sense.

"John, it's too hot," he whined. The combination of heat and thwarted desire made him nasty.

She stoppered his mouth with her hand. He ignored the violence in the gesture and kissed her moist palm. His eyes lidded with hopefulness, he rolled towards her, his body making a sucking sound as it unglued itself from the bare mattress. The sheets had drooped from their hospital corners; they wilted onto the floor.

John's right hand played piano on her ribs, and his mouth blew a piccolo on her breasts.

"Shit!" she yelled at him, leaping out of bed. "Fuck!" He had forced her to say her least favorite word in the world. She would never ever forgive him for that.

"Ever?" he said, angrily grabbing for her arm in the dark. "Ever?"

Her heart folded, flattened, folded again. The halves fluttered, blinked and opened. Her heart lifted up to the cloud-flowers in the sky.

"Ever!" She slapped him with the sound. "Ever! Ever!" She wished she had her clothes on. It was strange to make absolute statements in the nude.

He came home with a bouquet of flowers that she knew he had paid too much for. They were blue, and she guessed they were irises. *Irises* was her favorite name for flowers, so they had to be irises.

But as he handed them to her, she could not make out his words.

They were clean, bright sounds, but they meant nothing to her.

"What are you trying to say?" she kept asking. He spoke kindly, but in a language she had never heard before.

She pretended she understood. She took a big smell of the flowers. "Thank you, love." At the word *love*, her hands itched so fiercely that she was afraid she would drop the flowers.

He said something happily, again in sounds she could not ascribe meanings to.

"Come on, love," she asked his eyes; she spoke precisely as if she were talking to a foreigner or a willful child. "John, can you understand me?" She nodded her head to let him know that he should answer her by nodding his head if words failed him.

He shook his head, No.

She held him steady with both hands as if she were trying to nail him down into her world. "John!" she pleaded. "Please, love!"

He pointed to his ears and nodded. Volume wasn't the problem. He could hear her. "Babble babble." His lips were slow motion on each syllable.

He is saying *I love you*, she thought! "Babble," she mimicked him. "Babble babble babble babble." Maybe that meant, *I love you too*, in whatever tongue he was speaking.

He pointed to her, to himself. "Babble?"

She nodded wildly. Her valentine hairline, the heart in her ribs and all the ones on her sleeves twinkled like the pinchers of the crab in the sky. Maybe now they could start over, in silence.

When she left her husband, Yo wrote a note, *I'm going to my folks till my head-slash-heart clear*. She revised the note: *I'm needing some space, some time, until my head-slash-heart-slash-soul*—No, no, no, she didn't want to divide herself anymore, three persons in one Yo.

John, she began, then she jotted a little triangle before *John*. *Dear*, she wrote on a slant. She had read in a handwriting analysis book that this was the style of the self-assured. *Dear John, listen, we both know it's not working.*

"*It's?*" he would ask. "*It's*, meaning what?"

Yo crossed the vague pronoun out.

We are not working. You know it, I know it, we both know it, oh John, John, John. Her hand kept writing, automatically, until the page was filled with the dark ink of his name. She tore the note up and confettied it over her head, a rainfall of John's. She wrote him a short memo, *Gone*—then added—*to my folks.* She thought of signing it, Yolanda, but her real name no longer sounded like her own, so instead she scribbled his name for her, *Joe.*

Her parents were worried. She talked too much, yakked all the time. She talked in her sleep, she talked when she ate despite twenty-seven years of teaching her to keep her mouth shut when she chewed. She talked in comparisons, she spoke in riddles.

She ranted, her mother said to her father. Her father coughed, upset. She quoted famous lines of poetry and the opening sentences of the classics. How could anyone remember so much? her mother asked her sullen father. She was carried away with the sound of her voice, her mother diagnosed.

She quoted Frost; she misquoted Stevens; she paraphrased Rilke's description of love.

"Can you hear me!" Doctor Payne held his hands up to his mouth like a megaphone and made believe he was yelling over a great distance. "Can you hear me?"

She quoted to him from Rumi; she sang what she knew of "Mary Had a Little Lamb," mixing it up with "Baa Baa, Black Sheep."

The doctor thought it best if she checked into a small, private facility where he could keep an eye on her. For her own good:

round-the-clock care; nice grounds; arts and crafts classes; tennis courts; a friendly, unintimidating staff, no one in a uniform. Her parents signed the papers—"For your own good," they quoted the nice doctor to her. Her mother held her while a nurse camouflaged in street clothes filled a syringe. Yo quoted from *Don Quijote* in the original; she translated the passage on prisoners into instantaneous English.

The nurse stung her with an injection of tears. Yo went quiet for the first time in months, then burst into tears. The nurse rubbed a tiny cloud on her arm. "Please, honey, don't cry," her mother pleaded with her.

"Let her cry," the doctor advised. "It's a good sign, a very good sign."

"Tears, tears," Joe said, reciting again, *"tears from the depths of some profound despair."*

"Don't worry," the doctor said, coaching the alarmed parents. "It's just a poem."

"But men die daily for lack of what is found there," Yo quoted and misquoted, drowning in the flooded streams of her consciousness.

The signs got better. Yo fantasized about Doc. He would save her body-slash-mind-slash-soul by taking all the slashes out, making her one whole Yolanda. She talked to him about growth and fear and the self in transition and women's spiritual quest. She told him everything except that she was falling in love with him.

Was she ready for her parents? he asked.

Ready for her parents, she echoed.

Her parents stepped into the room, staging happiness. They tested her with questions about the food, the doctor, the weather, and the tile ashtray she had made in arts and crafts therapy.

She offered it to her mother.

Her mother cried. "I shouldn't cry."

"It's a good sign," Yo said, quoting Doc, then caught herself. Quoting others again, a bad sign.

Her father moved to the window and checked the sky. "When are you coming home?" the back asked Yo.

"Whenever she's ready to!" Her mother parted the hair from Yo's forehead.

And the valentine appeared again on the earth.

"I love you guys," Yo improvised. So what if her first original words in months were the most hackneyed. They were her own truth. "I do, I do," she singsang. Her mother looked a little worried as if she had bitten into something sour she had thought would be sweet.

"What happened, Yo?" her mother asked the hand she was patting a little later. "We thought you and John were so happy."

"We just didn't speak the same language," Yo said, simplifying.

"*Ay*, Yolanda." Her mother pronounced her name in Spanish, her pure, mouth-filling, full-blooded name, Yolanda. But then, it was inevitable, like gravity, like night and day, little apple-bites when God's back is turned, her name fell, bastardized, breaking into a half dozen nicknames—"*pobrecita* Yosita"— another nickname. "We love you." Her mother said it loud enough for two people's worth. "Don't we, Papi?"

"Don't we what, Mami?" Yo's father turned.

"Love her," his wife snapped.

"There's no question at all." Papi came towards Mami, or Yo.

"What is love?" Yo asks Dr. Payne; the skin on her neck prickles and reddens. She has developed a random allergy to certain words. She does not know which ones, until they are on the tip of her tongue and it is too late, her lips swell, her skin itches, her eyes water with allergic reaction tears.

The doctor studies her and smells the backs of his fingers. "What do you think it is, Joe? Love."

"I don't know." She tries to look him in the eyes, but she is afraid if she does, he will know, he will know.

"Oh, Joe," he consoles, "we constantly have to redefine the things that are important to us. It's okay not to know. When you find yourself in love again, you'll know what it is."

"Love," Yo murmurs, testing. Sure enough, the skin on her arm erupts into an ugly rash. "I guess you're right." She itches. "It's just scary not to know what the most important word in my vocabulary means!"

"Don't you think that's the challenge of being alive?"

"Alive," she echoes, as if she were relapsing to her old quoting days. Her lips burn. *Alive, love,* words she can use now only at a cost.

Yo's finger traces Doc's body on the metallic screen of the window as if she were making him up. Maybe she will try writing again, nothing too ambitious, a fun poem in the limerick mode. She'll call it, "Dennis' Racket," playing on the double meaning of the word *racket* as well as on his last name, Payne.

Deep within her, something stirs, an itch she can't get to.

"Indigestion," she murmurs, patting her belly. Perhaps not, she thinks, perhaps it is a personality phenomenon: the real Yolanda resurrecting on an August afternoon above the kempt green lawns of this private facility.

Her stomach hurts. She strokes wide I-am-hungry circles on her hospital smock. But the beating inside her is more desperate than hunger, a moth wild inside a lampshade.

It rises, a thrashing of wings, up through her trachea—until Yo retches. How tragic! At her age to die of a broken-heart attack. She tries to laugh, but instead of laughter, she feels ticklish wings unfolding like a fan at the base of her throat. They spread her mouth open as if she were screaming a name out over a great distance. A huge, black bird springs out; it perches on her bureau, looking just like the etching of the raven in Yo's first English poetry book.

She holds out her hand to befriend the dark bird.

It ignores her, and looks philosophically out the window at the darkening sky. Slowly its wings lift and fall, huge arcs rise and collapse, rise and collapse, up and down, up and down. Her hair is blown about her face. Dust hurries to corners. Curtains set sail from their windows.

It flies towards the window. "Oh my God! The screen!" Yo remembers in a moment of suspension of belief. "Have a little faith," she coaches herself, as the dark shape floats easily through the screen like smoke or clouds or figments of any sort. Out it flies, delighting in its new-found freedom, its dark hooded beak and tiny head drooping like its sex between arching wings.

Suddenly—it stops—midair. Delight and surprise are written all over its wing grin. It plummets down towards the sunning man on the lawn. Beak first, a dark and secret complex, a personality disorder let loose on the world, it plunges!

"Oh no," Yo wails. "No, not him!" She had thought that alone at her window on an August afternoon she would be far from where she could do any harm. And now, down it dives towards the one man she most wants immune to her words.

Yo screams as the hooked beak rips at the man's shirt and chest; the white figure on the lawn is a red sop.

Satiated, the dark bird rises and joins a rolling cluster of rain clouds in the northern sky.

Yo bangs on the screen. The man looks up, trying to guess a window. "Who is that?"

"Are you all right?" she cries out, liking her role as unidentified voice from the heavens.

"Who *is* that?" He stands, grabs the beach towel. The blood congeals into a long, red terrycloth rectangle. "Who is it?" He is annoyed at the prolonged guessing game.

"A secret admirer," she trills. "God."

"Heather?" he guesses.

"Yolanda," she murmurs to herself. "Yo," she shouts down at him. Who the hell is Heather, she wonders.

"Oh, Joe!" He laughs, waving his racket.

Her lips prickle and pucker. Oh no, she thinks, recognizing the first signs of her allergy—not my own name!

∎∎∎

The lawn is green and clean and quiet.

"Love," Yo enunciates, letting the full force of the word loose in her mouth. She is determined to get over this allergy. She will build immunity to the offending words. She braces herself for a double dose: *"Love, love,"* she says the words quickly. Her face is one itchy valentine. *"Amor."* Even in Spanish, the word makes a rash erupt on the backs of her hands.

Inside her ribs, her heart is an empty nest.

"Love." She rounds the sound of the word as if it were an egg to put into it. *"Yolanda."* She puts in another one.

She looks up at the thunderclouds. His tennis game is going to be rainchecked, all right. There isn't a sample of blue up there to remind her of the sky. So she says, *"Blue."* She searches for the right word to follow the blue of *blue*. *"Cry . . . why . . . sky . . ."* She gains faith as she says each word, and dares further: *"World . . . squirrel . . . rough . . . tough . . . love . . . enough . . ."*

The words tumble out, making a sound like the rumble of distant thunder, taking shape, depth, and substance. Yo continues: *"Doc, rock, smock, luck,"* so many words. There is no end to what can be said about the world.

The Rudy Elmenhurst Story

▼▲▼▲▼▲▼▲▼▲▼▲▼▲▼▲▼▲▼▲▼▲▼▲▼▲▼▲▼III▼▲▼▲▼

Yolanda

We took turns being the wildest. First one, then another, of us would confess our sins on vacation nights after the parents went to bed, and we had double-checked the hall to make sure there were "no Moors on the coast," an Island expression for the coast being clear. Baby Sister Fifi held that title the longest, though Sandi, with her good looks and many opportunities, gave her some competition. Several times Carla, the responsible eldest, did something crazy. But she always claimed she had done whatever it was she'd done to gain ground for us all. So her reigns of error smacked of good intentions and were never as juicy as Fifi's. To our "Wow, Fifi, how could you?!" Fifi gave us bad-girl grins and the catchphrase from the Alka-Seltzer commercial, "Try it, you'll like it!"

For a brief few giddy years, I was the one with the reputation among my sisters of being the wild one. I suppose it all started at boarding school when I began getting lots of callers, and though none of these beaus lasted long enough to even

be called relationships, my sisters mistook volume for vamp-
ishness. Back in those days I had what one teacher called "a
vivacious personality." I had to look up the word in the dictionary and was relieved to find out it didn't mean I had problems.
English was then still a party favor for me—crack open the
dictionary, find out if I'd just been insulted, praised, admonished, criticized. Those shy prep school guys at mixers with
their endearing long hands and blushing complexions, I could
make them laugh. I could make them believe they had really
engaged a girl in conversation. There wasn't a Saturday afternoon or Sunday after morning service that I didn't have callers.
A bunch of guys from our brother school would come down
the hill and hang out in our parlor to get away from their dor-
mitories, maybe sneaking a cigarette or a swig from a flask on
the walk over. At our front desk, they had to give a girl's name,
and quite a few gave mine. This had nothing to do with my
being attractive in any remarkable way. This was vivaciousness
through and through.

When I went away to college, my vivaciousness ultimately
worked against me. I'd meet someone, conversation would
flow, they'd come calling, but pretty soon afterwards, just as my
heart was beginning to throw out little tendrils of attachment,
they'd leave. I couldn't keep them interested. Why I couldn't
keep them interested was pretty simple: I wouldn't sleep with
them. By the time I went to college, it was the late sixties, and
everyone was sleeping around as a matter of principle. By then,
I was a lapsed Catholic; my sisters and I had been pretty well
Americanized since our arrival in this country a decade before,
so really, I didn't have a good excuse. Why I didn't just sleep

with someone as persistent as Rudy Elmenhurst is a mystery
I'm exploring here by picking it apart the way we learned to do
to each other's poems and stories in the English class where I
met Rudolf Brodermann Elmenhurst, the third.

Rudolf Brodermann Elmenhurst, the third, didn't show up
until ten minutes or so into the class. I, on the other hand, had
been the first to arrive, selecting a place around the seminar
table close to the door, but unfortunately since the table was
round, equally exposed. Others strolled in, the English jocks
at the school. I knew they were special from their jeans and
T-shirts, their knowing, ironic looks when obscure works of
literature were referred to. The girls didn't all knit during class
like education and socio majors. I'd already been writing on my
own for a while, but this was my first English class since I'd
talked my parents into letting me transfer to this co-ed college
last fall.

At my place around the seminar table I unpacked my notebook and every one of the required and recommended texts
which I had already bought, stacking them in front of me
like my credentials. Most of the other students were too cool
to have done anything hasty like purchase the books for the
course. The professor walked in, a young guy in a turtleneck
and jacket, the uniform of the *with it* professors of the day;
he had that edge of the untenured, too eager, too many hand-
outs, too many *please feel free*s on his syllabus, a home number as well as an office number. He called roll, acknowledging
most of the other students with nicknames and jokes and remarks, stumbling over my name and smiling falsely at me, a
smile I had identified as one flashed on "foreign students" to

show them the natives were friendly. I felt profoundly out of place. The only person I seemed to have anything in common with was the absent Rudolf Brodermann Elmenhurst, the third, who also had an odd name and who was out of it because he wasn't there.

We were into the logistics of how to make copies for workshops when a young man walked in, late. He was one of those guys who has just come through a bout of adolescent acne into a scarred, masculine, bad-boy face. A guy to be passed over by the beauties in our class looking for sweethearts. He had an ironic smile on his lips, and—a phrase I haven't heard in a while—bedroom eyes. A guy who would break your heart. But you wouldn't know all this if you went by the sound of his name—which I did, an immigrant's failing, literalism. I assumed he was late because he'd just whizzed in from his small barony somewhere in Austria.

The professor stopped the class. "Rudolf Brodermann Elmenhurst, the third, I presume?" Everybody laughed, this guy too. I admired that from the start, to be able to make such an entrance without blushing and stumbling and arraying the floor with your books and the contents of your pocketbook. He could take a joke, and put on such an ironic self-assured face no one felt bad laughing. The guy looked around and there was a space next to the territory I'd carved out for myself on the table with my pile of books. He came and sat down. I could tell he was looking me over, probably wondering who the hell I was, this intruder upon the sanctuary of English majors.

Class resumed. The professor started explaining again about what all he expected from us in the course. Later, he asked us to write down a response to a little poem he passed around. This guy with a name like a title leaned over and asked if I could lend him a piece of paper and a pen. I felt honored to be the one asked. I tore some pages out of my notebook, then rummaged in my pocketbook for another pen. I looked up with a sorry-eyed expression. "I don't have an extra pen," I whispered, complete sentences for whispers, that's what tells you I was still a greenhorn in this culture. This guy looked at me as if he didn't give a damn about a pen, and I was a fool to think so. It was such an intense look, I felt myself coloring. "That's okay," he mouthed, without really using his voice so I had to lip-read, his full lips puckering as if he were throwing little kisses at me. If I'd known what sexy feelings felt like I would have identified the shiver going down my spine and into my legs. He turned to his other neighbor, who didn't have a pen either. The word went round. Anyone have an extra pen? No one. There was a dearth of pens that day in class.

I sunk my hand back into my pocketbook. I was the proverbially overprepared student; I had to have a standby writing utensil. I felt something promising at the bottom of my purse and pulled it out: it was a teensy pencil from a monogrammed set my mother had given me for Christmas: a box of pencils "my color," red, and inscribed with my so-called name in gold letters: *Jolinda*. (My mother had tried for my own name Yolanda, but the company had substituted the Americanized, southernized *Jolinda*.) *Jolinda*, that's what this pencil used to say. In fact, it was so worn down, only the hook of the *J* was left. We didn't throw things away in my family. I used both sides of a piece of paper. I handed my find over to this guy. He took it and held it up as if to say, "What have we here?" His buddies around us chuckled. I felt shabby for having saved a pencil through so many sharpenings. At the end of class, I fled before he could turn around and give it back to me.

That night there was a knock on my door. I was in my night-gown already, doing our assignment, a love poem in the form of a sonnet. I'd been reading it out loud pretty dramatically, trying to get the accents right, so I felt embarrassed to be caught. I asked who it was. I didn't recognize the name. Rudy? "The guy who borrowed your pencil," the voice said through the closed door. Strange, I thought, ten-thirty at night. I hadn't caught on yet to some of the strategies. "Did I wake you up?" he wanted to know when I opened the door. "No, no," I said, laughing apologetically. This guy I had sworn never to talk to after he had embarrassed me in class, but my politeness-training ran on automatic. I excused myself for not asking him in. "I'm doing my homework." That wasn't an excuse in the circles he ran in. We stood at the door a long moment, he looking over my shoulder into my room for an invitation. "I just came to return your pencil." He held it out, a small red stub in his palm. "Just to return that?" I said, calling his bluff. He grinned, dimples making parenthesis at the corners of his lips as if his smile were a secret between us. "Yeah," he said, and again he had that intent look in his eye, and again he looked over my shoulder. I picked the pencil out of his palm and was glad it had been sharpened to a stub so he couldn't see my name in gold letters inscribed on the side. "Thank you," I said, shifting my weight on my feet and touching the door knob, little moves, polite preliminaries to closing the door.

He spoke up. "Can we have lunch sometime?"

"Sure, we can have lunch, sometime." The way I emphasized *sometime* it was hopeless. I didn't trust this guy, I didn't know how to read him. I had nothing in my vocabulary of human behavior to explain him. Ten minutes late to the first meeting of a class. I knock myself out to get him a pencil and he makes fun. Ten-thirty, he shows up at my door to return it, and asks me to have lunch with him.

"How about tomorrow before class," Rudy said.

"We don't have class tomorrow."

"That gives us time for a long lunch," he answered, real quick on his feet. I couldn't help being impressed. "Okay," I said, shaking my head. "Tomorrow, lunch."

We had lunch the next day, talked until supper, and then had supper. That's the way I remember relationships starting in college—those obsessive marathon beginnings. It was hard to go back to your little dorm room and do your homework after having been so absorbed in someone else. But that's just what I did, I went back and worked on my sonnet. It was a fourteen-line treatise on the nature of love, but the whole time I was writing down my abstractions, I was thinking about how Rudy listened, looking at my mouth, so that it was hard for me to pay attention to what I was saying. How he puckered his lips as if he were kissing each word goodbye. How his hand had touched the small of my back to steer me through a crowd of rowdy frat guys in the dining room. If we admire some people for their originality with words, others for their quirky inter-esting minds, then Rudy had to be admired for his sexy, in-stinctive way with his body. He was the kind of guy who could kiss you behind your ear and make you feel like you'd just had kinky sex.

The next day Rudy didn't turn in his sonnet. After class, while I packed up my luggage of schoolbooks, I heard him talking to the professor how he'd gotten stuck and couldn't think of anything. The professor was likable, it was the sixties, not having your creative juices flowing was understandable. Rudy could have until Monday to turn in his sonnet. We spent most of the weekend together, writing it, actually me writing down lines and crossing them off when they didn't scan or rhyme, and Rudy coming up with the ideas. It was the first pornographic poem I'd ever co-written; of course I didn't know it was pornographic until Rudy explained to me all the word plays and double meanings. "The coming of the spring upon the boughs," was the last line. That meant spring was ejaculating green leaves on the trees; the new crocuses were standing stiff on the lawn on account of they were turned on. I was shocked by all of this. I was a virgin; I wasn't one hundred per cent sure how sex worked. That anyone should put all of this into a poem, a place I'd reserved for deep feelings and lofty sentiments! I wonder now how much of Rudy's gutsiness was a veiled flirtation with me, who was obviously much taken with words and their meanings. I can't say; like I said, I hadn't learned yet some of the strategies one went through. But I was catching on.

I remember the close of each of those weekend nights as a prolonged farewell. It would start by my noting the time, midnight, one, one-thirty, and saying, "Well, I'm going to bed." Rudy would concur, "Me too," but then, he wouldn't move from his place at the foot of my bed next to my desk where I sat writing. It was a teensy dorm room. If you stood up to open the closet, you'd have to negotiate the desk so you wouldn't end up piled on the bed. "Me too." He smiled that ironic smile of his that always made me feel so foolish. Finally, I would just blurt out, "You've got to go, Rudy." He wouldn't say yes or no, or sorry to have stayed too long. He would just look at me with those bedroom eyes, and stand, as if he wasn't going out the door but coming—in both the old sense of the word and the new I had just learned—coming in from the cold outside for a night of lovemaking with his lady-lay. We stood at the door. Then he leaned over and kissed me behind the ear for goodbye.

It was that weekend too at one of our lingering departure scenes that I learned where he'd gotten his odd, ornate name. He'd had this crusty old grandfather he'd never met, from Germany, who'd left his unborn grandchild a trust fund with the proviso that he be named after the old man. "What if you'd been a girl?" I wondered.

"I wouldn't be having so much fun," Rudy said. By this time the kisses had migrated from behind my ear to my neck. I shivered when he put a necklace of them around me before departing.

Our next workshop, no one understood what my sublimated love sonnet was all about, but Rudy's brought down the house. Suddenly, it seemed to me, not only that the world was full of English majors, but of people with a lot more experience than I had. For the hundredth time, I cursed my immigrant origins. If only I too had been born in Connecticut or Virginia, I too would understand the jokes everyone was making on the last two digits of the year, 1969; I too would be having sex and smoking dope; I too would have suntanned parents who took me skiing in Colorado over Christmas break, and I would say things like "no shit," without feeling like I was imitating someone else.

Rudy and I began seeing each other regularly that spring. Besides class, we ate all our meals together, and on weekends, he'd asked me over to his dormitory for parties in his hall. His dorm was next to mine, the two buildings connected by an underground lounge which would fill weekends with good-natured, clean parties, much monitored by security. The real parties went on in the men's dorms. Mostly guys migrated from one room to another, smoking a little dope, drinking a lot. There were the heavy rooms for dropping acid or taking mushrooms. Candles flickered, incense burned in an unsuccessful attempt to cover the pungent smell of marijuana. The Beatles or Bob Dylan or The Mamas and the Papas blasted from stereos. It was a decadent atmosphere for me whose previous experience of dating had been mixers and parlor calls from boys at prep school. I'd go over to Rudy's, but I would drink only a sip or two of the Dixie cup he offered, and I wouldn't dare touch the drugs. I was less afraid of what they would do to my mind than I was of what Rudy might do to my body while I was under the influence.

He pooh-poohed my fears. For one thing, he said, without my consent, he couldn't do anything. "What about rape?" I asked, I wasn't a total bumpkin. "Jesus Christ," he said, shaking his head, disbelieving what he'd let himself in for with me. "I'm not going to fucking rape you!" I was hurt. I'd never been spoken to that way. If my father had heard a man use such obscenities before his daughters, he would have asked him to step outside where he would have defended my honor. Of course, I would have had to do a lot of explaining afterwards about what I was up to at midnight on a Saturday night in a man's dormitory with a cigarette in one hand and a Dixie cup of cheap wine in the other.

After some time in his buddies' rooms sitting in clusters, guys and their dates, Rudy and I migrated to his room. His bed was a mattress on the floor, the American flag draped over it for a coverlet, which even as a non-native, I thought most disrespectful. We would lie down under it, side by side, cuddling and kissing, Rudy's hand exploring down my blouse. But if he wandered any lower, I'd pull away. "No," I'd say, "don't." "Why not?" he'd challenge, or ironically or seductively or exasperatedly, depending on how much he'd imbibed, smoked, dropped. My own answers varied, depending on my current hangups, that's what Rudy called my refusals, hangups. Mostly I was afraid I'd get pregnant. "From getting felt up?" Rudy said with sarcasm. "*Ay*, Rudy," I'd plead, "don't say it that way."

"What do you mean, *don't say it that way*? A spade's a spade. This isn't a goddamn poetry class."

Perhaps if Rudy had acted a little more as if lovemaking were a workshop of sorts, things might have moved more swiftly toward his desired conclusion. But the guy had no sense of connotation in bed. His vocabulary turned me off even as I was beginning to acknowledge my body's pleasure. If Rudy had said, *Sweet lady, lay across my big, soft bed and let me touch your dear, exquisite body*, I might have felt up to being felt up.

But I didn't want to just be in the sack, screwed, balled, laid, and fucked my first time around with a man.

Rudy did have a honeymoon of patience with me at the start. He must have realized from his having had to explain to me so many references in his sonnet that I didn't know, as he put it, worth shit. To me, vagina, cervix, ovary were synonyms. Via diagrams he introduced me to my anatomy; he drew the little egg going down its hour glass into the sticky pocket of the uterus. He calculated when I'd last had my period, when I'd probably ovulated, whether a certain night was a safe time of the month. "You're not going to get pregnant"—all his lessons ended with the same point. But still I didn't want to sleep with him.

"Why? What's wrong with you, are you frigid or something?"

Now there was a worry. I'd just gotten over worrying I'd get pregnant from proximity, or damned by God should I die at that moment, and now I started wondering if maybe my upbringing had disconnected some vital nerves. "I just don't think it's right yet," I said.

"Jesus, we've been going out a month," Rudy said. "When's it going to be all right?"

"Soon," I promised, as if I knew.

But soon didn't happen soon enough. We had progressed to where I stayed the night, waking up early in the morning, not daring to move for fear I'd wake Rudy up in an amorous mood and end up in an early morning discussion of why not now. I scanned the room, as small as mine. Beside his bed I could see the pad with the hourglass shapes. I touched my belly to make sure I was still intact. On the cinderblock wall opposite the bed, Rudy had put up a bulletin board. There were pennants from his ski teams and photos of his family, all lined up on skis on top of a mountain. His parents looked so young and casual—like classmates. My own old world parents were still an embarrassment at parents' weekend, my father with his thick mustache and three-piece suit and fedora hat, my mother in one of her outfits she bought especially to visit us at school, everything overly matched, patent leather purse and pumps that would go back, once she was home, to plastic storage bags in her closet. I marveled at his youthful parents. No wonder Rudy didn't have hangups, no wonder his high school acne hadn't left him riddled with self-doubt, his name hadn't cowed him. They encouraged him, his parents, to have experiences with girls but to be careful. He had told them he was seeing "a Spanish girl," and he reported they said that should be interesting for him to find out about people from other cultures. It bothered me that they should treat me like a geography lesson for their son. But I didn't have the vocabulary back then to explain even to myself what annoyed me about their remark.

I met them only once right before spring break and ironically at the very close of my relationship with Rudy. What happened was the night before break started, Rudy and I had another one of our showdowns in his bed. Rudy turned on the light and sat up on his mattress, his back against the wall. He was nude—I, in my old long-sleeved flannel nightgown Rudy called a *nungown*. From the moonlight and streetlight coming in through the window, I saw his body beautifully sculpted by light and shadows. I did yearn for him, but I yearned for so much more along with that body, which I must have sensed

Rudy would never give me. He was worn down with frustration, he said. I was cruel. I didn't understand that unlike a girl, it was physically painful for guys not to have sex. He thought it was time to call it quits. I was tearful and pleading: I wanted to feel we were serious about each other before we made love. "Serious!" He made a face. "How about fun? Fun, you know?" What did that have to do with this momentous rending of the veil, I wondered. "You mean you don't think sex is fun?" Rudy faced me as if he were finally seeing the root of the problem. "Sure," I lied. "It's fun if it's right." But he shook his head. He had seen through me. "You know," he said, "I thought you'd be hot-blooded, being Spanish and all, and that under all the Catholic bullshit, you'd be really free, instead of all hung up like these cotillion chicks from prep schools. But Jesus, you're worse than a fucking Puritan." I felt stung to the quick. I got up and threw my coat over my nightgown, packed up my clothes, and left the room, half hoping he'd come after me and say he really did love me, he'd wait as long as I needed to after all.

But he didn't slip into my room and under my sheets and hold me tight against the empty, endless night. I hardly slept. I saw what a cold, lonely life awaited me in this country. I would never find someone who would understand my peculiar mix of Catholicism and agnosticism, Hispanic and American styles. Had I been raised with the tradition of stuffed animals, I would have hugged my bear or stuffed dog or rabbit, salting the ragged fur with my tears all night. Instead, I did something that even as a lapsed Catholic I still did for good luck on nights before exams. I opened my drawer and took out the crucifix I kept hidden under my clothes, and I put it under my pillow for the night. This large crucifix had been a "security blanket" I took to bed with me for years after coming to this country. I had slept with it so many nights that finally Jesus had come unglued, and I had to fasten him back on his cross with a rubber band.

Rudy did not come calling the next day. I bumped into him as he was leaving with his parents and I was exiting my dorm to take the taxi to the bus to my parents' in New York. I was sleepy and weepy and did not look back when I felt Rudy's eyes on me. His parents did most of the chatting, talking too slowly to me as if I wouldn't understand native speakers; they complimented me on my "accentless" English and observed that my parents must be so proud of me. When we said goodbye, I did glance up at Rudy, and though I was out in the cold, he was still in the bedroom with the look in his eyes.

After break, I didn't see much of Rudy. He didn't sit by me in class; his workshop poems became unaccountably straightforward and affectionate, out and out love poems. Was he trying to say he really had fallen in love with me? Then why didn't he stop by my room anymore? I started making excuses for him in my head. He had been there, but I wasn't in, and then he was too afraid to leave a note. He was too shy to come sit by me in class. Afraid, shy! Rudolf Brodermann Elmenhurst, the third! How we lie to ourselves when we've fallen in love with the wrong man.

Of course, I could have sought him out and told him how I felt about him. How I was frightened of sex with a man who called it *getting laid*. But I was still in the mode where the guy did all the courting and seeking out. I kept aloof, I waited, I fantasized, misleading myself. The copies of my poems Rudy handed back had on them brief, inane remarks I read and reread for double meaning. "Good," or "I don't get this line" or "Nice details." My copies of his poems went back to him with long, complimentary comments. I became more and more of a recluse, avoiding our old haunts for fear of running into him. But we rarely bumped into each other, and when we did, he always flashed me his cool, ironic smile and greeted me with an offhand, "How you doing?" I, on the other hand, was bristling with so much feeling, I pretended not to have seen him.

Spring dance approached. I don't know why I still thought Rudy would certainly end up going with me. This was the culminating romantic event of the school year on campus, and it seemed to me in my fantasy mode to be the perfect vehicle for our reconciliation. I played it out in my head. We would dance all night. We would talk and confess how much we had missed each other. I would go back to his dorm room with him. We would make love, my first time, and then, almost as if they were the different positions Rudy had told me about, we would screw and fuck and ball and get laid—all the synonyms Rudy preferred for referring to his sex.

In real life, the day approached, and then the night, and I was still hoping. The dance was in the lounge between the two dorms, and so, when I heard the band start up, I wandered down the stairs to a landing where I could watch, unobserved, the partiers. They were a motley group: the conservative frat guy types in tuxedos and their dates in fancy prom dresses, the new hippies in Indian paisleys, jeans and sneakers, and maybe for flare, an incongruous bow tie. I saw the figures dancing luridly, the lights flashing, the band going. They all seemed so caught up in a rhythm I didn't feel a part of. Then I saw Rudy come into the room, a glass in one hand, no doubt full of something spiked with alcohol or acid. My heart would have fluttered if there had been any time between the initial glimpse of his familiar figure and the sight of another figure clinging to him. I could hardly tell what she looked like, who she was, but by the way they were holding on to each other, leaning into each other's bodies, I knew, first off that she was the beloved of his poems, and second of all the beloved of his bed. Within weeks of breaking up with me! I was crushed. For the second time in our relationship, as a kind of closing frame to our first meeting which had ended in my flight out of the classroom, I fled up the stairs.

There's more to the story. There always is to a true story. About five years later, I was in grad school in upstate New York. I was a poet, a bohemian, et cetera. I'd had a couple of lovers. I was on birth control. I guessed I'd resolved the soul and sin thing by lapsing from my heavy-duty Catholic background, giving up my immortal soul for a blues kind of soul. Funky and low-down, the kind inspired by reading too much Carlos Castaneda and Rilke and Robert Bly and dropping acid with a guy who claimed to be my cosmic mate from a past life. I got this call one night from Rudy. His parents lived just down the road, and he had read that I was at the neighboring university in the Alumni Bulletin. Could he come over to see me? Sure, I said. When? Tonight, he said. Tonight was already about nine-thirty. Up to his same old tricks. But I was taken with the guy's persistence. Sure, I said, come on over.

He came on over. Brought an expensive bottle of wine. At

the door, I gave him a friendly hug, but he held on for longer. I got nervous and gabby. His bad boy always drove me to my vivacious good girl. I sat him down in my one chair and started to quiz him on his five years since graduation. He sighed a lot, stretched his legs, cracked his knuckles. Finally, he cut me off, said, Hey, Jesus Christ, I've waited five years, and you look like you've gotten past all your hang-ups. Let's just fuck. I threw him out. It still offended me that he didn't want to do anything but screw me, get that over with. Catholic or not, I still thought it a sin for a guy to just barge in five years later with a bottle of expensive wine and assume you'd drink out of his hand. A guy who had ditched me, who had haunted my sexual awakening with a nightmare of self-doubt. For a moment as I watched him get in his car and drive away, I felt a flash of that old self-doubt.

On the counter, he had left behind the bottle of wine. I had one of those unserious, cheap, grad school corkscrews. Those days we bought gallon jugs of Gallo with pull-out corks or screwed-on lids. I worked the corkscrew in as far as it would go. I wasn't very good at this. Each time I yanked the screw out, I got a spurt of cork, but the stub remained snug in the bottleneck. Finally, I worked it in so I could see the sharp point of the spiral through the glass neck at the bottom of the cork. I put the bottle between my legs and pulled so hard that not only did I jerk the crumbled cork out but I sprayed myself with expensive Bordeaux. "Shit," I thought, "this is not going to wash out." I held the bottle up to my mouth and drew a long messy swallow, as if I were some decadent wild woman who had just dismissed an unsatisfactory lover.

II

▼▲▼▲▼ⅢⅠ▼▲▼▲▼▲▼▲▼▲▼▲▼▲▼▲▼▲▼▲▼▲▼▲▼▲▼▲▼▲▼

1970–1960

A Regular Revolution

▼▲▼▲▼▲▼▲▼▲▼▲▼▲▼▲▼▲▼▲▼▲▼▲▼▲▼▲▼▲▼III▼▲▼▲▼

Carla, Sandi, Yoyo, Fifi

For three-going-on-four years Mami and Papi were on green cards, and the four of us shifted from foot to foot, waiting to go home. Then Papi went down for a trial visit, and a revolution broke out, a minor one, but still.

He came back to New York reciting the Pledge of Allegiance, and saying, "I am given up, Mami! It is no hope for the Island. I will become *un dominican-york.*" So, Papi raised his right hand and swore to defend the Constitution of the United States, and we were here to stay.

You can believe we sisters wailed and paled, whining to go home. We didn't feel we had the best the United States had to offer. We had only second-hand stuff, rental houses in one redneck Catholic neighborhood after another, clothes at Round Robin, a black and white TV afflicted with wavy lines. Cooped up in those little suburban houses, the rules were as strict as for Island girls, but there was no island to make up the difference. Then a few weird things happened. Carla met a pervert. At school, epithets ("spic," "greaseballs") were hurled our way.

Some girlfriend of Sandi's got her to try a Tampax, and Mami found out. Stuff like that, and soon she was writing away to preparatory schools (all-girls ones) where we would meet and mix with the "right kind" of Americans.

We ended up at school with the cream of the American crop, the Hoover girl and the Hanes twins and the Scott girls and the Reese kid who got incredible care packages once a week. You wouldn't be as gauche as to ask, "Hey, are you related to the guy who makes vacuum cleaners?" (You could see all those attachments just by the way Madeline Hoover turned her nose up at you.) Anyhow, we met the right kind of Americans all right, but they didn't exactly mix with us.

We had our own kind of fame, based mostly on the rich girls' supposition and our own silence. García de la Torre didn't mean a thing to them, but those brand-named beauties simply assumed that, like all third world foreign students in boarding schools, we were filthy rich and related to some dictator or other. Our privilege smacked of evil and mystery whereas theirs came in recognizable panty hose packages and candy wrappers and vacuum cleaner bags and Kleenex boxes.

But hey, we might be fish out of water, but at least we had escaped the horns of our dilemma to a silver lining, as Mami might say. It was a long train ride up to our prep school in Boston, and there *were* guys on that train. We learned to forge Mami's signature and went just about everywhere, to dance weekends and football weekends and snow sculpture weekends. We could kiss and not get pregnant. We could smoke and no great aunt would smell us and croak. We began to develop a taste for the American teenage good life, and soon, Island was old hat, man. Island was the hair-and-nails crowd, chaperones, and icky boys with all their macho strutting and unbuttoned shirts and hairy chests with gold chains and teensy gold cruci-fixes. By the end of a couple of years away from home, we had *more* than adjusted.

And of course, as soon as we had, Mami and Papi got all worried they were going to lose their girls to America. Things had calmed down on the Island and Papi had started making real money in his office up in the Bronx. The next decision was obvious: we four girls would be sent summers to the Island so we wouldn't lose touch with *la familia.* The hidden agenda was marriage to homeland boys, since everyone knew that once a girl married an American, those grandbabies came out jabber-ing in English and thinking of the Island as a place to go get a suntan.

The summer plan met with annual resistance from all four of us. We didn't mind a couple of weeks, but a *whole* summer? "Have you got anything better to do?" Mami questioned. Like yes, like *yes* we did, if she and Papi would only let us do it. But working was off-limits. (A boss hiring a young girl was after one thing only. Never mind if his name was Hoover.) Summer time was family time. Big time family time, a whole island of family, here a cousin, there a cousin, everywhere we turned a kissing cousin was puckering up at us.

Winters whenever one of us got out of line, Mami and Papi would march out the old "Maybe what you need *right now* is some time back home to help set you straight." We'd shape up pretty quick, or pretend to. Sometimes the parents upped the ante. It wouldn't be just the bad daughter who'd be shipped back, but *all four girls.*

By the time the three oldest were in college—we all started

out at the same all-girls one, of course—we had devised as sophisticated and complicated a code and underground system as Papi had when he and his group plotted against the dictator. The parents' habit was to call us on Friday or Saturday nights around ten right before the switchboard closed. We took turns "on duty" to catch those calls. But Mami and Papi were like *psychic*. They *always* directed the first call to the missing daughter, and when she wasn't in, they'd asked to talk to another missing daughter. The third, on-duty daughter would get the third call, in which the first question would be, "Where are your sisters?" At the library studying or in so-and-so's room getting tutored on her calculus. We kept most things from the old people, but sometimes they caught on and then we rotated the hot seat.

Fifi was on for smoking in the bathroom. (She always ran the shower, as if smoking were a noisy activity whose hullabaloo she had to drown out.)

Carla was on for experimenting with hair removal cream. (Mami threw a fit, saying that once you got started on that road, there was no stopping—the hairs would grow back thicker, uglier each time. She made it sound like drinking or drugs.)

Yoyo was on for bringing a book into the house, *Our Bodies, Our Selves*. (Mami couldn't quite put her finger on what it was that bothered her about the book. I mean, there were no men in it. The pictures all celebrated women and their bodies, so it wasn't technically about sex as she had understood it up to then. But there were women exploring "what their bodies were all about" and a whole chapter on lesbians. Things, Mami said, examining the pictures, to be ashamed of.)

Sandi was on when a visiting aunt and uncle dropped in for a visit at college early Sunday morning. (She wasn't back yet from her Saturday night calculus tutorial.)

It was a regular revolution: constant skirmishes. Until the time we took open aim and won, and our summers—if not our lives—became our own.

That last summer we were shipped home began like all the others. The night before the trip, we sisters stayed up late packing and gabbing. Sandi called her boyfriend long distance and, with her back turned to us, whispered things like "Me too." We got pretty punchy, imitating aunts and uncles and cousins we would be seeing the next day. Maybe it was a way of getting even with people who would have power over us all summer. We played with their names, translating them into literal English so they sounded ridiculous. Tía Concha became Aunt Conchshell, and Tía Asunción, Aunt Ascension; Tío Mundo was Uncle World; Paloma, our model cousin, turned into Pigeon, and for spite we surnamed her, accurately, Toed.

Around midnight, Mami came fussing down the hall to our bedrooms in those fuzzy slippers of hers with the bobby-socks and a roller cap on her head. "That's enough, girls," she said. "You have all morning tomorrow. You need your beauty dreams."

We turned our faces glum to reaffirm the forced nature of this trip.

And she gave us the little pep talk on family and how important roots were. Finally she went back to bed, and to sleep, or so we thought. We turned the volume down but stayed up talking.

Fifi held up a Baggy with dregs of greenish brown weed inside. "Okay, vote time," she said. "Do I or don't I take it."

"Don't do it," Carla said. Her nightwear was the antithesis of Mami's: in fact, Carla looked almost dressed up in her prim cotton nightgown. A yellow ribbon held her hair back from her face. "If we're caught at Customs we're in a shitload of trouble. And remember, now that Uncle World's in government, it would be all over the newspapers."

"Carla, you're such a priss," Sandi taunted her. "For one thing, now that Tío is a V.I.P., we won't have to go through Customs. Security will whisk us off, the Misses Garcías de la Torres." She waved her hand with a flourish as if she were introducing us to King Arthur's court.

"You could try the Kotex trick," Yoyo suggested, thinking it would be nice to have a little pot to smoke when things on the Island got dull. Pile a layer of Kotex above whatever you were trying to hide, the Island cousins once advised her, and the officers would shy from probing.

"Who uses Kotex anymore?" Fifi asked. "Would Tampax work?"

"Those guys probably wouldn't know what it was." Sandi slid one out of the box she was taking. She pantomined an investigation, ripping off the paper envelope and trying to bite off the end like our uncles did their cigars.

We burst out in the loud laughter we'd kept at bay since Mami exited. Soon enough, there were footsteps down the hall. Just before the door swung open, Fifi, who was still holding the Baggy of grass, tossed it behind a bookcase, where it lay forgotten in the haste of our final packing next morning before our noon plane.

Not three weeks on the Island had gone by when Mami called. Tía Carmen came padding out to the pool to tell us our mother was on her way from New York and that she intended to have a *long* talk with us. Tía admitted that yes, something was amiss, but she had promised our mother not to say what. Tía was superreligious, and we knew we wouldn't get it out of her if she'd given her word. By way of consolation, she counseled us to "examine your consciences."

We reviewed our recent sins with our girl cousins until late that night.

"All I can think of," Yoyo offered, "was they opened our mail."

"Or maybe our grades came?" Fifi suggested.

"Or the phone bill," Sandi added. Her boyfriend lived in Palo Alto.

"I think it's really unfair to leave us hanging." Carla's head was fretted with clips and bobbypins as if she were wired up for an experiment. Her hair turned frizzy on the Island, and every night she ironed it, then rolled it in a "tubie," using her head as large roller.

"Examine your consciences," Sandi said in a boogeyman voice.

"I have, I have," Fifi joked, "and the problem isn't I can't find anything to worry about but that I find so much." We spent the rest of the evening confessing to our giggly, over-chaperoned girl cousins the naughtinesses we had committed up in the home of the brave and the land of the free.

That almost-empty Baggy of grass behind the bureau never crossed our minds. Mami had a maid from the Island who lived with us in the States. She, Primitiva, had found the stash. Primi herself used Baggies in her practice of layman's *santería*, concocting powders and potions to make this ache or that rival woman go away. But why the girls would have a Baggy of oregano in their room was *un misterio* she deferred to her mistress to solve.

As we later reconstructed it from what Primi said, Mami's first reaction was anger that we had broken her rule against eating in our bedrooms. (Oregano qualified as food?) But when she opened the Baggy and took a sniff and poked her finger in and tasted a pinch and had Primitiva do the same, they were flabbergasted. The dreaded and illegal marijuana that was lately so much in the news! Mami was sure of it. And here she'd been, worried sick about protecting our virginity since we'd hit puberty in this land of wild and loose Americans, and vice had entered through an unguarded orifice at the other end.

Immediately, she contacted Tío Pedro, a psychiatrist "uncle by affection" with a practice in Jackson Heights. Tío Pedro was always consulted when one or the other of us daughters got into trouble. He identified the oregano most surely as grass, and got Mami free-associating about what else we might be up to. By the time she touched down on the Island forty-eight hours after finding the Baggy, we were all addicts, fallen women with married lovers and illegitimate babies on the way. One teensy hope she held on to was that a workman or a house guest had left the pot there. She had come to find out the truth, shielding Papi from the news and the heart attack he would surely die of if he knew.

Since we were caught by surprise, we didn't have a plan. At first, Carla made a vague attempt to discredit Tío Pedro by revealing how he always ended our sessions with long hugs and a pat on the butt. "He's a lech," she accused. "And besides, what does Saint Peter know of grass?"

"Grass?" Mami scowled. "This is marijuana."

Carla held her tongue.

Before we could come up with a better approach, Fifi surprised us by admitting that the Baggy was hers. Instantly, we all rallied to her guilty side. "It's mine too," Yoyo claimed. "And mine," Carla and Sandi chimed in.

Mami's eyes shifted from one to the other, each cry of *Mine!* confirming another bad daughter. She wore her tragic look of the Madonna with delinquent children. "All of you?" she asked in a low, shocked voice.

Fifi stepped forward. "I tell you it was me who put it there, I did it, and they"—she pointed to us—"they had nothing to do with it."

Technically, she was right. It was her Baggy. The rest of us had had dope only when our boyfriends rolled a joint or when, in a party of friends, a cigarette made its rounds, everyone drawing a toke. Still, there was something untoward about Fifi taking all the blame since our habit had been to share the good *and* the bad that came our way. She gave Mami an impassioned apology and argument—her sisters should not be punished along with her. Oddly enough, Mami consented. She asked us, though, not to tell Papi unless we wanted wholesale Island confinement. It's possible that Mami had her own little revolution brewing, and she didn't want to blow the whistle on her girls and thus call attention to herself.

Recently, she had begun spreading her wings, taking adult courses in real estate and international economics and business management, dreaming of a bigger-than-family-size life for herself. She still did lip service to the old ways, while herself nibbling away at forbidden fruit.

Anyhow, she agreed that the three oldest of us could go back to our school at the end of the summer. Fifi was given the choice of either staying on the Island for a year at Tía Carmen's or going back to the States, but not to her boarding school. She would have to live at home with Mami and Papi and attend the local Catholic school.

Fifi opted to stay. Better one of a dozen chaperoned cousins, she figured, than home alone with Mami and Papi breathing down her neck and Peter Pan with his hand on her ass. "Besides, I wanna try it out here. Maybe I'll like it," Fifi said, defending her choice to us. As the youngest of the four, she had had the least chance to bond to the Island before our abrupt exile almost a decade before. "And besides, the States aren't making me happy."

"You're in the middle of your adolescence, for God's sake!" Carla had decided to major in psych and had been giving all of us frequent free analysis. "You're supposed to be unhappy and confused. It means you're normal, well adjusted. This is just going to make it worse, I guarantee it!"

"Maybe it won't, maybe I'll surprise you," said Fifi.

"You'll be climbing these walls before the year is out," Carla warned.

We looked beyond the pool at the high stone wall. Down a ways one of the maids had draped her underclothes on the wall. In the cup of a brassiere, his little head hardly visible, a lizard was blowing out his throat as if he had just taken a toke and were holding it in until the small dazed cells of his brain zinged a hit.

By Christmas, we are wild for news of Fifi's exile. From Mami we hear that our sister is beautifully acclimated to life on the Island and taking classes in shorthand and typing at the Ford Foundation trade school. She's also seeing someone nice.

This, of course, is dangerous for the rest of us. With one successfully repatriated daughter, Papi might yank us all out of college and send us back. Not to mention that it's out and out creepy that Fifi, the maverick, is *so* changed. Carla, in fact, says it's a borderline schizoid response to traumatic cultural displacement.

The minute we step off the plane, we see Mami has not exaggerated. Fifi, there to meet us at the airport, is a jangle of bangles and a cascade of beauty parlor curls held back on one side very smartly by a big gold barrette. She has darkened her lashes with black mascara so that her eyes stand out as if she were slightly startled at her good luck. Fifi—who used to wear her hair in her trademark, two Indian braids that she pinned up in the heat like an Austrian milkmaid. Fifi—who always made a point of not wearing makeup or fixing herself up. Now she looks like the *after* person in one of those *before-after* makeovers in magazines. "*Elegante,*" Mami has said of Fifi's new style, but on our lips are other epithets. "She's turned into a S.A.P.," Yoyo mutters. A Spanish-American princess.

"My God, Fifi," we say in greeting, looking her over.

"Where's the party?" Sandi teases.

"If you can't say something nice—" Fifi begins, defensively. Her little patent leather pocketbook plaintively matches her pumps.

"Hey, hey!" We give her one of our huddle hugs. "Don't lose your sense of humor on us, come on! You look great!"

"Don't muss my hair," Fifi fusses, patting it down as if it were a hat. But she smiles. "Guess what, you guys?" She looks from one to the other of us.

"You're seeing someone nice," we chorus.

Fifi is taken aback, then laughs. "Ye Olde Grapevine, huh?" We nod. She goes on to explain that her someone nice is a cousin, Manuel Gustavo. "A *nice* cousin," she is quick to add.

"A cousin?" We know most of our cousins, and Manuel Gustavo is a new one on us.

"A closet cousin," Fifi says, searching her purse for a photo. "One of the illegitimates."

Right on! We sisters give each other the V for victory sign. It's still a guerrilla revolution after all! We were afraid that Fifi was caving in to family pressure and regressing into some nice third-world girl. But no way. She's still Ye Olde Fifi.

Fifi tells us the full story of Manuel Gustavo. His father is our father's brother, Tío Orlando, who has a half dozen children from *una mujer del campo*, a woman from the countryside around one of his ranches. Of course, Tía Fidelina, our uncle's wife, who is sweet and dedicated to *La Virgen*, "knows noth-

ing" about Tío Orlando's infidelities. But now that Manuel
Gustavo is at the manger door, so to speak, his father has to
come up with some explanation just short of immaculate con-
ception. Who is this young man who is seeing her niece? Tía
Fidelina wants to know. Where does he come from? What's his
family name? Another uncle, Ignacio, offers to take Manuel
Gustavo on as his own illegitimate son. He's never married
and is always getting ragged about being homosexual. So two
men are off the hook with one bastard. According to Fifi, the
alta sociedad, the high-class ladies of the oligarchy who form
a kind of club, not unlike a country club, are delighted by this
juicy bit of gossip.

"They have nothing better to do," she concludes, drawing up
her chin, above it all.

We take Manuel on as our own favorite cousin.

He looks like a handsome young double for Papi, and a lot
like us, the family eyebrows, the same high cheekbones, the
full, generous mouth. In short, he could be the brother we
never had. When he roars into the compound in his pickup,
all four of us run down the driveway to greet him with kisses
and hugs.

"Girls," Tía Carmen says, frowning, "that's no way to greet
a man."

"Yeah, you guys," Fifi agrees. "Get off him, he's mine!"

We laugh, but we keep fussing over him, waiting on him as
if we've never been to the States or read Simone de Beauvoir or
planned lives of our own.

But, as the days go by, Fifi grows withdrawn and watchful.

Daily, there are little standoffs and pouts and cold shoulders because one of us has put her arm around Manuel or has gotten involved in a too-lengthy conversation with him about the production of sugar cane.

To reassure her, we tone ourselves down and become more reserved with Manuel. From this new distance, we begin to get the long view, and it's not so pretty. Lovable Manuel is quite the tyrant, a mini Papi and Mami rolled into one. Fifi can't wear pants in public. Fifi can't talk to another man. Fifi can't leave the house without his permission. And what's most disturbing is that Fifi, feisty, lively Fifi, is letting this man tell her what she can and cannot do.

One day Fifi, who rarely reads anymore, becomes absorbed in one of the novels we brought along, and not a trashy one for once. Manuel Gustavo arrives, and when no one answers the door, comes in the back way. In the patio, all four of us are draped over lawn chairs reading. Fifi sees him and her face lights up. She is about to put aside her book, when Manuel Gustavo reaches down and lifts it out of her hands.

"This," Manuel Gustavo says, holding the book up like a dirty diaper, "is junk in your head. You have better things to do." He tosses the book on the coffee table.

Fifi pales, though her two blushed-on cheeks blush on. She stands quickly, hands on her hips, eyes narrowing, the Fifi we know and love. "You have no right to tell me what I can and can't do!"

"¿Que no?" Manuel challenges.

"No!" Fifi asserts.

One by one we three sisters exit, cheering Fifi on under our breaths. A few minutes later we hear the pickup roar down the driveway, and Fifi comes sobbing into the bedroom.

"Fifi, he asked for it," we say. "Don't let him push you around. You're a free spirit," we remind her.

But within the hour, Fifi is on the phone with Manuelito, pleading for forgiveness.

We nickname him M.G., a make of car we consider slightly sleazy, a car one of our older cousins might get his Papi to buy him to impress the Island girls. We rev up imaginary motors at the mention of his name. He's such a tyrant! Rrrrmm. He's breaking Fifi's spirit! Rrrrmm-rrrmm.

A few days after the book episode, Manuel Gustavo arrives for the noon meal, and since Fifi is still at her Spanish class, we decide to have a little talk with him.

Yoyo begins by asking him if he's ever heard of Mary Woll-stonecraft. How about Susan B. Anthony? Or Virginia Woolf?

"Friends of yours?" he asks.

For the benefit of an invisible sisterhood, since our aunts and girl cousins consider it very unfeminine for a woman to go around demonstrating for her rights, Yoyo sighs and all of us roll our eyes. We don't even try anymore to raise conscious-ness here. It'd be like trying for cathedral ceilings in a tunnel, or something. Once, we did take on Tía Flor, who indicated her large house, the well-kept grounds, the stone Cupid who had been re-routed so it was his mouth that spouted water. "Look at me, I'm a queen," she argued. "My husband has to go to work every day. I can sleep until noon, if I want. I'm going to protest for my *rights*?"

Yoyo turns Manuel's interview over to Carla, who's good at befriending with small talk. Yoyo calls it her therapist "softening-them-up-for-the-spill" mode. "Manuel, why do you feel so upset when Fifi is on her own?" Carla's manner is straight out of her Psych 101 textbook.

"Women don't do that here." Manuel Gustavo's foot, posed on his knee, shakes up and down. "Maybe you do things different in your United States of America." His tone is somewhere between a tease and a taunt. "But where does it get those *gringas*? Most of them divorce or stay *jamona*, with nothing better to do than take drugs and sleep around."

Sandi revs, "Rrrmm, rrrmm."

"Manuel," Carla pleads. "Women do have rights here too, you know. Even Dominican law grants that."

"Yes, women have rights," Manuel Gustavo agrees. A wry smile spreads on his face: he is about to say something clever. "But men wear the pants."

The revolution is on. We have one week left to win the fight for our Fifi's heart and mind.

Nights on the Island we go out, the gang of cousins, to the Avenida. It's the main drag, happily crowded with cars and horse-drawn buggies for tourists who want to ride in moonlight by the seashore. Hotels and night spots flood the sky with so much light, you can make out people's faces as you cruise by. The gossip mill turns. Marianela was out on Utcho with Claudio. Margarita looks too pregnant for only two months since the wedding. Get a load of Pilar's miniskirt with those huge legs of hers, you'd think some people would check their mirrors, geez.

We distribute ourselves in several cars, driven by boy cousins. We don't want stool pigeon chauffeurs along. We're off to the movies or to Capri's for an ice cream and just hanging out, the boys much exhorted to take care of the ladies. As the oldest, Carla must ride with Fifi in Manuel's pickup, *la chaperona*, at least until we're off compound grounds. Then she is dropped off at Capri's to join the rest of us. Fifi and Manuel steal off for some private time from the watchful eyes of the extended family. On these drives, they usually end up parking somewhere, only to neck and stuff, according to Fifi. She has admitted that the stuff is getting more and more to the point, and the problem is that she has no contraception. Anyone on the Island she might go to for pills or a diaphragm would know who she is and would surely rat on her to the family. And Manuel won't wear a rubber.

"He thinks it might cause impotence," Fifi says, smiling sweetly, cherishing his cute male ignorance.

"Jesus, Fifi!" Sandi sighs. "Tell him that *not* using one most surely can cause pregnancy." A pregnant Fifi would have to do what is always done in such cases on the Island—marry immediately and brace herself for the gossip when her "premature baby" comes out fat and fully grown.

We keep warning her and worrying over her until she promises us—on pain of our betrayal: "We'll tell on you, we will!"—that she won't have sex with Manuel unless she gets some contraception first. Which is highly unlikely. Where can she go for it on this fishbowl island?

But her word doesn't count for much after what happens one night.

■■■

We're sitting around at Capri's that night, bored. Fifi and Manuel have already taken off, and we've got a couple of hours to kill before they get back and we can return to the compound. We start brainstorming what to do: we can drive to Embassy Beach and go skinny-dipping. We can try to find our cousin of a cousin, Jorge, who often has a couple of joints and knows a voodoo priest who will tell us our futures after performing a scary animal sacrifice.

Our official escort Mundín vetoes both ideas. He's got a better one. We pile into his car, his three American cousins and his sister Lucinda, nagging him about what he's got in mind. He grins wickedly and drives us a little ways out of town to Motel Los Encantos, "motel" being the Island euphemism for a whore house. He pulls right in like he knows the place, honks the horn, asks the gatekeeper for a cabin, then heads for the one he's assigned. The garage door is opened by a waiting yardboy. Once we are out of the car, the yardboy pulls the garage door down and hands Mundín the key to the connected cabin.

"That way no one can tell who's here," Mundín explains in English. "This is the high-class motel, *la crème de la crème*, not to get too gross. Everyone would know everyone else's cars here." Mundín unlocks the door to the cabin and stands aside to let the ladies in. An unabashed king-size bed made up with a flowered bedspread stands in the dead center of the room. There are a couple of rolled pillows with tassels at the head of the bed. Covered with the same wishy-washy flowered material as the spread, the pillows evoke an Arab engineer more than a lord and master of the harem.

"Is this all?" we say, disappointed.

"What'd ya expect?" Mundín is nonplussed at our lack of proper titillation. After all, he has risked getting into a lot of trouble to show us the naughty face of the Island. Nice girls at a whore house! His mother would kill him!

Sandi puts her arm around Mundín and bumps hips. She is doing her Mae West imitation just as the yardboy comes in with a tray of rum and Cokes. He keeps his eyes on the tile floor as he goes from one to the other, proffering refreshments, as if to reassure us there will be no witnesses. As soon as he exits, we laugh. "I wonder what he thinks?" Carla shakes her head, just imagining it. Mundín wiggles his eyebrows. "How many taboos can we break here? Let's see." He enumerates: incest, group sex, lesbian sex, virgin sex—

"Virgin sex? Who're you talking about?" his sister Lucinda challenges with a hand on her hip.

"Yeah," we concur, hands on our hips, facing him, a line-up of feminists.

Mundín's eyes do a double blink. For all his liberal education in the States, and all his sleeping around there and here, and all his eager laughter when his Americanized cousins recount their misadventures, his own sister has to be pure. "Let's go." He hurries us after we finish our rum and Cokes. As we're backing out of our garage, a pickup passes behind us on the motel drive.

"Hey!" Yoyo cries out. "Is that Fifi and Manuel?"

Mundín chuckles. "Hey, hey! Way to go."

"Way to go, way to schmo," Sandi snaps. "That's our baby sister going in there with a guy who thinks condoms cause impotence."

"Go back in there after them!" Carla orders Mundín.

"She's got her rights too." Mundín laughs pointedly as he drives through the gate, which the boy is already closing on our taillights.

"This isn't funny," Carla warns as we consult in the bathroom back at Capri's. "She's not going to come back home on her own, she's brainwashed."

Sandi concurs. "I mean, they wouldn't need a motel room if they weren't sleeping together."

"After she promised," Carla says, nodding, aggrieved.

There, among the pink vanities with baskets of little towels and talcum powder and brushes, we come up with our plot. We reach out our hands and seal our pact. Yoyo rallies us with "¡Que viva la revolución!" On top of our motel rum and Cokes, we've had a few of Capri's famous frozen daiquiris. The young maid who has been listening to our English gibberish offers us a pink perfumed hand towel, which Sandi accepts and waves like the flag for our side.

Our last Saturday night on the Island, the compound folks sit on Tía Carmen's patio, reminiscing. Periodically, family stops by to say goodbye to our parents and deliver the packets of letters and bills they want mailed in the States. Now that Tío Mundo is in government, there are always other cabinet members and old friends coming over to shoptalk politics and ask for favors. The patio is sex segregated—the men sit to one side, smoking their cigars and tinkling their rum drinks. The women lounge on wicker armchairs by the wall lamps, exclaiming over whatever there is to be exclaimed about.

The young people take off for the Avenida, promising to be home early. Tonight, it's the regulars, Lucinda, Mundín, and Fifi and Manuel, of course, and the three of us. Carla does the usual chaperone duty in the pickup and then gets dropped off at Capri's. "They're having some big fight," she confesses when she joins us.

"What now?" Sandi asks.

"Same old thing," Carla sighs. "Fifi spent too much time talking to Jorge and her skirt is too short and her jersey too tight, blah, blah, blah."

"Rmm, rmm," Sandi and Yoyo rev.

Mundín laughs. "Serves you girls right."

We narrow our eyes at him. When he's in the States, where he went to prep school and is now in college, he's one of us, our buddy. But back on the Island, he struts and turns macho, needling us with the unfair advantage being male here gives him.

As usual, we're to wait for the lovers at Capri's. Twenty minutes before our curfew, they'll pick up Carla, and we'll all head home again like one big happy group of virgin cousins. But tonight, as we've agreed, we're staging a coup on the same Avenida where a decade ago the dictator was cornered and wounded on his way to a tryst with his mistress. It was a plot our father helped devise but did not carry through, since by then we had fled to the States. Tonight, we are blowing the lovers' cover. First step is to get Mundín to drive us home. Male loyalty is what keeps the macho system going, so Mundín will want to protect Manuel.

Lucinda works a version of her Kotex custom officer trick.

She complains to her brother that she's just gotten her period and needs to go home. "I've got terrible cramps," Lucinda moans.

"Can't you take something for it?" Mundín asks, inconvenienced and awed by the mysteries of the female body.

Lucinda nods. "It's at home, though."

Mundín shakes his head at his sister. Nevertheless, he is her protector. Ever since her quip at the motel, he's been watching her closely. "Okay, okay, I'll take you." He turns to us, his cousins. "You guys have to stay here and cover for Manuel."

"We can't stay here without you," we remind him. Rule *número uno*: Girls are not left unescorted in public. "We'll get in trouble, Mundín."

Mundín scowls. This is unexpected prissiness from us. "Well, I'll tell them I left you here with some cousins who showed. Then, I'll come back for you. By then Fifi and Manuel should be done."

Should be done. A cannon shot across the bow. No time for further delay. We smile three churlish Che Guevara smiles. "We're going with you."

"But what about Fifi and Manuel?" Mundín is flabbergasted. If everyone except Fifi and Manuel shows up at the compound, the lovers will be in deep trouble. Rule *número dos*: Girls are not to be left unchaperoned with their *novios*.

"We came with you, we stay with you. *We* don't want to get into trouble." Our good-girl voices don't quite convince our cousin.

"I won't do it!" Mundín folds his hands on the table.

We remind him of last night's outing to the motel. Should we mention that to his father? We know what sword of Damocles hangs over his head—an electric razor for the military school crewcut Mundín would have to get. For just as we, his American cousins, are threatened with Island confinement, military school is what's in store for Mundín should he step out of line.

He looks us straight in the eyes. "What are you girls up to?" he fires at us. We meet his look with bulletproof smiles, stone faces on which, with his myopic macho vision, he can't make out the writing on the walls.

The compound driveway looks like a Mercedes Benz car lot. A Jeep and two Japanese cars say some of the younger generation are also here. Lucinda spots Tía Fidelina and Tío Orlando's pale salmon Mercedes. "This is going to be *muy* interesting," she whispers.

The patio is packed with relatives. Mundín hurries over to the men's side, knowing the first bomb will explode among the women. We sisters go on our rounds, kissing all the aunts. Tía Fidelina's milky dark eyes are almost totally sightless. "And which one is the *novia*?" she asks, squinting at her nieces.

"Yes," Mami agrees. "Where is Fifi?"

"With Manuel," Sandi offers smoothly. Her tone implies we have no problem with that.

"*Where* are they?" Mami asks more emphatically.

Carla shrugs. "How should she know?"

There is an embarrassed silence in which the words *her reputation* are as palpable as if someone had hung a wedding dress in the air. Tía Carmen sighs. Tía Fidelina unfolds her fan of overly-gorgeous roses. Tía Flor smiles wildly at the rest of us and asks us if *we* had a nice time. Mami looks past the crowd at Papi, over there happily exchanging dictatorship stories with the other men.

Steely-faced, she stands up and nods for us to follow her. The three of us single-file behind Mami into Tía Carmen's bedroom again, the scene of Mami's courtroom. Tía comes along, counseling patience.

Once the door is closed, Mami loses her temper. First, she berates Carla, who as the oldest was in charge and had orders to stick with Mundín and Fifi as their in-car chaperone. Then, we get chapter and verse on being bad daughters. Finally, she swears, in front of our aunt, that Fifi is going back with us. "If your father should find out!" Our mother shakes her head, reviewing the consequences. Rather anticlimactically, she adds, "A disgrace to the family."

"*Ya, ya.*" Tía Carmen lifts her hand for her sister-in-law to stop. "These girls have lived so long away, they have gotten American ways."

"American ways!" Mami cries. "Fifi's been living here for six months. That's no excuse."

"There must be an explanation." Tía Carmen changes course. "Let's not anticipate where the coconut will fall when the hurricane hasn't hit yet," she advises.

Mami shakes her head conclusively. "If she can't behave herself here, she goes back with us, period! I'm not going to send them anymore to cause trouble!"

Tía Carmen puts her arms around us. "Don't forget, these are my girls, too. And they're good girls, no trouble at all. What would I do"—she looks up at us—"if I didn't get to have them with me every year?"

We look at each other, and then, drop our gaze to hide our confusion. We are free at last, but here, just at the moment the gate swings open, and we can fly the coop, Tía Carmen's love revives our old homesickness. It's like this monkey experiment Carla read about in her clinical psych class. These baby monkeys were kept in a cage so long, they wouldn't come out when the doors were finally left open. Instead, they stayed inside and poked their arms through the bars for their food, just out of reach.

It is close to midnight when we hear the pickup laboring up the driveway. Out on the patio, the visiting relatives have left, and only the compound folks remain, talking in low, preoccupied voices. In our bedroom, we have been defending ourselves to each other. We all know Fifi was headed for trouble with M.G. "She's only sixteen," we keep exclaiming. She thought she could be all Island. We know better.

But still, we feel rotten when a pale Fifi marches into our bedroom awhile later after a grueling interrogation in Tía Carmen's bedroom.

She says nothing to us but opens the closet and begins packing all her clothes. For a moment we panic. Is she going to elope with Manuel?

"What are you doing, Fifi?" Yoyo asks.

Fifi continues to pack from a pile of clothes she has emptied out of her drawers onto the floor. Silence.

"Fifi?" Carla touches her shoulder. "What happened?" She means, of course, out in the patio or even—since the dull, absent look on Fifi's face implies more—before.

Fifi turns to us, her eyes are red and weepy. "Traitors," she says. The sound of her suitcase latching closed gives the accusation an eerie finality. At the door, she raises her chin proudly, and then we hear her steps echoing down the hall to our cousin Carmencita's room.

We look at each other as if to say, "She'll get over it." Meaning Manuel, meaning her fury at us, meaning her fear of her own life. Like ours, it lies ahead of her like a wilderness just before the first explorer sets foot on the virgin sand.

Daughter of Invention

▼▲▼▲▼▲▼▲▼▲▼▲▼▲▼▲▼▲▼▲▼▲▼▲▼▲▼▲▼III▼▲▼▲▼

Mami, Papi, Yoyo

For a period after they arrived in this country, Laura García tried to invent something. Her ideas always came after the sightseeing visits she took with her daughters to department stores to see the wonders of this new country. On his free Sundays, Carlos carted the girls off to the Statue of Liberty or the Brooklyn Bridge or Rockefeller Center, but as far as Laura was concerned, these were men's wonders. Down in housewares were the true treasures women were after.

Laura and her daughters would take the escalator, marveling at the moving staircase, she teasing them that this might be the ladder Jacob saw with angels moving up and down to heaven. The moment they lingered by a display, a perky saleslady approached, no doubt thinking a young mother with four girls in tow fit the perfect profile for the new refrigerator with automatic defrost or the heavy duty washing machine with the prewash soak cycle. Laura paid close attention during the demonstrations, asking intelligent questions, but at the last minute saying she would talk it over with her husband. On the drive home, try as they might, her daughters could not engage their mother in conversation, for inspired by what she had just seen, Laura had begun inventing.

She never put anything actual on paper until she had settled her house down at night. On his side of the bed her husband would be conked out for an hour already, his Spanish newspapers draped over his chest, his glasses propped up on his bedside table, looking out eerily at the darkened room like a disembodied bodyguard. In her lighted corner, pillows propped behind her, Laura sat up inventing. On her lap lay one of those innumerable pads of paper her husband brought home from his office, compliments of some pharmaceutical company, advertising tranquilizers or antibiotics or skin cream. She would be working on a sketch of something familiar but drawn at such close range so she could attach a special nozzle or handier handle, the thing looked peculiar. Her daughters would giggle over the odd doodles they found in kitchen drawers or on the back shelf of the downstairs toilet. Once Yoyo was sure her mother had drawn a picture of a man's you-know-what; she showed her sisters her find, and with coy, posed faces they inquired of their mother what she was up to. *Ay*, that was one of her failures, she explained to them, a child's double-compartment drinking glass with an outsized, built-in straw.

Her daughters would seek her out at night when she seemed to have a moment to talk to them: they were having trouble at school or they wanted her to persuade their father to give them permission to go into the city or to a shopping mall or a movie—in broad daylight, Mami! Laura would wave them out of her room. "The problem with you girls . . ." The problem boiled down to the fact that they wanted to become Americans and their father—and their mother, too, at first—would have none of it.

"You girls are going to drive me crazy!" she threatened, if they kept nagging. "When I end up in Bellevue, you'll be safely sorry!"

She spoke in English when she argued with them. And her English was a mishmash of mixed-up idioms and sayings that showed she was "green behind the ears," as she called it.

If her husband insisted she speak in Spanish to the girls so they wouldn't forget their native tongue, she'd snap, "When in Rome, do unto the Romans."

Yoyo, the Big Mouth, had become the spokesman for her sisters, and she stood her ground in that bedroom. "We're not going to that school anymore, Mami!"

"You have to." Her eyes would widen with worry. "In this country, it is against the law not to go to school. You want us to get thrown out?"

"You want us to get killed? Those kids were throwing stones today!"

"Sticks and stones don't break bones," she chanted. Yoyo could tell, though, by the look on her face, it was as if one of those stones the kids had aimed at her daughters had hit her. But she always pretended they were at fault. "What did you do to provoke them? It takes two to tangle, you know."

"Thanks, thanks a lot, Mom!" Yoyo stormed out of that room and into her own. Her daughters never called her *Mom* except when they wanted her to feel how much she had failed them in this country. She was a good enough Mami, fussing and scolding and giving advice, but a terrible girlfriend parent, a real failure of a Mom.

Back she went to her pencil and pad, scribbling and tsking and tearing off sheets, finally giving up, and taking up her *New York Times*. Some nights, though, if she got a good idea, she rushed into Yoyo's room, a flushed look on her face, her tablet of paper in her hand, a cursory knock on the door she'd just thrown open. "Do I have something to show you, Cuquita!"

This was Yoyo's time to herself, after she finished her homework, while her sisters were still downstairs watching TV in the basement. Hunched over her small desk, the overhead light turned off, her desk lamp poignantly lighting only her paper, the rest of the room in warm, soft, uncreated darkness, she wrote her secret poems in her new language.

"You're going to ruin your eyes!" Laura began, snapping on the overly bright overhead light, scaring off whatever shy passion Yoyo, with the blue thread of her writing, had just begun coaxing out of a labyrinth of feelings.

"Oh, Mami!" Yoyo cried out, her eyes blinking up at her mother. "I'm writing."

"*Ay*, Cuquita." That was her communal pet name for whoever was in her favor. "Cuquita, when I make a million, I'll buy you your very own typewriter." (Yoyo had been nagging her mother for one just like the one her father had bought to do his order forms at home.) "Gravy on the turkey" was what she called it when someone was buttering her up. She buttered and poured. "I'll hire you your very own typist."

Down she plopped on the bed and held out her pad. "Take

a guess, Cuquita?" Yoyo studied the rough sketch a moment. Soap sprayed from the nozzle head of a shower when you turned the knob a certain way? Instant coffee with creamer already mixed in? Time-released water capsules for your potted plants when you were away? A keychain with a timer that would go off when your parking meter was about to expire? (The ticking would help you find your keys easily if you mislaid them.) The famous one, famous only in hindsight, was the stick person dragging a square by a rope—a suitcase with wheels? "Oh, of course," Yoyo said, humoring her. "What every household needs: a shower like a car wash, keys ticking like a bomb, luggage on a leash!" By now, it had become something of a family joke, their Thomas Edison Mami, their Benjamin Franklin Mom.

Her face fell. "Come on now! Use your head." One more wrong guess, and she'd show Yoyo, pointing with her pencil to the different highlights of this incredible new wonder. "Remember that time we took the car to Bear Mountain, and we re-ah-lized that we had forgotten to pack an opener with our pick-a-nick?" (Her daughters kept correcting her, but she insisted this was how it should be said.) "When we were ready to eat we didn't have any way to open the refreshments cans?" (This before fliptop lids, which she claimed had crossed her mind.) "You know what this is now?" Yoyo shook her head. "Is a car bumper, but see this part is a removable can opener. So simple and yet so necessary, eh?"

"Yeah, Mami. You should patent it." Yoyo shrugged as her mother tore off the scratch paper and folded it, carefully, corner to corner, as if she were going to save it. But then, she tossed it in the wastebasket on her way out of the room and gave a little laugh like a disclaimer. "It's half of one or two dozen of another."

None of her daughters was very encouraging. They resented her spending time on those dumb inventions. Here they were trying to fit in America among Americans; they needed help figuring out who they were, why the Irish kids whose grandparents had been micks were calling them spics. Why had they come to this country in the first place? Important, crucial, final things, and here was their own mother, who didn't have a second to help them puzzle any of this out, inventing gadgets to make life easier for the American Moms.

Sometimes Yoyo challenged her. "Why, Mami? Why do it? You're never going to make money. The Americans have already thought of everything, you know that."

"Maybe not. Maybe, just maybe, there's something they've missed that's important. With patience and calm, even a burro can climb a palm." This last was one of her many Dominican sayings she had imported into her scrambled English.

"But what's the point?" Yoyo persisted.

"Point, point, does everything need a point? Why do you write poems?"

Yoyo had to admit it was her mother who had the point there. Still, in the hierarchy of things, a poem seemed much more important than a potty that played music when a toilet-training toddler went in its bowl.

They talked about it among themselves, the four girls, as they often did now about the many puzzling things in this new country.

"Better she reinvents the wheel than be on our cases all the time," the oldest, Carla, observed. In the close quarters of an American nuclear family, their mother's prodigious energy was becoming a real drain on their self-determination. Let her have a project. What harm could she do, and besides, she needed that acknowledgement. It had come to her automatically in the old country from being a de la Torre. "García de la Torre," Laura would enunciate carefully, giving her maiden as well as married name when they first arrived. But the blank smiles had never heard of her name. She would show them. She would prove to these Americans what a smart woman could do with a pencil and pad.

She had a near miss once. Every night, she liked to read *The New York Times* in bed before turning off her light, to see what the Americans were up to. One night, she let out a yelp to wake up her husband beside her. He sat bolt upright, reaching for his glasses which in his haste, he knocked across the room. "*¿Qué pasa? ¿Qué pasa?*" What is wrong? There was terror in his voice, the same fear she'd heard in the Dominican Republic before they left. They had been watched there; he was followed. They could not talk, of course, though they had whispered to each other in fear at night in the dark bed. Now in America, he was safe, a success even; his Centro de Medicina in the Bronx was thronged with the sick and the homesick yearning to go home again. But in dreams, he went back to those awful days and long nights, and his wife's screams confirmed his secret fear: they had not gotten away after all; the SIM had come for them at last.

"*Ay*, Cuco! Remember how I showed you that suitcase with

little wheels so we should not have to carry those heavy bags when we traveled? Someone stole my idea and made a million!" She shook the paper in his face. "See, see! This man was no *bobo!* He didn't put all his pokers on a back burner. I kept telling you, one of these days my ship would pass me by in the night!" She wagged her finger at her husband and daughters, laughing all the while, one of those eerie laughs crazy people in movies laugh. The four girls had congregated in her room. They eyed their mother and each other. Perhaps they were all thinking the same thing, wouldn't it be weird and sad if Mami did end up in Bellevue?

"*¡Ya, ya!*" She waved them out of her room at last. "There is no use trying to drink spilt milk, that's for sure."

It was the suitcase rollers that stopped Laura's hand; she had weathervaned a minor brainstorm. And yet, this plagiarist had gotten all the credit, and the money. What use was it trying to compete with the Americans: they would always have the head start. It was their country, after all. Best stick close to home. She cast her sights about—her daughters ducked—and found her husband's office in need. Several days a week, dressed professionally in a white smock with a little name tag pinned on the lapel, a shopping bag full of cleaning materials and rags, she rode with her husband in his car to the Bronx. On the way, she organized the glove compartment or took off the address stickers from the magazines for the waiting room because she had read somewhere how by means of these stickers drug addict patients found out where doctors lived and burglarized their homes looking for syringes. At night, she did the books, filling in columns with how much money they had made that day. Who had time to be inventing silly things!

She did take up her pencil and pad one last time. But it was to help one of her daughters out. In ninth grade, Yoyo was chosen by her English teacher, Sister Mary Joseph, to deliver the Teacher's Day address at the school assembly. Back in the Dominican Republic growing up, Yoyo had been a terrible student. No one could ever get her to sit down to a book. But in New York, she needed to settle somewhere, and since the natives were unfriendly, and the country inhospitable, she took root in the language. By high school, the nuns were reading her stories and compositions out loud in English class.

But the spectre of delivering a speech brown-nosing the teachers jammed her imagination. At first she didn't want to and then she couldn't seem to write that speech. She should have thought of it as "a great honor," as her father called it. But she was mortified. She still had a slight accent, and she did not like to speak in public, subjecting herself to her classmates' ridicule. It also took no great figuring to see that to deliver a eulogy for a convent full of crazy, old, overweight nuns was no way to endear herself to her peers.

But she didn't know how to get out of it. Night after night, she sat at her desk, hoping to polish off some quick, noncommittal little speech. But she couldn't get anything down.

The weekend before the assembly Monday morning Yoyo went into a panic. Her mother would just have to call in tomorrow and say Yoyo was in the hospital, in a coma.

Laura tried to calm her down. "Just remember how Mister Lincoln couldn't think of anything to say at the Gettysburg, but then, bang! *Four score and once upon a time ago,*" she began reciting. "Something is going to come if you just relax. You'll see, like the Americans say, *Necessity is the daughter of invention.* I'll help you."

That weekend, her mother turned all her energy towards helping Yoyo write her speech. "Please, Mami, just leave me alone, please," Yoyo pleaded with her. But Yoyo would get rid of the goose only to have to contend with the gander. Her father kept poking his head in the door just to see if Yoyo had "fulfilled your obligations," a phrase he had used when the girls were younger and he'd check to see whether they had gone to the bathroom before a car trip. Several times that weekend around the supper table, he recited his own high school valedictorian speech. He gave Yoyo pointers on delivery, notes on the great orators and their tricks. (Humbleness and praise and falling silent with great emotion were his favorites.)

Laura sat across the table, the only one who seemed to be listening to him. Yoyo and her sisters were forgetting a lot of their Spanish, and their father's formal, florid diction was hard to understand. But Laura smiled softly to herself, and turned the lazy Susan at the center of the table around and around as if it were the prime mover, the first gear of her attention.

That Sunday evening, Yoyo was reading some poetry to get herself inspired: Whitman's poems in an old book with an engraved cover her father had picked up in a thrift shop next to his office. *I celebrate myself and sing myself. . . . He most honors my style who learns under it to destroy the teacher.* The poet's words shocked and thrilled her. She had gotten used to the nuns, a literature of appropriate sentiments, poems with a message, expurgated texts. But here was a flesh and blood man, belching and laughing and sweating in poems. *Who touches this book touches a man.*

That night, at last, she started to write, recklessly, three, five pages, looking up once only to see her father passing by the hall on tiptoe. When Yoyo was done, she read over her words, and her eyes filled. She finally sounded like herself in English!

As soon as she had finished that first draft, she called her mother to her room. Laura listened attentively while Yoyo read the speech out loud, and in the end, her eyes were glistening too. Her face was soft and warm and proud. "*Ay*, Yoyo, you are going to be the one to bring our name to the headlights in this country! That is a beautiful, beautiful speech I want for your father to hear it before he goes to sleep. Then I will type it for you, all right?"

Down the hall they went, mother and daughter, faces flushed with accomplishment. Into the master bedroom where Carlos was propped up on his pillows, still awake, reading the Dominican papers, already days old. Now that the dictatorship had been toppled, he had become interested in his country's fate again. The interim government was going to hold the first free elections in thirty years. History was in the making, freedom and hope were in the air again! There was still some question in his mind whether or not he might move his family back. But Laura had gotten used to the life here. She did not want to go back to the old country where, de la Torre or not, she was only a wife and a mother (and a failed one at that, since she had never provided the required son). Better an independent nobody than a high-class houseslave. She did not come straight out and disagree with her husband's plans. Instead, she fussed with him about reading the papers in bed, soiling their sheets with those poorly printed, foreign tabloids. "*The Times* is not that bad!" she'd claim if her husband tried to humor her by saying they shared the same dirty habit.

The minute Carlos saw his wife and daughter filing in, he put his paper down, and his face brightened as if at long last his wife had delivered the son, and that was the news she was bringing him. His teeth were already grinning from the glass of water next to his bedside lamp, so he lisped when he said, "Eh-speech, eh-speech!"

"It is so beautiful, Cuco," Laura coached him, turning the sound on his TV off. She sat down at the foot of the bed. Yoyo stood before both of them, blocking their view of the soldiers in helicopters landing amid silenced gun reports and explosions. A few weeks ago it had been the shores of the Dominican Republic. Now it was the jungles of Southeast Asia they were saving. Her mother gave her the nod to begin reading.

Yoyo didn't need much encouragement. She put her nose to the fire, as her mother would have said, and read from start to finish without looking up. When she concluded, she was a little embarrassed at the pride she took in her own words. She pretended to quibble with a phrase or two, then looked questioningly to her mother. Laura's face was radiant. Yoyo turned to share her pride with her father.

The expression on his face shocked both mother and daughter. Carlos's toothless mouth had collapsed into a dark zero.

His eyes bored into Yoyo, then shifted to Laura. In barely audible Spanish, as if secret microphones or informers were all about, he whispered to his wife, "You will permit her to read *that*?"

Laura's eyebrows shot up, her mouth fell open. In the old country, any whisper of a challenge to authority could bring the secret police in their black V.W.'s. But this was America. People could say what they thought. "What is wrong with her speech?" Laura questioned him.

"What ees wrrrong with her eh-speech?" Carlos wagged his head at her. His anger was always more frightening in his broken English. As if he had mutilated the language in his fury— and now there was nothing to stand between them and his raw, dumb anger. "What is wrong? I will tell you what is wrong. It show no gratitude. It is boastful. *I celebrate myself*? *The best student learns to destroy the teacher*?" He mocked Yoyo's plagiarized words. "That is insubordinate. It is improper. It is disrespecting of her teachers—" In his anger he had forgotten his fear of lurking spies: each wrong he voiced was a decibel higher than the last outrage. Finally, he shouted at Yoyo, "As your father, I forbid you to make that eh-speech!"

Laura leapt to her feet, a sign that *she* was about to deliver her own speech. She was a small woman, and she spoke all her pronouncements standing up, either for more projection or as a carry-over from her girlhood in convent schools where one asked for, and literally, took the floor in order to speak. She stood by Yoyo's side, shoulder to shoulder. They looked down at Carlos. "That is no tone of voice—" she began.

But now, Carlos was truly furious. It was bad enough that

his daughter was rebelling, but here was his own wife joining forces with her. Soon he would be surrounded by a houseful of independent American women. He too leapt from the bed, throwing off his covers. The Spanish newspapers flew across the room. He snatched the speech out of Yoyo's hands, held it before the girl's wide eyes, a vengeful, mad look in his own, and then once, twice, three, four, countless times, he tore the speech into shreds.

"Are you crazy?" Laura lunged at him. "Have you gone mad? That is her speech for tomorrow you have torn up!"

"Have *you* gone mad?" He shook her away. "You were going to let her read that . . . that insult to her teachers?"

"Insult to her teachers!" Laura's face had crumpled up like a piece of paper. On it was written a love note to her husband, an unhappy, haunted man. "This is America, Papi, America! You are not in a savage country anymore!"

Meanwhile, Yoyo was on her knees, weeping wildly, collecting all the little pieces of her speech, hoping that she could put it back together before the assembly tomorrow morning. But not even a sibyl could have made sense of those tiny scraps of paper. All hope was lost. "He broke it, he broke it," Yoyo moaned as she picked up a handful of pieces.

Probably, if she had thought a moment about it, she would not have done what she did next. She would have realized her father had lost brothers and friends to the dictator Trujillo. For the rest of his life, he would be haunted by blood in the streets and late night disappearances. Even after all these years, he cringed if a black Volkswagen passed him on the street. He feared anyone in uniform: the meter maid giving out parking tickets, a museum guard approaching to tell him not to get too close to his favorite Goya.

On her knees, Yoyo thought of the worst thing she could say to her father. She gathered a handful of scraps, stood up, and hurled them in his face. In a low, ugly whisper, she pronounced Trujillo's hated nickname: "Chapita! You're just another Chapita!"

It took Yoyo's father only a moment to register the loathsome nickname before he came after her. Down the halls they raced, but Yoyo was quicker than he and made it into her room just in time to lock the door as her father threw his weight against it. He called down curses on her head, ordered her on his authority as her father to open that door! He throttled that doorknob, but all to no avail. Her mother's love of gadgets saved Yoyo's hide that night. Laura had hired a locksmith to install good locks on all the bedroom doors after the house had been broken into once while they were away. Now if burglars broke in again, and the family were at home, there would be a second round of locks for the thieves to contend with.

"Lolo," she said, trying to calm him down. "Don't you ruin my new locks."

Finally he did calm down, his anger spent. Yoyo heard their footsteps retreating down the hall. Their door clicked shut. Then, muffled voices, her mother's rising in anger, in persuasion, her father's deeper murmurs of explanation and self-defense. The house fell silent a moment, before Yoyo heard, far off, the gun blasts and explosions, the serious, self-important voices of newscasters reporting their TV war.

A little while later, there was a quiet knock at Yoyo's door, followed by a tentative attempt at the door knob. "Cuquita?" her mother whispered. "Open up, Cuquita."

"Go away," Yoyo wailed, but they both knew she was glad her mother was there, and needed only a moment's protest to save face.

Together they concocted a speech: two brief pages of stale compliments and the polite commonplaces on teachers, a speech wrought by necessity and without much invention by mother and daughter late into the night on one of the pads of paper Laura had once used for her own inventions. After it was drafted, Laura typed it up while Yoyo stood by, correcting her mother's misnomers and mis-sayings.

Yoyo came home the next day with the success story of the assembly. The nuns had been flattered, the audience had stood up and given "our devoted teachers a standing ovation," what Laura had suggested they do at the end of the speech.

She clapped her hands together as Yoyo recreated the moment. "I stole that from your father's speech, remember? Remember how he put that in at the end?" She quoted him in Spanish, then translated for Yoyo into English.

That night, Yoyo watched him from the upstairs hall window, where she'd retreated the minute she heard his car pull up in front of the house. Slowly, her father came up the driveway, a grim expression on his face as he grappled with a large, heavy cardboard box. At the front door, he set the package down carefully and patted all his pockets for his house keys. (If only he'd had Laura's ticking key chain!) Yoyo heard the snapping open of locks downstairs. She listened as he struggled to maneuver the box through the narrow doorway. He called her name several times, but she did not answer him.

"My daughter, your father, he love you very much," he explained from the bottom of the stairs. "He just want to protect you." Finally, her mother came up and pleaded with Yoyo to go down and reconcile with him. "Your father did not mean to harm. You must pardon him. Always it is better to let bygones be forgotten, no?"

Downstairs, Yoyo found her father setting up a brand new electric typewriter on the kitchen table. It was even better than her mother's. He had outdone himself with all the extra features: a plastic carrying case with Yoyo's initials decaled below the handle, a brace to lift the paper upright while she typed, an erase cartridge, an automatic margin tab, a plastic hood like a toaster cover to keep the dust away. Not even her mother could have invented such a machine!

But Laura's inventing days were over just as Yoyo's were starting up with her school-wide success. Rather than the rolling suitcase everyone else in the family remembers, Yoyo thinks of the speech her mother wrote as her last invention. It was as if, after that, her mother had passed on to Yoyo her pencil and pad and said, "Okay, Cuquita, here's the buck. You give it a shot."

Trespass

▼▲▼▲▼▲▼▲▼▲▼▲▼▲▼▲▼▲▼▲▼▲▼▲▼▲▼▲▼▲▼▲▼III▼▲▼▲▼

Carla

The day the Garcías were one American year old, they had a celebration at dinner. Mami had baked a nice flan and stuck a candle in the center. "Guess what day it is today?" She looked around the table at her daughters' baffled faces. "One year ago today," Papi began orating, "we came to the shores of this great country." When he was done misquoting the poem on the Statue of Liberty, the youngest, Fifi, asked if she could blow out the candle, and Mami said only after everyone had made a wish.

What do you wish for on the first celebration of the day you lost everything? Carla wondered. Everyone else around the table had their eyes closed as if they had no trouble deciding. Carla closed her eyes too. She should make an effort and not wish for what she always wished for in her homesickness. But just this last time, she would let herself. "Dear God," she began. She could not get used to this American wish-making without bringing God into it. "Let us please go back home, please," she half prayed and half wished. It seemed a less and less likely prospect. In fact, her parents were sinking roots here. Only a month ago, they had moved out of the city to a neighborhood on Long Island so that the girls could have a yard to play in, so Mami said. The little green squares around each look-alike house seemed more like carpeting that had to be kept clean than yards to play in. The trees were no taller than little Fifi. Carla thought yearningly of the lush grasses and thick-limbed, vine-ladened trees around the compound back home. Under the *amapola* tree her best-friend cousin, Lucinda, and she had told each other what each knew about how babies were made. What is Lucinda doing right this moment? Carla wondered.

Down the block the neighborhood dead-ended in abandoned farmland that Mami read in the local paper the developers were negotiating to buy. Grasses and real trees and real bushes still grew beyond the barbed-wire fence posted with a big sign: PRI-VATE, NO TRESPASSING. The sign had surprised Carla since "for-give us our trespasses" was the only other context in which she had heard the word. She pointed the sign out to Mami on one of their first walks to the bus stop. "Isn't that funny, Mami? A sign that you have to be good." Her mother did not under-stand at first until Carla explained about the Lord's Prayer. Mami laughed. Words sometimes meant two things in English too. This trespass meant that no one must go inside the prop-erty because it was not public like a park, but private. Carla nodded, disappointed. She would never get the hang of this new country.

Mami walked her to the bus stop for her first month at her new school over in the next parish. The first week, Mami even rode the buses with her, transferring, going and coming, twice a day, until Carla learned the way. Her sisters had all been enrolled at the neighborhood Catholic school only one block away from the house the Garcías had rented at the end of the summer. But by then, Carla's seventh grade was full. The nun who was the principal had suggested that Carla stay back a year in sixth grade, where they still had two spaces left. At twelve, though, Carla was at least a year older than most sixth graders, and she felt mortified at the thought of having to repeat yet another year. All four girls had been put back a year when they arrived in the country. Sure, Carla could use the practice with her English, but that also meant she would be in the same grade as her younger sister, Sandi. That she could not bear. "Please," she pleaded with her mother, "let me go to the other school!" The public school was a mere two blocks beyond the Catholic school, but Laura García would not hear of it. Public schools, she had learned from other Catholic parents, were where juvenile delinquents went and where teachers taught those new crazy ideas about how we all came from monkeys. No child of hers was going to forget her family name and think she was nothing but a kissing cousin to an orangutan.

Carla soon knew her school route *by heart*, an expression she used for weeks after she learned it. First, she walked down the block by heart, noting the infinitesimal differences between the look-alike houses: different color drapes, an azalea bush on the left side of the door instead of on the right, a mailbox or door with a doodad of some kind. Then by heart, she walked the long mile by the deserted farmland lot with the funny sign. Finally, a sharp right down the service road into the main thoroughfare, where by heart she boarded the bus. "A young lady señorita," her mother pronounced the first morning Carla set out by herself, her heart drumming in her chest. It was a long and scary trek, but she was too grateful to have escaped the embarrassment of being put back a year to complain.

And as the months went by, she neglected to complain about an even scarier development. Every day on the playground and in the halls of her new school, a gang of boys chased after her, calling her names, some of which she had heard before from the old lady neighbor in the apartment they had rented in the city. Out of sight of the nuns, the boys pelted Carla with stones, aiming them at her feet so there would be no bruises. "Go back to where you came from, you dirty spic!" One of them, standing behind her in line, pulled her blouse out of her skirt where it was tucked in and lifted it high. "No titties," he snickered. Another yanked down her socks, displaying her legs, which had begun growing soft, dark hairs. "Monkey legs!" he yelled to his pals.

"Stop!" Carla cried. "Please stop."

"Eh-stop!" they mimicked her. "Plees eh-stop."

They were disclosing her secret shame: her body was changing. The girl she had been back home in Spanish was being shed. In her place—almost as if the boys' ugly words and taunts had the power of spells—was a hairy, breast-budding grownup no one would ever love.

Every day, Carla set out on her long journey to school with a host of confused feelings. First of all, there was this body whose daily changes she noted behind the closed bathroom door until one of her sisters knocked that Carla's turn was over. How she wished she could wrap her body up the way she'd heard Chinese girls had their feet bound so they wouldn't grow big. She would stay herself, a quick, skinny girl with brown eyes and a braid down her back, a girl she had just begun to feel could get things in this world.

But then, too, Carla felt relieved to be setting out towards her very own school in her proper grade away from the crowding that was her family of four girls too close in age. She could come home with stories of what had happened that day and not have a chorus of three naysayers to correct her. But she also felt dread. There, in the playground, they would be waiting for her—the gang of four or five boys, blond, snotty-nosed, freckled-faced. They looked bland and unknowable, the way all Americans did. Their faces betrayed no sign of human warmth. Their eyes were too clear for cleaving, intimate looks. Their pale bodies did not seem real but were like costumes they were wearing as they played the part of her persecutors.

She watched them. In the classroom, they bent over workbooks or wore scared faces when Sister Beatrice, their beefy, no-nonsense teacher, scolded them for missing their homework. Sometimes Carla spied them in the playground, looking through the chain link fence and talking about the cars parked on the sidewalk. To Carla's bafflement, those cars had names beyond the names of their color or size. All she knew of their family car, for instance, was that it was a big black car where all four sisters could ride in the back, though Fifi always made a fuss and was allowed up front. Carla could also identify Volkswagens because that had been the car (in black) of the secret police back home; every time Mami saw one she made the sign of the cross and said a prayer for Tío Mundo, who had not been allowed to leave the Island. Beyond Volkswagens and medium blue cars or big black cars, Carla could not tell one car from the other.

But the boys at the fence talked excitedly about Fords and Falcons and Corvairs and Plymouth Valiants. They argued over how fast each car could go and what models were better than others. Carla sometimes imagined herself being driven to school in a flashy red car the boys would admire. Except there was no one *to* drive her. Her immigrant father with his thick mustache and accent and three-piece suit would only bring her more ridicule. Her mother did not yet know how to drive. Even though Carla could imagine owning a very expensive car, she could not imagine her parents as different from what they were. They were, like this new body she was growing into, givens.

One day when she had been attending Sacred Heart about a month, she was followed by a car on her mile walk home from the bus stop. It was a lime green car, sort of medium sized, and with a kind of long snout, so had it been a person, Carla would have described it as having a long nose. A long-nosed, lime-green car. It drove slowly, trailing her. Carla figured the driver was looking for an address, just as Papi drove slowly and got honked at when he was reading the signs of shops before stopping at a particular one.

A blat from the horn made Carla jump and turn to the car, now fully stopped just a little ahead of her. She could see the driver clearly, from the shoulders up, a man in a red shirt about the age of her parents—though it was hard for Carla to tell with Americans how old they were. They were like cars to her, identifiable by the color of their clothes and a general age group—a little kid younger than herself, a kid her same age, a teenager in high school, and then the vast indistinguishable group of American grownups.

This grownup American man about her parents' age beckoned for her to come up to the window. Carla dreaded being asked directions since she had just moved into this area right before school started, and all she knew for sure was the route home from the bus stop. Besides, her English was still just classroom English, a foreign language. She knew the neutral bland things: how to ask for a glass of water, how to say good morning and good afternoon and good night. How to thank someone and say they were welcomed. But if a grownup American of indeterminable age asked her for directions, invariably speaking too quickly, she merely shrugged and smiled an inane smile. "I don't speak very much English," she would say in a small voice by way of apology. She hated having to admit this since such an admission proved, no doubt, the boy gang's point that she didn't belong here.

As Carla drew closer, the driver leaned over and rolled down the passenger door window. Carla bent down as if she were about to speak to a little kid and peeked in. The man smiled a friendly smile, but there was something wrong with it that Carla couldn't put her finger on: this smile had a bruised, sorry quality as if the man were someone who'd been picked on all his life, and so his smiles were appeasing, not friendly. He was wearing his red shirt unbuttoned, which seemed normal given the warm Indian-summer day. In fact, if Carla's legs hadn't begun to grow hairs, she would have taken off her school-green knee socks and walked home bare-legged.

The man spoke up. "Whereyagoin?" he asked, running all his words together the way the Americans always did. Carla was, as usual, not quite sure if she had heard right.

"Excuse me?" she asked politely, leaning into the car to hear the man's whispery voice better. Something caught her eye. She looked down and stared, aghast.

The man had tied his two shirtends just above his waist and was naked from there on down. String encircled his waist, the loose ends knotted in front and then looped around his penis. As Carla watched, his big blunt-headed thing grew so that it filled and strained at the lasso it was caught in.

"Where ya' going?" His voice had slowed down when he spoke this time, so that Carla definitely understood him. Her eyes snapped back up to his eyes.

"Excuse me?" she said again dumbly.

He leaned towards the passenger door and clicked it open. "C'moninere." He nodded towards the seat beside him. "C'm'on," he moaned. He cupped his hand over his thing as if it were a flame that might blow out.

Carla clutched her bookbag tighter in her hand. Her mouth hung open. Not one word, English or Spanish, occurred to her. She backed away from the big green car, all the while keeping her eyes on the man. A pained, urgent expression was deepening on his face like a plea that Carla did not know how to answer. His arm pumped at something Carla could not see, and then after much agitation, he was still. The face relaxed into something like peacefulness. The man bowed his head as if in prayer. Carla turned and fled down the street, her book-bag banging against her leg like a whip she was using to make herself go faster, faster.

Her mother called the police after piecing together the breathless, frantic story Carla told. The enormity of what she had seen was now topped by the further enormity of involving the police. Carla and her sisters feared the American police almost as much as the SIM back home. Their father, too, seemed uneasy around policemen; whenever a cop car was behind them in traffic, he kept looking at the rearview mirror and insisting on silence in the car so he could think. If officers stood on the sidewalk as he walked by, he bowed ingratiatingly at them. Back home, he had been tailed by the secret police for months and the family had only narrowly escaped capture their last day on the Island. Of course, Carla knew American policemen were "nice guys," but still she felt uneasy around them.

The doorbell rang only minutes after Carla's mother had called the station. This was a law-abiding family neighborhood, and no one wanted a creep like this on the loose among so many children, least of all the police. As her mother answered the door, Carla stayed behind in the kitchen, listening with a racing heart to her mother's explanation. Mami's voice was high and hesitant and slightly apologetic—a small, accented woman's voice among the booming, impersonal American male voices that interrogated her.

"My daughter, she was walking home—"

"Where exactly?" a male voice demanded.

"That street, you know?" Carla's mother must have pointed. "The one that comes up the avenue, I don't know the name of it."

"Must be the service road," a nicer male voice offered.

"Yes, yes, the service road." Her mother's jubilant voice seemed to conclude whatever had been the problem.

"Please go on, ma'am."

"Well, my daughter, she said this, this crazy man in this car—" Her voice lowered. Carla heard snatches: something, something "to come in the car—"

"Where's your daughter, ma'am?" the male voice with authority asked.

Carla cringed behind the kitchen door. Her mother had promised that she would not involve Carla with the police but would do all the talking herself.

"She is just a young girl," her mother excused Carla.

"Well, ma'am, if you want to file charges, we have to talk to her."

"File charges? What does that mean, file charges?"

There was a sigh of exasperation. A too-patient voice with dividers between each word explained the legal procedures as if repeating a history lesson Carla's mother should have learned long before she had troubled the police or moved into this neighborhood.

"I don't want any trouble," her mother protested. "I just think this is a crazy man who should not be allowed on the streets."

"You're absolutely right, ma'am, but our hands are tied unless you, as a responsible citizen, help us out."

Oh no, Carla groaned, now she was in for it. The magic words had been uttered. The Garcías were only legal residents, not citizens, but for the police to mistake Mami for a citizen was a compliment too great to spare a child discomfort. "Carla!" her mother called from the door.

"What's the girl's name?" the officer with the voice in charge asked.

Her mother repeated Carla's full name and spelled it for the officer, then called out again in her voice of authority, "Carla Antonia!"

Slowly, sullenly, Carla wrapped herself around the kitchen door, only her head poking out and into the hallway. "¿Sí, Mami?" she answered in a polite, law-abiding voice to impress the cops.

"Come here," her mother said, motioning. "These very nice officers need for you to explain what you saw." There was an apologetic look on her face. "Come on, Cuca, don't be afraid."

"There's nothing to be afraid of," the policeman said in his gruff, scary voice.

Carla kept her head down as she approached the front door, glancing up briefly when the two officers introduced themselves. One was an embarrassingly young man with a face no older than the boys' faces at school on top of a large, muscular man's body. The other man, also big and fair-skinned, looked older because of his meaner, sharp-featured face like an animal's in a beast fable a child knows by looking at the picture not to trust. Belts were slung around both their hips, guns poking out of the holsters. Their very masculinity offended and threatened. They were so big, so strong, so male, so American.

After a few facts about her had been established, the mean-faced cop with the big voice and the pad asked her if she would answer a few questions. Not knowing she could refuse, Carla nodded meekly, on the verge of tears.

"Could you describe the vehicle the suspect was driving?"

She wasn't sure what a vehicle was or a suspect, for that matter. Her mother translated into simpler English, "What car was the man driving, Carla?"

"A big green car," Carla mumbled.

As if she hadn't answered in English, her mother repeated for the officers, "A big green car."

"What make?" the officer wanted to know.

"Make?" Carla asked.

"You know, Ford, Chrysler, Plymouth." The man ended his catalogue with a sigh. Carla and her mother were wasting his time.

"*¿Qué clase de carro?*" her mother asked in Spanish, but of course she knew Carla wouldn't know the make of a car. Carla shook her head, and her mother explained to the officer, helping her save face, "She doesn't remember."

"Can't she talk?" the gruff cop snapped. The boyish-looking one now asked Carla a question. "Carla," he began, pronouncing her name so that Carla felt herself coated all over with something warm and too sweet. "Carla," he coaxed, "can you please describe the man you saw?"

All memory of the man's face fled. She remembered only the bruised smile and a few strands of dirty blond hair laid carefully over a bald pate. But she could not remember the word for bald and so she said, "He had almost nothing on his head."

"You mean no hat?" the gentle cop suggested.

"Almost no hair," Carla explained, looking up as if she had taken a guess and wanted to know if she was wrong or right.

"Bald?" The gruff cop pointed first to a hairy stretch of wrist beyond his uniform's cuff, then to his pink, hairless palm.

"Bald, yes." Carla nodded. The sight of the man's few dark hairs had disgusted her. She thought of her own legs sprouting dark hairs, of the changes going on in secret in her body, turning her into one of these grownup persons. No wonder the high-voiced boys with smooth, hairless cheeks hated her. They could see that her body was already betraying her.

The interrogation proceeded through a description of the man's appearance, and then the dreaded question came.

"What did you see?" the boy-faced cop asked.

Carla looked down at the cops' feet. The black tips of their shoes poked out from under their cuffs like the snouts of wily animals. "The man was naked all down here." She gestured with her hand. "And he had a string around his waist."

"A string?" The man's voice was like a hand trying to lift her chin to make her look up, which is precisely what her mother did when the man repeated, "A string?"

Carla was forced to confront the cop's face. It was indeed an adult version of the sickly white faces of the boys in the playground. This is what they would look like once they grew up. There was no meanness in this face, no kindness either. No recognition of the difficulty she was having in trying to describe what she had seen with her tiny English vocabulary. It was the face of someone in a movie Carla was watching ask her, "What was he doing with the string?"

She shrugged, tears peeping at the corners of her eyes.

Her mother intervened. "The string was holding up this man's—"

"Please, ma'am," the cop who was writing said. "Let your daughter describe what she saw."

Carla thought hard for what could be the name of a man's genitals. They had come to this country before she had reached puberty in Spanish, so a lot of the key words she would have been picking up in the last year, she had missed. Now, she was learning English in a Catholic classroom, where no nun had ever mentioned the words she was needing. "He had a string around his waist," Carla explained. By the ease with which the man was writing, she could tell she was now making perfect sense.

"And it came up to the front"—she showed on herself—"and here it was tied in a—" She held up her fingers and made the sign for zero.

"A noose?" the gentle cop offered.

"A noose, and his thing—" Carla pointed to the policeman's crotch. The cop writing scowled. "His thing was inside that noose and it got bigger and bigger," she blurted, her voice wobbling.

The friendly cop lifted his eyebrows and pushed his cap back on his head. His big hand wiped the small beads of sweat that had accumulated on his brow.

Carla prayed without prayer that this interview would stop now. What she had begun fearing was that her picture—but who was there to take a picture?—would appear in the paper the next day and the gang of mean boys would torment her with what she had seen. She wondered if she could report them now to these young officers. "By the way," she could say, and the gruff one would begin to take notes. She would have the words to describe them: their mean, snickering faces she knew by heart. Their pale look-alike sickly bodies. Their high voices squealing with delight when Carla mispronounced some word they coaxed her to repeat.

But soon after her description of the incident, the interview ended. The cop snapped his pad closed, and each officer gave Carla and her mother a salute of farewell. They drove off in their squad car, and all down the block, drapes fell back to rest, half-opened shades closed like eyes that saw no evil.

For the next two months before Carla's mother moved her to the public school close to home for the second half of her seventh grade, she took Carla on the bus to school and was there at the end of the day to pick her up. The tauntings and chasings stopped. The boys must have thought Carla had complained, and so her mother was along to defend her. Even during class times, when her mother was not around, they now ignored her, their sharp, clear eyes roaming the classroom for another victim, someone too fat, too ugly, too poor, too different. Carla had faded into the walls.

But their faces did not fade as fast from Carla's life. They trespassed in her dreams and in her waking moments. Sometimes when she woke in the dark, they were perched at the foot of her bed, a grim chorus of urchin faces, boys without bodies, chanting without words, "Go back! Go back!"

So as not to see them, Carla would close her eyes and wish them gone. In that dark she created by keeping her eyes shut, she would pray, beginning with the names of her own sisters, for all those she wanted God to especially care for, here and back home. The seemingly endless list of familiar names would coax her back to sleep with a feeling of safety, of a world still peopled by those who loved her.

Snow

▼▲▼▲▼▲▼▲▼▲▼▲▼▲▼▲▼▲▼▲▼▲▼▲▼▲▼▲▼▲▼III▼▲▼▲▼

Yolanda

O ur first year in New York we rented a small apartment with a Catholic school nearby, taught by the Sisters of Charity, hefty women in long black gowns and bonnets that made them look peculiar, like dolls in mourning. I liked them a lot, especially my grandmotherly fourth grade teacher, Sister Zoe. I had a lovely name, she said, and she had me teach the whole class how to pronounce it. *Yo-lan-da.* As the only immigrant in my class, I was put in a special seat in the first row by the window, apart from the other children so that Sister Zoe could tutor me without disturbing them. Slowly, she enunciated the new words I was to repeat: *laundromat, corn flakes, subway, snow.*

Soon I picked up enough English to understand holocaust was in the air. Sister Zoe explained to a wide-eyed classroom what was happening in Cuba. Russian missiles were being assembled, trained supposedly on New York City. President Kennedy, looking worried too, was on the television at home, explaining we might have to go to war against the Communists. At school, we had air-raid drills: an ominous bell would go off and we'd file into the hall, fall to the floor, cover our heads with our coats, and imagine our hair falling out, the bones in our arms going soft. At home, Mami and my sisters and I said a rosary for world peace. I heard new vocabulary: *nuclear bomb, radioactive fallout, bomb shelter.* Sister Zoe explained how it would happen. She drew a picture of a mushroom on the blackboard and dotted a flurry of chalkmarks for the dusty fallout that would kill us all.

The months grew cold, November, December. It was dark when I got up in the morning, frosty when I followed my breath to school. One morning as I sat at my desk daydreaming out the window, I saw dots in the air like the ones Sister Zoe had drawn—random at first, then lots and lots. I shrieked, "Bomb! Bomb!" Sister Zoe jerked around, her full black skirt ballooning as she hurried to my side. A few girls began to cry.

But then Sister Zoe's shocked look faded. "Why, Yolanda dear, that's snow!" She laughed. "Snow."

"Snow," I repeated. I looked out the window warily. All my life I had heard about the white crystals that fell out of American skies in the winter. From my desk I watched the fine powder dust the sidewalk and parked cars below. Each flake was different, Sister Zoe had said, like a person, irreplaceable and beautiful.

Floor Show

▼▲▼▲▼▲▼▲▼▲▼▲▼▲▼▲▼▲▼▲▼▲▼▲▼▲▼▲▼▲▼III▼▲▼▲▼

Sandi

"**N**o elbows, no Cokes, only milk or—" Mami paused. Which of her four girls could fill in the blank of how they were to behave at the restaurant with the Fannings?

"No elbows on the table," Sandi guessed.

"She already said that," Carla accused.

"No fighting, girls!" Mami scolded them all and continued The Epistle. "Only milk or ice water. And I make your orders. Is that clear?"

The four braided and beribboned heads nodded. At moments like this when they all seemed one organism—*the four girls*—Sandi would get that yearning to wander off into the United States of America by herself and never come back as the second of four girls so close in age.

This time, though, she nodded. Mami's tone of voice did not invite contradiction. The procedures of this dinner out with the important Fannings had been explained to the girls so many times in the last few days and particularly today that there really was no point in clowning around to get their mother to be more lenient.

"Mami, just please don't order anything I don't like, please?" Sandi pleaded. She had always been a fussy eater, and now that they had come to the States, it seemed as if there were twice as many inedible foods that could be piled high on her plate.

"No fish, Mami," Carla reminded her. "I get sick to my stomach."

"And nothing with mayonnaise," Yoyo added. "I can't eat—"

"Girls!" Their mother lifted up her hands like an Island traffic policeman, halting their requests. On her face was the panicked look she had worn ever since they had arrived in New York three months ago after a narrow escape from the secret police. At the least provocation, she would burst out crying, lose her temper, or threaten to end up in Bellevue, the place, she had learned, where crazy people were sent in this country.

"Can't you make a little effort tonight?" Her mother's voice was so sad that the youngest, Fifi, began to cry. "I don't want to go," she moaned. "I don't want to go."

"But why on earth not?" Mami asked, her face brightening. She seemed genuinely mystified, as if she hadn't terrorized them for days into thinking of this outing as equivalent to going to the doctor for their booster shots. "It's going to be such fun. The Fannings are taking us to a special Spanish restaurant that was written up in a magazine. You girls will like it, I'm sure. And there's going to be a floor show—"

"What's that?" Sandi, who had lost interest in pleading for a reasonable menu and had been fiddling with the ribbon in her hair, looked up. "Floor show?"

A playful expression came on their mother's face. She lifted her shoulders, curled her arms over head and clapped her hands, then stamped her feet, fast, fast, fast on the floor as if she were putting out a fire. "Flamenco dancing! ¡Olé! Remember the dancers?" Sandi nodded. They had all been enthralled by the folk dancers from Madrid at the Dominican World's Fair last year. As Mami began to explain that this restaurant had shows of Spanish dancers as well as yummy Spanish food, a series of thumps sounded on the floor from below.

The girls glanced at each other and looked towards their mother, who rolled her eyes. "La Bruja," she explained. "I forgot." The old woman in the apartment below, who had a helmet of beauty parlor blue hair, had been complaining to the super since the day the family moved in a few months ago. The Garcías should be evicted. Their food smelled. They spoke too loudly and not in English. The kids sounded like a herd of wild burros. The Puerto Rican super, Alfredo, came to their door almost daily. Could Mrs. García turn the radio down? Could Mrs. García maybe keep the girls more in line? The neighbor downstairs had been awakened by the clatter of their shoes on the floor.

"If I keep them any more in line," their mother began—and then Sandi heard her mother's voice breaking. "We have to walk around. We have to breathe."

Alfredo surveyed the fourth floor lobby behind his back, then murmured under his breath. "I understand, I understand." He shrugged his shoulders, helpless. "It is a difficult place, this country, before you get used to it. You have to not take things personal." He brightened his voice at the end, but Sandi's mother merely nodded quietly.

"And how are my little señoritas?" Alfredo called over Mrs. García's shoulders. The girls forced smiles as they had been taught, but Sandi, in revenge, also crossed her eyes. She did not like Alfredo; something about the man's overfriendliness and his speaking to them in English even though they all knew Spanish made her feel uneasy. La Bruja downstairs she thought of as the devil—her being below them made sense. When Sandi played Toro, bullfighting Yoyo with a towel, she would shout after each successful scrape with death, *¡OLE!* and stamp her feet in triumph, lifting her right hand to the crowd. She always had a bad conscience afterwards, but she couldn't help herself. One day soon after they had moved in, La Bruja had stopped her mother and the girls in the lobby and spat out that ugly word the kids at school sometimes used: "Spics! Go back to where you came from!"

As soon as Papi came home from his shift at the hospital, he showered, singing a favorite Island song that made the girls giggle as they slipped on their party dresses. They were already in a giddy mood from an inspired discovery that the Fannings' name sure sounded like the word for a person's bottom they had recently learned in the playground at school. "We're going to eat with the fannies," one sister would say to make the others laugh. Papi emerged from the bathroom combing his dark wet curls flat. He looked at the girls and winked. "Your Papi is a dashing man, eh?" He posed in front of the hall mirror, turning this way and that. "A handsome man, your Papi."

The girls indulged him with cries of "*Ay,* Papi." This was the first time in New York that they had seen their father in a lighthearted mood. Mostly he worried about *la situación* back home. Some uncles were in trouble. Tío Mundo had been jailed, and Tío Fidelio was maybe dead. Papi had not been able to get an American doctor's license—some hitch about his foreign education—and the money was running out. Dr. Fanning was trying to help out by lining up jobs, but first Papi needed to pass his licensing exam. It had been Dr. Fanning who had arranged the fellowship that had allowed them all to get out of the old country. And now, the good doctor and his wife had invited the whole family out to an expensive restaurant in the city as a treat. The Fannings knew the Garcías could not afford such a luxury these days. They were such nice people, that was the truth, Mami said, they gave you hope that maybe at the bottom Americans were kind souls.

"But you must behave," Mami said, going back to the same old Epistle. "You must show them what a nice family you come from."

As Mami and Papi finished dressing, the girls watched, fussing at their tights, an uncomfortable new article of clothing. These things bunched at the ankles and sagged at the crotch so you always felt as if your pants might be falling down. They made you feel like those bandaged mummies in the museum. If you unwrapped them, Sandi had pondered, misting the glass case with her breath, would they still be dark Egyptians or would their skin have turned pale after such long bondage— like American skin under all these heavy clothes for the winter that was just starting?

Sandi leaned her elbows on the vanity and watched her mother comb her dark hair in the mirror. Tonight Mami was turning back into the beauty she had been back home. Her face was pale and tragic in the lamplight; her bright eyes shone like amber held up to the light. She wore a black dress with a scoop back and wide shoulders so her long neck had the appearance of a swan gliding on a lake. Around her neck sparkled her good necklace that had real diamonds. "If things get really bad," Mami sometimes joked grimly, "I'll sell the necklace and earrings Papito gave me." Papi always scowled and told her not to speak such nonsense.

If things ever get that bad, Sandi thought, she would sell her charm bracelet with the windmill that always got caught on her clothing. She would even cut her hair and sell it—a maid back home had told her that girls with good hair could always do that. She had no idea who would buy it. She had not seen hair for sale in the big department stores Mami sometimes took them through on outings "to see this new country." But Sandi would make the needed sacrifices. Tonight, she thought, with the rich Fannings, she would present herself as the daughter willing to make these sacrifices. Maybe they would adopt her, and give her an allowance like other American girls got, which Sandi would then pass on to her real family. Provided she could see them periodically, that would not be a bad life, being an only child in a fine, rich, childless American family.

Downstairs, the doorman, Ralph, who had himself come from a country called Ireland as a boy, stood by the opened door and gave each young lady a sweeping bow as she passed by. He always flirted with the girls, calling them the Misses Garcías as if they were rich people's children. Mami often quipped that Ralph probably made more money than Papi on his fellowship. Thank God their grandfather was helping them out. "Without

Papito," Mami confided in her girls, swearing them never to repeat this to their father, "without Papito, we would have to go on welfare." Welfare, they knew, was what people in this country got so they wouldn't turn into beggars like those outside La Catedral back home. It was Papito who paid the rent and bought them their winter clothes and spoiled them once with an outing to Lincoln Center to see the doll-like ballerinas dancing on their toes.

"Will you be needing a taxi tonight, Doc?" Ralph asked their father as he did every time the family came out all dressed up. Usually, Papi said, "No, thank you, Ralph," and the family turned the corner and took a bus. Tonight, though, to Sandi's surprise, her father splurged. "Yes, please, Ralph, a Checker for all my girls." Sandi could not get over how happy her father seemed. She slipped her hand into his, and he gave it a squeeze before he released it. He was not a man to show public affection on foreign soil.

As the taxi sped along, Mami had to repeat the address for the driver because the man could not understand Papi's accent. Sandi realized with a pang one of the things that had been missing in the last few months. It was precisely this kind of special attention paid to them. At home there had always been a chauffeur opening a car door or a gardener tipping his hat and a half dozen maids and nursemaids acting as if the health and well-being of the de la Torre-García children were of wide public concern. Of course, it was usually the de la Torre boys, not the girls, who came in for special consideration. Still, as bearers of the de la Torre name, the girls were made to feel important.

The restaurant had a white awning with its name EL FLA-MENCO in brilliant red letters. A doorman, dressed up as a dignitary with a flaming red band across his white ruffled shirt, opened the car door for them. A carpet on the sidewalk led into the reception foyer, from which they could see into a large room of tables dressed up with white tablecloths and napkins folded to look like bishops' hats. Silverware and glasses gleamed like ornaments. Around the occupied tables handsome waiters gathered, their black hair slicked back into bullfighters' little ponytails. They wore cummerbunds and white shirts with ruffles on the chest—beautiful men like the one Sandi would someday marry. Best of all were the rich, familiar smells of garlic and onion and the lilting cadence of Spanish spoken by the dark-eyed waiters, who reminded Sandi of her uncles.

At the entrance to the dining room, the maître d' explained that Mrs. Fanning had called to say she and her husband were on their way, to go ahead and sit down and order some drinks. He led them, a procession of six, to a table right next to a platform. He pulled out all their chairs, handed them each an opened menu, then bowed and backed away. Three waiters descended on the table, filling water glasses, adjusting silverware and plates. Sandi sat very still and watched their beautiful long fingers fast at work.

"Something to drink, señor?" one of them said, addressing Papi.

"Can I have a Coke?" Fifi piped up, but then backed down when her mother and her sisters eyed her. "I'll have chocolate milk."

Their father laughed good-naturedly, aware of the waiting waiter. "I don't think they have chocolate milk. Cokes is fine for tonight. Right, Mami?"

Mami rolled her eyes in mock exasperation. She was too beautiful tonight to be their mother and to impose the old rules. "Have you noticed," she whispered to Papi when the waiter had left with the drink orders. The girls drew in to hear. Mami was the leader now that they lived in the States. *She* had gone to school in the States. *She* spoke English without a heavy accent. "Look at the menu. Notice how there aren't any prices? I bet a Coke here is a couple of dollars."

Sandi's mouth dropped open. "A couple of dollars!"

Her mother hushed her with an angry look. "Don't embarrass us, please, Sandi!" she said, and then laughed when Papi reminded her that Spanish was not a secret language in this place.

"*Ay*, Mami." He covered her hand briefly with his. "This is a special night. I want us to have a good time. We need a celebration."

"I suppose," Mami said, sighing. "And the Fannings are paying."

Papi's face tightened.

"There's nothing to be ashamed of," Mami reminded him. "When they were our guests back home, we treated them like royalty."

That was true. Sandi remembered when the famous Doctor Fanning and his wife had come down to instruct the country's leading doctors on new procedures for heart surgery. The tall, slender man and his goofy wife had been guests in the family compound. There had been many barbecues with the driveway lined with cars and a troop of chauffeurs under the palm trees exchanging news and gossip.

When the drinks arrived, Papi made a funny toast, in Spanish and loud enough for the waiters' benefit, but they were all too professional, and if they did overhear, no one chuckled. Just as they all lifted their glasses, Mami leaned into the table. "They're here." Sandi turned to see the maître d' heading in their direction with a tall, dressed-up woman, and behind her, a towering, preoccupied-looking man. It took a moment to register that these were the same human beings who had loitered around the pool back on the Island, looking silly in sunglasses and sunhats, noses smeared with suntan cream, and speaking a grossly inadequate Spanish to the maids.

A flutter of hellos and apologies ensued. Papi stood up, and Sandi, not knowing what manners were called for, stood up too, and was eyed by her mother to sit back down. The doctor and his wife lingered over each girl, "trying to get them straight," and remembering how each one had been only this tall when last they had seen them. "What little beauties!" Dr. Fanning teased. "Carlos, you've got quite a harem here!" The four girls watched their father's naughty smile tilt on his face.

For the first few minutes the adults exchanged news. Dr. Fanning told how he had spoken with a friend who was the manager of an important hotel that needed a house doctor. The job was a piece of cake, Dr. Fanning explained, mostly keeping rich widows in Valium, but heck, the pay was good. Sandi's father looked down at his plate, grateful, but also embarrassed to be in such straits and to be so beholden.

The Fannings' drinks arrived. Mrs. Fanning drank hers down in several greedy swallows, then ordered another. She had been quiet during the flurry of arrival, but now she gushed questions, raising her eyebrows and pulling long faces when Mrs. García explained that they had not been able to get any news from the family ever since the news blackout two weeks back.

Sandi studied the woman carefully. Why had Dr. Fanning, who was tall and somewhat handsome, married this plain, bucktoothed woman? Maybe she came from a good family, which back home was the reason men married plain, bucktoothed women. Maybe Mrs. Fanning came with all the jewelry she had on, and Dr. Fanning had been attracted by its glittering the way little fishes are if you wrap tinfoil on a string and dangle it in the shallows.

Dr. Fanning opened his menu. "What would everyone like? Girls?" This was the moment they had been so carefully prepared for. Mami would order for them—they were not to be so rude or forward as to volunteer a special like or dislike. Besides, as Sandi tried reading the menu, with the help of her index finger, sounding out syllables, she did not recognize the names of dishes listed.

Her mother explained to Dr. Fanning that she would order two *pastelones* for the girls to share.

"Oh, but the seafood here is so good," the doctor pleaded, looking at her from above his glasses, which had slipped down on his nose like a schoolteacher's. "How about some paella, girls, or *camarones a la vinagreta*?"

"They don't eat shrimp," their mother said, and Sandi was grateful to her for defending them from this dreaded, wormy food. On the other hand, Sandi would have been glad to order something different and all to herself. But she remembered her mother's warnings.

"Mami," Fifi whispered, "what's *pastolone*?"

"*Pastelón*, Cuca." Mami explained it was a casserole like Chucha used to make back home with rice and ground beef. "It's very good. I know you girls will like it." Then she gave them a pointed look they understood to mean, they *must* like it.

"Yes," they said nicely when Dr. Fanning asked if *pastelón* was indeed what they wanted.

"Yes, what?" Mami coached.

"Yes, thank you," they chorused. The doctor laughed, then winked knowingly at them.

Their orders in and fresh drinks on the table, the grown-ups fell into the steady drone of adult conversation. Now and again the changed cadence of a story coming through made Sandi lean forward and listen. Otherwise, she sat quietly, playing with sugar packets until her mother made her stop. She watched the different tables around theirs. All the other guests were white and spoke in low, unexcited voices. Americans, for sure. They could have eaten anywhere, Sandi thought, and yet they had come to a *Spanish* place for dinner. La Bruja was wrong. Spanish was something other people paid to be around.

Her eye fell on a young waiter whose job seemed to be to pour water into the goblets at each table when they ran low. Every time she caught his eye, she would glance away embarrassed, but with boredom she grew bolder. She commenced a little flirtation; he smiled, and each time she smiled back, he approached with his silver pitcher to refill her water glass. Her mother noticed and said in coded scolding, "Their well is going to run dry."

In fact, Sandi had drunk so much water that, she explained quietly to Mami, she was going to have to go to the toilet. Her mother cast her another of her angry looks. They had been cautioned against making any demands tonight during dinner. Sandi squirmed at her seat, unwilling to go, unless she could be granted a smiling permission.

Papi offered to accompany her. "I could use the men's room myself." Mrs. Fanning also stood up and said she could stand to leave behind a little something. Dr. Fanning gave her a warning look, not too different from the one Sandi's mother had given her.

The three of them trooped to the back of the restaurant where the maître d' had directed, and down a narrow flight of stairs, lit gloomily by little lamps hung in archways. In the poorly lit basement Mrs. Fanning squinted at the writing on the two doors. "*Damas? Caballeros?*" Sandi checked an impulse to correct the American lady's pronunciation. "Hey there, Carlos, you're going to have to translate for me so I don't end up in the wrong room with you!" Mrs. Fanning rolled her hips in a droll way like someone trying to keep up a Hula-Hoop.

Papi looked down at his feet. Sandi had noticed before that around American women he was not himself. He rounded his shoulders and was stiffly well-mannered, like a servant. "Sandi will show you," he said, putting his daughter between himself and Mrs. Fanning, who laughed at his discomfort. "Go ahead then, sugar pie." Sandi held open the door marked DAMAS for the American lady. As Mrs. Fanning turned to follow, she leaned towards Sandi's father and brushed her lips on his.

Sandi didn't know whether to stand there foolishly or dash in and let the door fall on this uncomfortable moment. Like her father, she looked down at her feet, and waited for the giggling lady to sweep by her. Even in the dimly lit room, Sandi could see her father's face darken with color.

Sandi and Mrs. Fanning found themselves in a pretty little parlor with a couch and lamps and a stack of perfumed towels. Sandi spied the stalls in an adjoining room and hurried into one, releasing her bladder. Relieved, she now felt the full and shocking weight of what she had just witnessed. A married American woman kissing her father!

As she let herself out of her stall, she heard Mrs. Fanning still active in hers. Quickly, she finished hitching up her silly tights, then swished her hands under the faucet, beginning to dry them on her dress, but remembering after an initial swipe, the towels. She took one from the stack, wiped her hands and tapped at her face as she had seen Mami do with the powder puff. Looking at herself in the mirror, she was surprised to find a pretty girl looking back at her. It was a girl who could pass as American, with soft blue eyes and fair skin, looks that were traced back to a great-great grandmother from Sweden at every family gathering. She lifted her bangs—her face was delicate like a ballerina's. It struck her impersonally as if it were a judgment someone else was delivering, someone American and important, like Dr. Fanning: she was pretty. She had heard it said before, of course, but the compliment was always a group compliment to all the sisters, so Sandi thought this was a politeness friends of her parents said about daughters just as they tended to say "They're so big" or "They're so smart" about sons. Being pretty, she would not have to go back to where she came from. Pretty spoke both languages. Pretty belonged in this country to spite La Bruja. As she studied herself, the stall door behind her opened in the mirror. Sandi let her bangs fall and rushed out of the room.

Her father was waiting in the anteroom, pacing nervously, his hands worrying the change in his pocket. "Where is she?" he whispered.

Sandi pointed back in the room with her chin.

"That woman is drunk," he whispered, crouching down beside Sandi. "But I can't insult her, imagine, our one chance in this country." He spoke in the serious, hushed voice he had used with Mami those last few days in the old country. "*Por favor*, Sandi, you're a big girl now. Not a word of this to your mother. You know how she is these days."

Sandi eyed him. This was the first time her father had ever asked her to do something sneaky. Before she had time to respond, the bathroom door swung open. Her father stood up. Mrs. Fanning called out, "Why, here you are, sugar!"

"Yes, here we are!" her father said in a too cheerful voice. "And we must better get back to the table before they send the marines!" He smiled archly, as if he had just thought up this quip he had been making for weeks.

Mrs. Fanning threw her head back and laughed. "Oh, Carlos!"

Her father joined the American lady's phony laughter, then stopped abruptly when he noticed Sandi's eyes on him. "What are you waiting for?" He spoke in a stern voice, nodding towards the stairs. Sandi glanced away, hurt. Mrs. Fanning laughed again and led the way up the narrow winding stairs. It was like coming up out of a dungeon, Sandi decided. She would tell her sisters this and make them wish they had gone to the bathroom as well, though truly, Sandi wished she had herself never strayed from the table. She wouldn't have seen what she could not now hope to forget.

At the table, the young waiter tucked the chair in for her. He was still lovely, his skin so smooth and of a rich olive color, his hands long and slender like those of angels in illustrations, holding their choir books. But this man could very well lean forward just as Mrs. Fanning had done downstairs. He could try to kiss *her*, Sandi, on the lips. She did not let her glance fall in his direction again.

Instead, she studied the Fannings intently for clues as to their mysterious behavior. One thing she noticed was that Mrs. Fanning drank a lot of wine, and each time she nodded to the waiter to fill her glass, Dr. Fanning said something to her out of the corner of his mouth. At one point when the waiter leaned toward her empty glass, Dr. Fanning covered it with his hand. "That's enough," he snapped, and quickly the waiter leaned away again.

"What a party fart," Mrs. Fanning observed, loud enough for the table to hear, though "fart" was not a word the girls recognized. Mami instantly began to fuss at Sandi and her sisters, pretending that the exchange of angry whispering between the Fannings was not taking place. But little Fifi could not be distracted from the scene at the end of the table: she stared wide-eyed at the bickering Fannings, and then over at Mami with a serious look of oncoming tears. Mami winked at her, and smiled a high-watt smile to reassure the little girl that these Americans need not be taken seriously.

Blessedly, their platters of food appeared, borne by a cortege of waiters, directed by the busybody maître d'. The tension dispelled as the two couples took small, pensive bites of their different servings. Compliments and evaluations erupted all around the table. Sandi found most of the things on her plate inedible. But there was a generous decorative lettuce leaf under which much of the goopy meat and greasy rice could be tucked away.

Tonight she felt beyond either of her parents: she could tell that they were small people compared to these Fannings. She had herself witnessed a scene whose disclosure could cause trouble. What did she care if her parents demanded that she eat all of her *pastelón*. She would say, just as an American girl might, "I don't wanna. You can't make me. This is a free country."

"Sandi, look!" It was her father, trying to befriend her. He was pointing towards the stage where the lights were dimming. Six señoritas in long, fitted dresses with flaring skirts and castanets in their hands flounced onto the stage. The guitarist came on and strummed a summoning tune. Beautiful men in toreador outfits joined their ladies. They stamped their feet for hello, and the ladies stamped back, Hello! Six and six, *damas* and *caballeros*, they went through a complicated series of steps, the women's castanets clacking a teasing beat, the men echoing their partners' moves with sultry struts, and foot stomps. These were not the dainty and chaste twirls and curtseys of the ballerinas at Lincoln Center. These women looked, well—Sandi knew no other way to put it—they looked as if they wanted to take their clothes off in front of the men.

Yoyo and Fifi were closest to the stage, but Mami let Carla and Sandi pull their chairs around in a cluster and join their sisters. The dancers clapped and strutted, tossing their heads boldly like horses. Sandi's heart soared. This wild and beautiful dance came from people like her, Spanish people, who danced the strange, disquieting joy that sometimes made Sandi squeeze Fifi's hand hard until she cried or bullfight Yoyo with a towel until both girls fell in a giggling, exhausted heap on the floor that made La Bruja beat her ceiling with a broom handle.

"The girls are having such fun," she heard her mother confide to Mrs. Fanning.

"Me too," the American lady observed. "These guys are something else. Hey, Lori, watch that one's tight tights."

"Very nice," Sandi's mother said a little stiffly.

Dr. Fanning hissed at his wife. "That's enough, Sylvia."

As the show progressed, Sandi could see that the dancers' faces were becoming beaded with sweat. Wet patches spread under their arms, and their smiles were strained. Still they were beautiful as first one couple then another came forward in solo dances. Then the men withdrew, and from somewhere they acquired roses, which they presented to their partners. The women began a dance in which the roses were held in their mouths, and their castanets clacked a merciless thank you to the men.

Behind Sandi, a chair scraped the floor, another fell over, and two figures hurled by. It was Mrs. Fanning with Dr. Fanning giving chase! She scrambled up onto the platform, clapping her hands over her head, Dr. Fanning lunging at but missing her as she escaped onto center stage. The dancers good-naturedly made way. Dr. Fanning did not follow, but with an angry shrug of his shoulders, headed back to their table.

"Let her enjoy herself," Sandi's mother said. Her voice was full of phony good cheer. "She is just having a good time."

"She's had too much to drink is what she's had," the doctor snapped.

The restaurant came alive with the American lady's clowning. She was a good ham, bumping her hips up against the male dancers and rolling her eyes. The diners laughed and clapped. The management, sensing a good moment, gave her a spotlight, and the guitarist came forward, strumming a popular American tune with a Spanish flair. One of the male dancers partnered Mrs. Fanning—who advanced as the dancer withdrew in a pantomine of a cartoon chase. The diners roared their approval.

All but Sandi. Mrs. Fanning had broken the spell of the wild and beautiful dancers. Sandi could not bear to watch her. She turned her chair around to face the table and occupied herself with her water glass, twisting the stem around, making damp links on the white cloth.

To a round of applause, Mrs. Fanning was escorted back to the table by her partner. Sandi's father stood up and pulled her chair out for her.

"Let's go." Dr. Fanning turned, looking for the waiter to ask for the check.

"Ah, come on, sugar, loosen up, will ya?" his wife coaxed

him. One of the dancers had given the American lady her rose, and Mrs. Fanning now tried to stick it in her husband's lapel. Dr. Fanning narrowed his eyes at her, but before he could speak, the table was presented with a complimentary bottle of champagne from the management. As the cork popped, a few of the customers in adjoining tables applauded and lifted their glasses up in a toast to Mrs. Fanning.

"A toast to all of us!" Mrs. Fanning held up her glass. "Come on, girls," she urged them. Sandi's sisters lifted their water glasses and clinked the American lady's.

"Sandi!" her mother said. "You too."

Reluctantly, Sandi lifted her glass.

Dr. Fanning held up his glass and tried to inject a pointed seriousness into the moment: "To you, the Garcías. Welcome to this country." Now her parents lifted their glasses, and in her father's eyes, Sandi noted gratitude and in her mother's eyes a moistness that meant barely checked tears.

As Dr. Fanning spoke to one of the waiters, a dancer approached the table, carrying a large straw basket with a strap that went around her neck. She tipped the basket towards the girls and smiled a wide, warm smile at the two men. Inside the basket were a dozen dark-haired Barbie dolls dressed like Spanish señoritas. The dancer held up a doll and puffed out the skirt of its dress so that it opened prettily like a fully blown flower.

"Would you like one?" she asked little Fifi. The woman spoke in English, but her voice was heavily accented like Dr. García's.

Fifi nodded eagerly, then looked over at her mother, who was eyeing the little girl. Slowly Fifi shook her head. "No?" the dancer said in a surprised voice, lifting up her eyebrows. She looked at the other girls, her eye falling on Sandi. "You would like one?"

Sandi, of course, remembered the much-repeated caution to the girls that they should not ask for any special dishes or treats of any sort. The Garcías could not afford extras, and they did not want to put their hosts in the embarrassing position of having to spend money out of largesse. Sandi stared at the small doll. She was a perfect replica of the beautiful dancers, dressed in a long, glittery gown with a pretty tortoise shell comb in her hair, from which cascaded a tiny, lacy mantilla. On her feet were strapped tiny black heels such as the dancers had worn. Sandi ignored her mother's fierce look and reached out for the doll.

With the tip of her painted fingernail, the dancer salesgirl showed the miniature maracas the doll was holding. Sandi felt such tenderness as when a new mother uncurls the tiny fists of a newborn. She turned to her father, ignoring her mother's glare. "Papi, can I have her?" Her father looked up at the pretty salesgirl and smiled. Sandi could tell he wanted to make an impression. "Sure," he nodded, adding, "Anything for my girl." The salesgirl smiled.

Instantly the cry from the other three: "Me too, Papi! Me too!"

Her mother reached over and took the doll from Sandi's hands. "Absolutely not, girls." She shook her head at the dancer, who had since reached in her basket and extracted three more dolls.

Meanwhile the check had been brought, and Dr. Fanning was reviewing the items, stacking bills on a little tray. As he did so, Papi gazed down at the tablecloth. Back in the old country, everyone fought for the honor of paying. But what could he do in this new country where he did not even know if he had enough cash in his pocket to make good on buying the four dolls that he was now committed to provide for his girls.

"You know the rules!" Mami hissed at them.

"Please, Mami, please," Fifi begged, not understanding that the woman's offer of a doll did not mean they were free.

"No!" Mami said sharply. "And no more discussion, girls." The edge on her voice made Mrs. Fanning, who had been absently collecting her things, look up. "What's going on?" she asked the girls' mother. "Nothing," Mami said, and smiled tensely.

Sandi was not going to miss her chance. This woman had kissed her father. This woman had ruined the act of the beautiful dancers. The way Sandi saw it, this woman owed her something. "We want one of those dolls." Sandi pointed to the basket in which the dancer was rearranging the rejected dolls.

"Sandi!" her mother cried.

"Why, I think that's a swell idea! A souvenir!" Mrs. Fanning motioned the dancer back, who approached the table with her full cargo. "Give each of these girls a doll and put it on the bill. Sugar"—she turned to her husband, who had finished clapping the small folder closed—"hold your horses."

"I will not permit—" Papi sat forward, reaching in his back pocket for his wallet.

"Nonsense!" Mrs. Fanning hushed him. She touched his

hand to prevent him from opening his wallet.

Papi flinched and then tried to disguise his reaction by pretending to shake her hand away. "I pay this."

"Don't take his money," Mrs. Fanning ordered the dancer, who smiled noncommittedly.

"Hey," Dr. Fanning said, agreeing with his wife. "We wanted to get the girls something, but heck, we didn't know what. This is perfect." He peeled four more tens from his wad. Papi exchanged a helpless look with Mami.

While her sisters fussed over which of the dolls to choose, Sandi grabbed the one dressed exactly like the dancers in the floor show. She stood the Barbie on the table and raised one of the doll's arms and pulled the other out so that the doll was frozen in the pose of the Spanish dancers.

"You are much too kind," her mother said to Mrs. Fanning, and then in a hard voice with the promise of later punishment, she addressed the four girls, "What do you say?"

"Thank you," Sandi's sisters chorused.

"Sandi?" her mother said.

Sandi looked up. Her mother's eyes were dark and beautiful like those of the little dancer before her. "Yes, Mami?" she asked politely, as if she hadn't heard the order.

"What do you say to Mrs. Fanning?"

Sandi turned to the woman whose blurry, alcoholic eyes and ironic smile intimated the things Sandi was just beginning to learn, things that the dancers knew all about, which was why they danced with such vehemence, such passion. She hopped her dancer right up to the American lady and gave her a bow. Mrs. Fanning giggled and returned an answering nod.

Sandi did not stop. She pushed her doll closer, so that Mrs. Fanning aped a surprised, cross-eyed look. Holding her new doll right up to the American woman's face and tipping it so that its little head touched the woman's flushed cheek, Sandi made a smacking sound.

"*Gracias*," Sandi said, as if the Barbie doll had to be true to her Spanish costume.

III

▼▲▼▲▼IIII▼▲▼▲▼▲▼▲▼▲▼▲▼▲▼▲▼▲▼▲▼▲▼▲▼▲▼▲▼▲▼▲▼▲▼

1960–1956

The Blood of the Conquistadores

▼▲▼▲▼▲▼▲▼▲▼▲▼▲▼▲▼▲▼▲▼▲▼▲▼▲▼▲▼▲▼▲▼III▼▲▼▲▼

Mami, Papi, the Four Girls

I

C arlos is in the pantry, getting himself a glass of water from the filtered spout when he sees the two men walking up the driveway. They are dressed in starched khaki. Each wears reflector sunglasses, and the gleam off the frames matches the gleam off the buckles on their holsters. Except for the guns, they could be foremen coming to collect on a bill or to supervise a job that other men will sweat over. But the guns give them away.

Beside him, the old cook Chucha is fussing with a coaster for his glass. The gesture of his head towards the window alerts her. She looks up and sees the two men. Very slowly, so that in their approach they will not catch a movement at the window, Carlos lifts his finger to his lips. Chucha nods. Step by careful step, he backs out of the room, and once he is in the hall where there are no windows to the driveway, he makes a mad dash towards the bedroom. He passes the patio, where the four girls are playing Statues with their cousins.

They are too intent on their game to notice the blur of his body running by. But Yoyo, just frozen in a spin, happens to look up and see him.

Again, he puts his finger to his lips. Yoyo cocks her head, intrigued.

"Yoyo!" one of the cousin cries. "Yoyo moved!"

The argument erupts just as he reaches the bedroom door. He hopes Yoyo will keep her mouth shut. Surely the men will question her when they go through the house. Children and servants are two groups they always interrogate.

In the bedroom, he opens the large walk-in closet and the inside light comes on. When he shuts the door, it goes off. He reaches for the flashlight and beams it on. Far off, he hears the children arguing, then the chiming of the doorbell. His heart is going so fast that he feels as if something, not his heart, is trapped inside. Easy now, easy.

He pushes to the back of the closet behind a row of Laura's dresses. He is comforted by the talc smell of her housedresses mixed with the sunbaked smell of her skin, the perfumy smell of her party dresses. He makes sure he does not disturb the arrangement of her shoes on the floor, but steps over them and disengages the back panel. Inside is a cubicle with a vent that opens out above the shower in the bathroom. Air and a little light. A couple of towels, a throw pillow, a sheet, a chamber pot, a container of filter water, aspirin, sleeping pills, even a San Judas, patron of impossible causes, that Laura has tacked to the inside wall. The small revolver Vic has smuggled in for him—just in case—is wrapped snugly in an extra shirt, a dark colored shirt, and a dark colored pair of pants for escaping at night. He steps inside, sets the flashlight on the floor, and snaps the panel back, closing himself in.

When she sees her father dash by, Yoyo thinks he is playing one of his games that nobody likes, and that Mami says are in poor taste. Like when he says, "You want to hear God speak?" and you have to press his nose, and he farts. Or when he asks over and over even after you say *white*, "What color was Napoleon's white horse?" Or when he gives you the test of whether or not you inherited the blood of the Conquistadores, and he holds you upside down by your feet until all the blood goes to your head, and he keeps asking, "Do you have the blood of the Conquistadores?" Yoyo always says no, until she can't stand it anymore because her head feels as if it's going to crack open, and she says yes. Then he puts her right side up and laughs a great big Conquistador laugh that comes all the way from the green, motherland hills of Spain.

But Papi is not playing a game now because soon after he runs by in hide-and-seek, the doorbell rings, and Chucha lets in those two creepy-looking men. They are coffee-with-milk color and the khaki they wear is the same color as their skin, so they look all beige, which no one would ever pick as a favorite color. They wear dark mirror glasses. What catches Yoyo's eye are their holster belts and the shiny black bulge of their guns poking through.

Now she knows guns are illegal. Only *guardias* in uniform can carry them, so either these men are criminals or some kind of secret police in plain clothes Mami has told her about who could be anywhere at anytime like guardian angels, except they don't keep you from doing bad but wait to catch you doing it. Mami has joked with Yoyo that she better behave because if these secret police see her doing something wrong, they will take her away to a prison for children where the menu is a list of everything Yoyo doesn't like to eat.

Chucha talks very loud and repeats what the men say as if she were deaf. She must be wanting Papi to hear from wherever he is hiding. This must be serious like the time Yoyo told their neighbor, the old general, a made-up story about Papi having a gun, a story which turned out to be true because Papi did really have a hidden gun for some reason. The nursemaid Milagros told on Yoyo telling the general that story, and her parents hit her very hard with a belt in the bathroom, with the shower on so no one could hear her screams. Then Mami had to meet Tío Vic in the middle of the night with the gun hidden under her raincoat so it wouldn't be on the premises in case the police came. That was very serious. That was the time Mami still talks about when "you almost got your father killed, Yoyo."

Once the men are seated in the living room off the inside patio, they try to lure the children into conversation. Yoyo does not say a word. She is sure these men have come on account of that gun story she told when she was only five and before anyone told her guns were illegal.

The taller man with the gold tooth asks Mundín, the only boy here, where his father is. Mundín explains his father is probably still at the office, and so the man asks him where his mother is, and Mundín says he thinks she is home.

"The maid said she was not at home," the short one with a broad face says in a testy voice. It is delicious to watch him realize a moment later that he is in the wrong when Mundín says, "You mean Tía Laura. But see, I live next door."

"Ahhh," the short one says, stretching the word out, his mouth round like the barrel of the revolver he has emptied and is passing around so the children can all hold it. Yoyo takes it in her hand and looks straight into the barrel hole, shuddering. Maybe it is loaded, maybe if she shot her head off, everyone would forgive her for having made up the story of the gun.

"So which of you girls live here?" the tall one asks. Carla raises her hand as if she were at school. Sandi also raises her hand like a copycat and tells Yoyo and Fifi to raise their hands too.

"Four girls," the fat one says, rolling his eyes. "No boys?" They shake their heads. "Your father better get good locks on the door."

A worried look flashes across Fifi's face. A few days ago she turned the small rod on her bedroom doorknob by mistake and then couldn't figure out how to pop it back and unlock the door. A workman from Papito's factory had to come and take out the whole lock, making a hole in the door, and letting the hysterical Fifi out. "Why locks?" she asks, her bottom lip quivering.

"Why?!" The chubby one laughs. The roll of fat around his waist jiggles. "Why?!" he keeps repeating and breaking out in fresh chuckles. "Come here, *cielito lindo*, and let me show you why your Papi has to put locks on the door." He beckons to Fifi with his index finger crooked. Fifi shakes her head no, and begins to cry.

Yoyo wants to cry, too, but she is sure if she does, the men will get suspicious and take her father away and maybe the whole family. Yoyo imagines herself in a jail cell. It would be like Felicidad, Mamita's little canary, in her birdcage. The guards would poke in rifles the way Yoyo sometimes pokes Felicidad with sticks when no one in the big house is looking. She gets herself so scared that she is on the brink of tears when she hears the car in the drive, and knows it must be, it must be. "Mami's here!" she cries out, hoping this good news will stop her little sister's tears.

The two men exchange a look and put their revolvers back into their holsters.

Chucha, grim-faced as always, comes in and announces loudly, "Doña Laura is home." As she exits, she lets drop a fine powder. Her lips move the whole time as if she were doing her usual sullen, under-her-breath grumbling, but Yoyo knows she is casting a spell that will leave the men powerless, becalmed.

As Laura nears her driveway, she honks the horn twice to alert the guard to open the gate, but surprisingly, it is already open. Chino is standing outside the little gatehouse talking to a man in khaki. Up ahead, Laura sees the black V.W., and her heart plummets right down to her toes. Next to her in the passenger seat it has taken her months to convince the young country girl to ride in, Imaculada says, *"Doña, hay visita."*

Laura plays along, controlling the tremor of her voice. "Yes, company." She stops and motions for Chino to come to the car. *"¡Qué hay, Chino!"*

"They are looking for Don Carlos," Chino says tensely. He

lowers his voice and looks over at Imaculada, who looks down at her hands. "They have been here for awhile. There are two more waiting in the house."

"I'll talk to them," Laura says to Chino, whose slightly slanted eyes have earned him his nickname. "And you go over to Doña Carmen's and tell her to call Don Victor and tell him to come right over and pick up his tennis shoes. Tennis shoes, you hear?" Chino nods. He can be trusted to put two and two together. Chino has been with the family forever—well, only a little less than Chucha, who came when Laura's mother was pregnant with Laura. Chino calls to the man in khaki, who flicks his cigarette onto the lawn behind him, and approaches the car. As Laura greets him, she sees Chino cutting across the lawn towards Don Mundo's house.

"Doña, excuse our dropping in on you," the man is saying with false politeness that seems as if it is being wastefully squeezed from a tube. "We need to ask Doctor García a few questions, and at the *clínica*, they told us he was home. Your boy"—Boy! Chino is over fifty—"he says *el doctor* is not home yet, so we will wait until he shows up. Surely, he is on his way—" The guard looks up at the sky, shielding his eyes: the sun is dead center above him, noon, time for dinner, time for every man to sit down at his table and break bread and say grace to God and Trujillo for the plenty the country is enjoying.

"By all means, wait for him, but please not under this hot sun." Laura switches into her grand manner. The grand manner will usually disarm these poor lackeys from the countryside, who have joined the SIM, most of them, in order to put money in their pockets, food and rum in their stomachs, and guns at their hips. But deep down, they are still boys in rags bringing down coconuts for *el patrón* when he visits his *fincas* with his family on Sundays.

"You must come in and have something cold to drink."

The man bows his head, grateful. But no, he must stay put, orders. Laura promises to send him down a cold beer and drives up to the house. She wonders if Carmen has been able to get hold of Victor. At the first sign of trouble, Victor said, get in touch, code phrase is *tennis shoes*. He is good for his word. It wasn't his fault the State Department chickened out of the plot they had him organize. And he has promised to get the men out safely. All but Fernando, of course. *Pobrecito* ending up the way he did, hanging himself by his belt in his cell to keep from giving out the others' names under the tortures Trujillo's henchmen were administering. Fernando, a month in his grave, San Judas protect us all.

At the door she directs Imaculada to unload the groceries and be sure to take the man down at the gate a Presidente, the common beer they all like. Then she crosses herself and enters the house. In the living room, the two men rise to greet her; Fifi runs to her in tears; Yoyo is right behind, all eyes, looking frightened. Laura is raising her girls American style, reading all the new literature, so she knows she shouldn't have beaten Yoyo that time the girl gave them such a scare. But you lose your head in this crazy hellhole, you do, and different rules apply. Now, for instance, she is thinking of doing something wild and mad, sinking down in a swoon the way women used to in old movies when they wanted to distract attention from some trouble spot, unbuttoning her blouse and offering the men pleasure if they'll let her husband and babies escape.

"Gentlemen, please," Laura says, urging them to sit down, and then she eyeballs the kids to leave the room. They all do, except Yoyo and Fifi, who hold on to either side of her, not saying a word.

"Is there some problem?" Laura begins.

"We just have a few questions to ask Don Carlos. Are you expecting him for the noon meal?"

At this moment, a way to delay these men comes to her. Vic is on his way, she hopes, and he'll know how to handle this mess.

"My husband had a tennis game today with Victor Hubbard." She says the name slowly so that it will register. "The game probably ran a little late. Make yourselves at home, please. My house, your house," she says, reciting the traditional Dominican welcome.

She excuses herself a moment to prepare a tray of little snacks they urge her not to trouble herself to prepare. In the pantry, Chucha is alone since Imaculada has gone off to serve the guard his beer. The old black woman and the young mistress exchange looks. "Don Carlos," Chucha mouths, "in the bedroom." Laura nods. She knows now where he is, and although it spooks her that he is within a few feet of these men, sealed in the secret compartment, she is also grateful that he is so close by she could almost reach out and touch him.

Back in the living room, she serves the men a tray of fried plantain chips and peanuts and *casabe* and pours each one a Presidente in the cheap glasses she keeps for servants. Seeing

.

the men eye the plates, she remembers the story that Trujillo forces his cooks to taste his food before he eats. Laura breaks off a piece of *casabe* for Fifi on one side of her, and another for Yoyo. Then she herself takes a handful of peanuts and puts them, like a schoolgirl, one by one in her mouth. The men reach out their hands and eat.

When the phone rings at Doña Tatica's, she feels the sound deep inside her sore belly. Bad news, she thinks. Candelario, be at my side. She picks the phone up as if it had claws, and announces in a small voice, so unlike hers, *"Buenos días, El Paraíso, para servirle."*

The voice on the other end is the American's secretary, a no-nonsense, too-much-schooling-in-her-voice woman who does not return Tatica's *buenos días*. Embassy business, the voice snaps, "Please call Don Vic to the phone." Tatica echoes the secretary's snippiness: "I cannot disturb him." But the voice gloats back, *"Urgente,"* and Tatica must obey.

She heads across the courtyard towards *casita* #6. Large enough already inside her broad, caramel-colored body, Tatica renders herself dramatically larger by always dressing in red, a *promesa* she has made to her *santo*, Candelario, so he will cure her of the horrible burning in her gut. The doctor went in and cut out some of her stomach and all of her woman machinery, but Candelario stayed, filling that empty space with spirit. Now whenever trouble is coming, Tatica feels a glimmer of the old burning in the centipede trail on her belly. Something pretty bad is on its way because with each step Tatica takes, the pain roils in her gut, trouble coming to full term.

Under the *amapola* tree, the yardboy is lounging with the American's chauffeur. When he sees her, quick he busies himself clipping a sorry-looking hedge. The chauffeur calls out, *Buenos días, doña Tatica*, and tips his cap at Tatica who lifts her head high above his riffraff. *Casita #6*, Don Victor's regular cabin, is straight ahead. The air conditioner is going. Tatica will have to pound hard with strength she does not have so her knock will be heard.

At the door she pauses. Candelario, she pleads as she lifts her hand to knock, for the burning has spread. *"Urgente,"* she calls out, meaning her own condition now, for her whole body feels bathed in a burning pain as if her flame-colored dress were itself on fire.

A goddamn bang comes at the goddamn door. *"Teléfono, urgente, señor Hubbard."* Vic does not lose a beat, but calls out, *"Un minuto,"* and finishes first. He shakes his head at the sweet giggling thing and says, *"Excusez, por favor."* Half the time he doesn't know whether he's using his CIA crash course in Spanish or his prep school Latin or his college French. But dicks and dollars are what talk in El Paraíso anyway.

When he first got to this little hot spot, Vic didn't know how hot it would be. Immediately, he looked up his old classmate Mundo, who comes from one of those old wealthy families who send their kids to the States to prep school, and the boys on to college. Old buddy introduced him around till he knew every firebrand among the upper-class fellas the State Department wanted him to groom for revolution. Fellas got him fixed up with Tatica, who has kept him in the little girls he likes, hot little numbers, dark and sweet like the little cups of *cafecito* so full of goddam caffeine and Island sugar you're shaking half the day.

Vic dresses quickly, and as soon as his clothes are on, he is all business. *"Hasta luego,"* he says, waving to the little girl sitting up and pouting prettily. "Behave yourself," he jokes. Naughtily, she lifts her little chin. Really, they are so cute.

He opens the door unto a crumbling Tatica, two hundred pounds going limp in his arms. He looks up and sees over her shoulder his chauffeur and the yardboy rushing to his aid. Behind him, above the air conditioner's roar, he can hear the little girl shout Doña Tatica's name, and as if summoned back from the hellhole of her pain, Tatica's eyes roll up, her mouth parts. *"Teléfono, urgente, Embajada,"* she whispers to Don Vic, and he takes off, leaving her to collapse into the arms of her own riffraff.

Vic goes first to Mundo's house, since the call came from Carmen, and finds her in the patio with endless kiddies having their noon meal at the big table. Carmen rushes towards him. *"Gracias a Dios, Vic,"* she says for hello. A sweetheart, this little lady, not bad legs either. Unfortunately, the nuns got to her young, and Vic has nodded himself silly several times to catechism lessons disguised as dinner conversations. He wonders if it shows all over him where he's been, and grins, thinking back on the sweet little number not much older than some of the little sirens sitting around the table now. "Tío Vic, Tío Vic," they call out. Honestly, lash me to a lamppost, he thinks.

Quick look around the table. No sign of Mundo. Maybe he's had to take refuge in the temporary holding closet Vic advised him and the others to construct? He smiles comfortingly at Carmen, whose smile back is a grimace of fear. "In the study," she directs him.

The kids keep calling for Tío Vic to come over to the lunch table they are not allowed to leave. He waves at them and says, "Carry on, troops," as he goes by. Over his shoulder, he hears Carmen call after him, "Have you eaten, Victor?" These Latin women, even when the bullets are flying and the bombs are falling, they want to make sure you have a full stomach, your shirt is ironed, your handkerchief is fresh. It's what makes the nice girls from polite society great hostesses, and the girls at Tatica's such obliging lovers.

He taps on the door, says his name, waits, says it again, a little louder this time since the air conditioner is going. The door opens eerily as if by itself since no one admits him. He enters, the door closes behind him, a gun's safety clicks off. "Whoa, fellas," he calls out, lifting his hands to show he's their unarmed, honest-to-god buddy. The jalousies have all been closed, and the men are spread around the room as if assuming lookout posts. Mundo comes out from behind the door, and Fidelio, the nervous one, stands by the bookshelves, pulling books in and out as if they were levers that might work their safe escape out of this frightening moment. Mateo squats, as if lighting a fire. Standing by different windows are the rest of the guys. Jesus, they look like a bunch of scared rabbits.

"Thought you might be SIM," Mundo says, explaining his withdrawn gun. He pulls a chair out for his buddy. The chairs in his study bear the logo from their alma mater, Yale, which Vic notes the family mispronounces as *jail*.

"What's up?" Vic asks in his heavily-accented Spanish.

"Trouble," says Mundo. "With a capital T."

Vic nods. "We're on," he says to the group. "*Operación Zapatos Tenis.*" Then he does what he has always done ever since back in Indiana as a boy the shit first began hitting fan: he cracks his knuckles and grins.

Carla and Sandi are having their lunch at Tía Carmen's house, which is not breaking the rules because, number one, Mami told them to SCRAM with her widened eyes, and number two, the rule is that unless you're grounded, you can eat at any aunt's house if you let Mami know first, which goes back to number one, that Mami told them to SCRAM, and it is already almost an hour since they should have eaten back home.

Something is fishy like when Mami walks in on them and they quick hide what they don't want her to see, and she clips her nose together with her fingers and says, "I smell a rat." Fishy is Tío Mundo arriving for lunch, then not even sitting down but going straight to his study, and then *all* the uncles coming like there's going to be a party or a big family decision about Mamita's drinking or about Papito's businesses while he's away. Tía Carmen jumps up each time the doorbell rings, and when she returns, she asks them the same question she's just asked them—"So you were playing Statues and the two men came?" Mundín is jabbering away about the gun he got to hold. Every time he mentions it, Carla can see a shiver go through Tía's body like when there's a draft up at the house in the mountains and all the aunts wear pretty shawls. Today, though, it's so hot, the kids got to go in the pool in the morning right before Statues, and Tía says if they're very good, they might be able to go in again after their digestion is completed. Twice in the pool in one day and Tía has the shivers in this heat. Something very fishy is going on.

Tía rings the little silver bell, and Adela comes out and clears all the plates, and brings dessert, which always includes the Russell Stover box with the painted-on bow. When the box goes around, you have to figure out by eyesight alone which one you think will have the nut inside or caramel or coconut, hoping that you won't be surprised when you bite in by some squishy center you want to spit out.

The Russell Stover box is pretty low because no one has been to the United States lately to buy chocolates. Papito and Mamita left right after Christmas as usual but haven't come back. And it's August already. Mami says that's because of Mamita's health, and having to see specialists, but Carla has heard whispers that Papito has resigned his United Nations post and so is not very well liked by the government right now. Every once in a while *guardias* roar in on their jeeps, jump out, and surround Papito's house, and then Chino always comes running and tells Mami, who calls Tío Vic to tell him to come pick up his tennis shoes. Carla has never seen Tío Vic bring any kind of shoes to the house but the pockmarked ones he wears. He always comes in one of those limousines Carla's only seen at weddings and when Trujillo goes by in a motorcade. Tío Vic talks to the head *guardia* and gives him some money, and they all climb back in their jeeps and roar away. It's really kind of neat, like a movie. But Mami says they're not to tell their friends about it. "No flies fly into a closed mouth," she explains when Carla asks, "Why can't we tell?"

The Russell Stover box has gone all the way around back to Tía, who takes out one of the little papery molds, and sighs when the kids argue about who will get it. Tío Vic comes out, grinning, and ruffles Mundín's hair, puts his hand on Tía's shoulder and asks the whole table, "So who wants to go to New York? Who wants to see the Empire State Building?" Tío Vic always talks to them in English so that they get practice. "How about the Statue of Liberty?"

At first, the cousins look around at each other, not wanting to embarrass themselves by calling out, "Me! Me!" and then having Tío Vic cry, "April Fool!" But tentatively Carla, and then Sandi, and then Lucinda raise their hands. Like a chain reaction, hand after hand goes up, some still holding Russell Stover chocolates. "Me, me, I want to go, I want to go!" Tío Vic lifts up his hands, palms out, to keep their voices down. When they are all quiet, waiting for him to pick the winners, he looks down at Tía Carmen beside him and says, "How about it, Carmen? Wanna go?" And the kids all chant, "Yes, Tía, yes!" Carla, too, until she notes that her aunt's hands are shaking as she fits the lid on the empty Russell Stover box.

Laura is terrified she is going to say something she mustn't. These two thugs have been quizzing her for half an hour. Thank God for Yoyo and Fifi hanging on her, whining. She makes a big deal of asking them what they want, of getting them to recite for the company, and trying to get sullen little Fifi to smile for the obnoxious fat man.

Finally—what a relief! There's Vic crossing the lawn with Carla and Sandi on each hand. The two men turn and, almost reflexively, their hands travel to their holsters. Their gesture reminds her of a man fondling his genitals. It might be this vague sexuality behind the violence around her that has turned Laura off lovemaking all these months.

"Victor!" she calls out, and then in a quieter voice she cues the men as if she does not want them to embarrass themselves by not knowing who this important personage is. "Victor Hubbard, consul at the Embajada Americana. Excuse me, señores." She comes down the patio and gives Vic a little peck on the cheek, whispering as she does, "I've told them he's been playing tennis with you." Vic gives her the slightest nod, all the while grinning as if his teeth were on review.

Effusively, Laura greets Carla and Sandi. "My darlings, my sweet Cuquitas, have you eaten?" They nod, watching her closely, and she sees with a twinge of pain that they are quickly picking up the national language of a police state: every word, every gesture, a possible mine field, watch what you say, look where you go.

With the men, Victor is jovial and back-patting, asking twice for their names, as if he means to pass on a compliment or a complaint. The men shift hams, nervous for the first time, Laura notes gleefully. "The doctor, we have come to ask him a few questions, but he seems to have disappeared."

"Not at all," Vic corrects them. "We were just playing tennis. He'll be home any minute." The men sit up, alert. Vic goes on to say that if there is some problem, perhaps he can straighten things out. After all, the doctor is a personal friend. Laura watches their reactions as Vic tells them news that is news to her. The doctor has been granted a fellowship at a hospital in the United States, and he, Victor, has just heard the family's papers have received clearence from the head of Immigration. So, why would the good doctor get into any trouble.

So, Laura thinks. So the papers have cleared and we are leaving. Now everything she sees sharpens as if through the lens of loss—the orchids in their hanging straw baskets, the row of apothecary jars Carlos has found for her in old druggists' throughout the countryside, the rich light shafts swarming with a golden pollen. She will miss this glorious light warming the inside of her skin and jeweling the trees, the grass, the lily pond beyond the hedge. She thinks of her ancestors, those fair-skinned Conquistadores arriving in this new world, not knowing that the gold they sought was this blazing light. And look at what they started, Laura thinks, looking up and seeing gold flash in the mouth of one of the *guardias* as it spreads open in a scared smile.

This morning when the fag at the corner sold them their *lotería* tickets, he said, "Watch yourselves, the flames of your *santos* burn just above your heads. The hand of God descends and some are lifted up, but some"—he looked from Pupo to Checo—"some are cast away." Pupo took heed and crossed himself, but Checo twisted the fag's arm behind his back and threatened to give his manhood the hand of God. It scares Pupo the meanness that comes out of Checo's mouth, as if they weren't both *campesino* cousins, ear-twisted to church on Sundays by mothers who raised them on faith and whatever grew in their little plot of dirt.

But the fag *lotería* guy was right. The day began to surprise them. First, Don Fabio calls them in. Special assignment: they are to report on this García doctor's comings and goings. Next thing Pupo knows Checo is driving the jeep right up to the García house and doing this whole search number that is not following orders. Point is, though, that if something comes out of the search, their enterprise will be praised and they will be decorated and promoted. If nothing turns up and the family has connections, then back they go to the prison beat, cleaning interrogation rooms and watering down the cells the poor, scared bastards dirty with their loss of self-control.

From the minute they enter the house Pupo can tell by the way the old Haitian woman acts that this is a stronghold of something, call it arms, call it spirits, call it money. When the woman arrives, she is nervous and grasshoppery, smiling falsely, dropping names like a trail of crumbs to the powerful. Mostly, she mentions the red-haired gringo at the embassy. At first Pupo thinks she's just bluffing and he's already congratulating Checo and himself for uncovering something hot. But then, sure enough, the red-haired gringo appears before them, two more doll-girls in either hand.

"Who is your supervisor?" The gringo's voice has an edge. When Checo informs him, the American throws back his head, "Oh, Fabio, of course!" Pupo sees Checo's mouth stretch in a rubberband smile that seems as if it may snap. They have detained a lady from an important family. They have maybe barked up the wrong tree. All Pupo knows is Don Fabio is going to have a heyday on their already scarred backs.

"I'll tell you what," the American consul offers them. "Why don't I just give old Fabio a call right now." Pupo lifts his shoulders and ducks his head as if just the mention of his superior's name could cause his head to roll. Checo nods, "*A sus órdenes*."

The American calls from the phone in the hall where Pupo can hear him talking his marbles-in-his-mouth Spanish. There is a silence in which he must be waiting to be connected, but then his voice warms up. "Fabio, about this little misunderstanding. Tell you what, I'll talk to Immigration myself, and I'll have the doctor out of the country in forty-eight hours." On the other end Don Fabio must have made a joke because the American breaks out in laughter, then calls Checo to the phone so his supervisor can speak with him. Pupo hears his comrade's rare apologetic tone. "*Sí, sí, cómo no, don Fabio, inmediatamente.*"

Pupo sits among these strange white people, ashamed and cornered. Already he is feeling the whip coming down like judgment on his bared back. They are all strangely quiet, listening to Checo's voice full of disclaimer, and when he falls silent, only to their own breathing as the hand of God draws closer. Whether it will pick up the saved or cast out the lost is unclear yet to Pupo, who picks up his empty glass and, for comfort, tinkles the ice.

While the men were saying their goodbyes at the door, Sandi stayed on the couch sitting on her hands. Fifi and Yoyo clustered around Mami, balling up her skirt with holding on, Fifi wailing every time the big fat guard bent down for a goodbye kiss from her. Carla, knowing better as the oldest, gave her hand to the men and curtsied the way they'd been taught to do for guests. Then, everyone came back to the living room, and

Mami rolled her eyes at Tío Vic the way she did when she was on the phone with someone she didn't want to talk to. Soon, she had everyone in motion: the girls were to go to their bedrooms and make a stack of their best clothes and pick one toy they wanted to take on this trip to the United States. Nivea and Milagros and Mami would later pack it for them. Then, Mami disappeared with Tío Vic into her bedroom.

Sandi followed her sisters into their side-by-side bedrooms. They stood in a scared little huddle, feeling strangely careful with each other. Yoyo turned to her. "What are you taking?" Fifi had already decided on her baby doll and Carla was going through her private box of jewelry and mementos. Yoyo fondled her revolver.

It was strange how when held up to the absolute phrase— *the one toy I really want*—nothing quite filled the hole that was opening wide inside Sandi. Not the doll whose long hair you could roll and comb into hairdos, not the loom for making pot holders that Mami was so thankful for, not the glass dome that you turned over and pretty flakes fell on a little red house in the woods. Nothing would quite fill that need, even years after, not the pretty woman she would surprise herself by becoming, not the prizes for her schoolwork and scholarships to study now this and now that she couldn't decide to stay with, not the men that held her close and almost convinced her when their mouths came down hard on her lips that this, this was what Sandi had been missing.

From the dark of the closet Carlos has heard tones, not content; known presences, not personalities. He wonders if this might be what he felt as a small child before the impressions and tones and presences were overlaid by memories, memories which are mostly others' stories about his past. He is the youngest of his father's thirty-five children, twenty-five legitimate, fifteen from his own mother, the second wife; he has no past of his own. It is not just a legacy, a future, you don't get as the youngest. Primogeniture is also the clean slate of the oldest making the past out of nothing but faint whispers, presences, and tones. Those tenuous, tentative first life-impressions have scattered like reflections in a pond under the swirling hand of an older brother or sister saying, I remember the day you ate the rat poison, Carlos, or, I remember the day you fell down the stairs. . . .

He has heard Laura in the living room speaking with two men, one of them with a ripply, tricky voice, the other with a coarser voice, a thicker laugh, a big man, no doubt. Fifi is there and Yoyo as well. The two other girls disappeared in a jabber of cousins earlier. Fifi whines periodically, and Yoyo has recited something for the men, he can tell from the singsong in her voice. Laura's voice is tense and bright like a newly sharpened knife that every time she speaks cuts a little sliver from her self-control. Carlos thinks, She will break, she will break, San Judas, let her not break.

Then, in that suffocating darkness, having to go but not daring to pee in the chamber pot for fear the men might hear a drip in the walls—though God knows, he and Mundo soundproofed this room enough so that there is no ventilation at all—in that growing claustrophobia, he hears her say distinctly, "Victor!" Sure enough, momentarily the monotone, garbled voice of the American consul nears the living room. By now, of course, they all know his consulship is only a front—Vic is, in fact, a CIA agent whose orders changed midstream from *organize the underground and get that SOB out* to *hold your horses, let's take a second look around to see what's best for us.*

When he hears the bedroom door open, Carlos puts his ear up against the front panel. Steps go into the bathroom, the shower is turned on, and then the fan to block out any noise of talk. The immediate effect is that fresh air begins to circulate in the tiny compartment. The closet door opens, and then Carlos hears her breathing close by on the other side of the wall.

II

I'm the one who doesn't remember anything from that last day on the Island because I'm the youngest and so the other three are always telling me what happened that last day. They say I almost got Papi killed on account of I was so mean to one of the secret police who came looking for him. Some weirdo who was going to sit me on his hard-on and pretend we were playing Ride the Cock Horse to Banbury Cross. But then whenever we start talking last-day-on-the-Island memories, and someone says, "Fifi, you almost got Papi killed for being so rude to that gestapo guy," Yoyo starts in on how it was she who almost got Papi killed when she told that story about the gun years before our last day on the Island. Like we're all competing, right? for the most haunted past.

I can tell you one thing I do remember from right before

we left. There was this old lady, Chucha, who had worked in Mami's family forever and who had this face like someone had wrung it out after washing it to try to get some of the black out. I mean, Chucha was super wrinkled and Haitian blue-black, not Dominican *café-con-leche* black. She was real Haitian too and that's why she couldn't say certain words like the word for parsley or anyone's name that had a *j* in it, which meant the family was like camp, everyone with nicknames Chucha could pronounce. She was always in a bad mood—not exactly a bad mood, but you couldn't get her to crack a smile or cry or anything. It was like all her emotions were spent, on account of everything she went through in her young years. Way back before Mami was even born, Chucha had just appeared at my grandfather's doorstep one night, begging to be taken in. Turns out it was the night of the massacre when Trujillo had decreed that all black Haitians on our side of the island would be executed by dawn. There's a river the bodies were finally thrown into that supposedly still runs red to this day, fifty years later. Chucha had escaped from some canepickers' camp and was asking for asylum. Papito took her in, poor skinny little thing, and I guess Mamita taught her to cook and iron and clean. Chucha was like a nun who had joined the convent of the de la Torre clan. She never married or went anywhere even on her days off. Instead, she'd close herself up in her room and pray for any de la Torre souls stuck up in purgatory.

Anyhow, that last day on the Island, we were in our side-by-side bedrooms, the four girls, setting out our clothes for going to the United States. The two creepy spies had left, and Mami and Tío Vic were in the bedroom. They were telling Papi, who was hidden in this secret closet, about how we would all be leaving in Tío Vic's limo for the airport for a flight he was going to get us. I know, I know, it sounds like something you saw on "Miami Vice," but all I'm doing is repeating what I've heard from the family.

But here's what I do remember of *my* last day on the Island. Chucha came into our bedrooms with this bundle in her hands, and Nivea, who was helping us pack, said to her in a gruff voice, "What do you want, old woman?" None of the maids liked Chucha because they all thought she was kind of below them, being so black and Haitian and all. Chucha, though, just gave Nivea one of her spelling looks, and all of sudden, Nivea remembered that she had to iron our outfits for wearing on the airplane.

Chucha started to unravel her bundle, and we all guessed she was about to do a little farewell voodoo on us. Chucha always had a voodoo job going, some spell she was casting or spirit she was courting or enemy she was punishing. I mean, you'd open a closet door, and there, in the corner behind your shoes, would sit a jar of something wicked that you weren't supposed to touch. Or you'd find a candle burning in her room right in front of someone's picture and a little dish with a cigar on it and red and white crepe streamers on certain days crisscrossing her room. Mami finally had to give her a room to herself because none of the other maids wanted to sleep with her. I can see why they were afraid. The maids said she got mounted by spirits. They said she cast spells on them. And besides, she slept in her coffin. No kidding. We were forbidden to go into her room to see it, but we were always sneaking back there to take a peek. She had her mosquito net rigged up over it, so it didn't look that strange like a real uncovered coffin with a dead person inside.

At first, Mami wouldn't let her do it, sleep in her coffin, I mean. She told Chucha civilized people had to sleep on beds, coffins were for corpses. But Chucha said she wanted to prepare herself for dying and couldn't one of the carpenters at Papito's factory measure her and build her a wooden box that would serve as her bed for now and her coffin later. Mami kept saying, Nonsense, Chucha, don't get tragic.

The thing was, you couldn't stand in Chucha's way even if you were Mami. Soon there were jars in Mami's closet, and her picture from when she was a baby being held by Chucha was out on Chucha's altar with mints on a little tin dish, and a constant votary candle going. Inside of a week, Mami relented. She said poor Chucha never asked for a blessed thing from the family, and had always been so loyal and good, and so, heavens to Betsy, if sleeping in her coffin would make the old woman happy, Mami would have a nice box built for her, and she did. It was plain pine, like Chucha wanted it, but inside, Mami had it lined in purple cushiony fabric, which was Chucha's favorite color, and bordered with white eyelet.

So here's the part I remember about that last day. Once Nivea left the room, Chucha stood us all up in front of her. "Chachas—" she always called us that, from *muchachas*, girls, which is how come we had ended up nicknaming her a play echo of her name for us, Chucha.

"You are going to a strange land." Something like that, I mean, I don't remember the exact words. But I do remember the piercing look she gave me as if she were actually going inside my head. "When I was a girl, I left my country too and never went back. Never saw father or mother or sisters or brothers. I brought only this along." She held the bundle up and finished unwrapping it from its white sheet. It was a statue carved out of wood like the kind I saw years later in the anthro textbooks I used to pore over, as if staring at those little talismanic wooden carvings would somehow be my madeleine, bringing back my past to me like they say tasting that cookie did for Proust. But the textbook gods never triggered any four-volume memory in my head. Just this little moment I'm recalling here.

Chucha stood this brown figure up on Carla's vanity. He had a grimacing expression on his face, deep grooves by his eyes and his nose and lips, as if he were trying to go but was real constipated. On top of his head was a little platform, and on it, Chucha placed a small cup of water. Soon, on account of the heat, I guess, that water started evaporating and drops ran down the grooves carved in that wooden face so that the statue looked as if it were crying. Chucha held each of our heads in her hands and wailed a prayer over us. We were used to some of this strange stuff from daily contact with her, but maybe it was because today we could feel an ending in the air, anyhow, we all started to cry as if Chucha had finally released her own tears in each of us.

They are gone, left in cars that came for them, driven by pale Americans in white uniforms with gold braids on their shoulders and on their caps. Too pale to be the living. The color of zombies, a nation of zombies. I worry about them, the girls, Doña Laura, moving among men the color of the living dead.

The girls all cried, especially the little one, clutching onto my skirts, Doña Laura weeping so hard into her handkerchief that I insisted on going back to her bureau and getting her a fresh one. I did not want her to enter her new country with a spent handkerchief because I know, I know what tears await her there. But let her be spared the knowledge that will come in time. That one's nerves have never been strong.

They have left—and only the silence remains, the deep and empty silence in which I can hear the voices of my *santos* settling into the rooms, of my *loa* telling me stories of what is to come.

After the girls and Doña Laura left with the American zombie whites, I heard a door click in the master bedroom, and I went out to the corridor to check for intruders. All in black, I saw the *loa* of Don Carlos putting his finger to his lips in mockery of the last gesture I had seen him make to me that morning. I answered with a sign and fell to my knees and watched him leave through the back door out through the guava orchard. Soon afterwards, I heard a car start up. And then the deep and empty silence of the deserted house.

I am to close up the house, and help over at Doña Carmen's until they go too, and then at Don Arturo's, who also is to go. Mostly, I am to tend to this house. Dust, give the rooms an airing. The others except for Chino have been dismissed, and I have been entrusted with the keys. From time to time, Don Victor, when he can get away from his young girls, will stop by to see to things and give me my monthly wages.

Now I hear the voices telling me how the grass will grow tall on the unkempt lawns; how Doña Laura's hanging orchids will burst their wire baskets, their frail blossoms eaten by bugs;

how the birdcages will stand empty, the poor having poached the *tórtolas* and *guineas* that Don Carlos took so much trouble to raise; how the swimming pools will fill with trash and leaves and dead things. Chino and I will be left behind in these decaying houses until that day I can see now—when I shut my eyes—that day the place will be overrun by *guardias*, smashing windows and carting off the silver and plates, the pictures and the mirror with the winged babies shooting arrows, and the chairs with medallions painted on back, the box that makes music, and the magic one that gives pictures. They will strip the girls' shelves of the toys their grandmother brought them back from that place they were always telling me about with the talcum powder flowers falling out of the clouds and the buildings that touch Damballah's sky, a bewitched and unsafe place where they must now make their lives.

I have said prayers to all the *santos*, to the *loa*, and to the Gran Poder de Dios, visiting each room, swinging the can of cleaning smoke, driving away the bad spirits that filled the house this day, and fixing in my head the different objects and where they belong so that if any workman sneaks in and steals something I will know what is gone. In the girls' rooms I remember each one as a certain heaviness, now in my heart, now in my shoulders, now in my head or feet; I feel their losses pile up like dirt thrown on a box after it has been lowered into the earth. I see their future, the troublesome life ahead. They will be haunted by what they do and don't remember. But they have spirit in them. They will invent what they need to survive.

They have left, and the house is closed and the air is blessed. I lock the back door and pass the maid's room, where I see

Imaculada and Nivea and Milagros packing to leave at dawn. They do not need my goodbyes. I go in my own room, the one Doña Laura had special made for me so I could be with my *santos* at peace and not have to bear the insolence and annoyance of young girls with no faith in the spirits. I clean the air with incense and light the six candles—one for each of the girls, and one for Doña Laura, whose diapers I changed, and one for Don Carlos. And then, I do what I always do after a hard day, I wash my face and arms in *agua florida*. I throw out the water, saying the prayer to the *loa* of the night who watch with bright eyes from the darkened sky. I part the mosquito netting and climb into my box, arranging myself so that I am facing up, my hands folded on my waist.

Before sleep, for a few minutes, I try to accustom my flesh to the burial that is coming. I reach up for the lid and I pull it down, closing myself in. In that hot and tight darkness before I lift the lid back up for air, I shut my eyes and lie so still that the blood I hear pounding and the heart I hear knocking could be something that I have forgotten to turn off in the deserted house.

The Human Body

▼▲▼▲▼▲▼▲▼▲▼▲▼▲▼▲▼▲▼▲▼▲▼▲▼▲▼▲▼▲▼▲▼III▼▲▼▲▼

Yoyo

Back then, we all lived side by side in adjoining houses on a piece of property which belonged to my grandparents. Every kid in the family was paired up with a best-friend cousin. My older sister, Carla, and my cousin Lucinda, the two oldest cousins, had a giggly, gossipy girlfriendship that made everyone else feel left out. Sandi had Gisela, whose pretty ballerina name we all envied. Baby sister Fifi and my sweet-natured cousin Carmencita were everyone's favorites, a helpful little pair, good for errands, turning jump ropes, and being captured when the large communal yard we played in was transformed into the old West by cowboy Mundín and cowgirl me. We were the only boy-girl pair, and as we grew older, Mami and Mundín's mother, Tía Carmen, encouraged a separation between us.

But that was hard to effect. In our family compound, there was no keeping anyone from anyone else. When one cousin caught the measles or mumps, we were all quarantined together so as to get that childhood illness over and done with.

We lived in each other's houses, staying for meals at whatever table we were closest to when dinner was put out, heading home only to take our baths and go to bed (or to get punished, like the time the report reached our mothers' ears that Yoyo and Mundín had shattered Tía Mimí's crystal-ball garden decoration with their slingshots. "That's a lie," we defended ourselves. "We broke it with the rake, trying to knock down some guavas!" Or the time that Yoyo and Mundín had used Lucinda's and Carla's nail polish to paint blood on their wounds. Or that time Yoyo and Mundín tied up Fifí and tiny Carmencita to the water tower near the back of the property and forgot them there).

Beyond those shacks, through a guava orchard Tía Mimí had planted, lived my grandparents, in a great big house we went to for Sunday dinners whenever they were home. Mostly, they were far away in New York City, where my grandfather had some position in the United Nations. A kindly, educated old man with a big white Panama hat who worried mostly about his digestion, my grandfather entertained no political ambitions. But the tyrant who had seized power was jealous of anyone with education and money, and so Papito was often sent out of the country on a bogus diplomatic post. When Papito returned home, the property would be overrun by the *guardia* in "routine searches for your own protection." Always after those searches, the family would miss silverware, cigarettes, small change, cuff links, and earrings left lying about. "Better that than our lives," my grandfather would console my grandmother, who wanted to leave the country again immediately.

But what did we kids know of all that back in those days? The height of violence for us was on the weekly television Western imported from Hollywood and dubbed clumsily in Spanish. Rin Tin Tin barked in sync, but the cowboys kept talking long after their mouths were closed. When the gun reports sounded, the villains already lay in a puddle of blood. Mundín and I craned our necks forward, wanting to make sure that the bad guys were really dead. As for the violence around us, the guards' periodic raids, the uncles whose faces no longer appeared at the yearly holiday gatherings, we believed the slogan at station identification—"God and Trujillo are taking care of you."

When the U.N. post was first conferred on him, my grandfather balked: he wanted no part of the corrupt regime. But, my grandmother's tyrannical constitution brought its own kind of pressure to bear on him; as she grew older, she was always ill: aches, migraines, moodiness that only expensive specialists in the States would know how to cure. The illnesses—so the underground family gossip went—were caused by the fact that Mamita had been a very beautiful young woman, and she had never fully recovered from losing her looks. My grandfather, whom everyone called a saint, pampered her in everything and tolerated her willfulness, so that the saying among the family was that Papito was so good, "he pees holy water." Mamita, furious at hearing her husband canonized at her expense, took her revenge. She brought home a large jar of holy water from the cathedral. One Sunday during the weekly family dinner, my mother caught her preparing my grandfather's whiskey-

and-water with holy water from the jar. "Damn it!" my grandmother gloated. "You all say he pees holy water, well he's been peeing it all right!"

In New York, my grandfather developed stomach ailments, and from then on all the foods in the world were divided into those that agreed and those that did not agree with Papito. My grandmother supervised his menu religiously, feeling guilty perhaps about earlier things she had run through his system.

When they did return from their New York City trips, Mamita brought back duffle bags full of toys for her grandchildren. Once she brought me a noisy drum and once a watercolor set and paintbrushes of different thicknesses for expressing the grand and fine things in the world. My American cowgirl outfit was an exact duplicate—except for the skirt—of Mundín's cowboy one.

My mother disapproved. The outfit would only encourage my playing with Mundín and the boy cousins. It was high time I got over my tomboy phase and started acting like a young lady señorita. "But it *is* for girls," I pointed out. "Boys don't wear skirts." Mamita threw her head back and laughed. "This one is no fool. She's as smart as Mimí even if she doesn't get it from books."

On her latest trip to New York City, my grandmother had taken her unmarried daughter, Mimí, along. Mimí was known as "the genius in the family" because she read books and knew Latin and had attended an American college for two years before my grandparents pulled her out because too much education might spoil her for marriage. The two years seemed to have done sufficient harm, for at twenty-eight, Mimí was an "old maid."

"The day Tía Mimí marries, cows will fly," we cousins teased. I did not think any less of my aunt for being single. In fact, as a tomboy, I had every intention of following in her footsteps. But Tía Mimí used her free time so poorly, she might as well have been married. She read and read, and for breaks, she tended an incredible Eden of a garden, then read some more.

"She reads tons and tons of books!" My mother rolled her eyes, for her sister's accomplishments could only be measured by weight, not specifics. Poor old maid Tía Mimí. I hoped soon she'd be able to rope someone into marrying her. I was not in the least bit interested in acquiring a new uncle or in wearing a dress for the occasion, but it would be worth putting up with both inconveniences to see a cow fly.

As we cousins feared, Mamita came back from this latest trip with Tía Mimí's idea of fun. Instead of the usual oversized, cheap, gaudy, noise-making, spoiling-your-clothes, wasting-your-mind toys, that duffle bag was lined with school supplies and flashcards and workbooks and puzzle-size boxes whose covers announced: MASTERING ARABIC NUMERALS, THE WONDERS OF NATURE, A B C OF READING, MORE SOUNDS TO SAY. Mundín and I exchanged a grim biting-the-bullet look as our gifts were handed to us.

I got a book of stories in English I could barely read but with interesting pictures of a girl in a bra and long slip with a little cap on her head that had a tassel dangling down. Mundín fared much better, I thought, with a see-through doll whose top half lifted off. Inside were blue and pink and light brown tubes and coils and odd-shaped pellets which all fit together like a puzzle. Tía Mimí explained the toy was called The Human Body. She had picked it out for Mundín because recently, in one of those after-dinner sessions in which aunts and uncles polled the children on what they were planning to do with themselves when they grew up, Mundín had expressed an interest in the medical profession. Everyone thought that was very good of him and proved he had a good heart after all, but Mundín had confided in me later that he was mostly interested in giving needles and cutting people open on the operating table.

We examined The Human Body doll while Tía Mimí read out loud from a little booklet that came with it about the different organs and what each was good for. After we'd learned to put them together so the heart wasn't tangled in the intestines and the lungs didn't face the spine, Mundín commenced grumbling. "A doll, why'd she get me a stupid doll?"

I disliked them too, but this doll was better than a reading book, and you could own it with self-respect, seeing as it was a boy with guts. But I was surprised that along with his other organs, this boy didn't have what in those days I called "a pee-er." I'd seen them on little naked beggar boys at the market and once on my grandfather, who peed holy water, when I walked in on him in the bathroom ministering to his need. But this doll was as smooth between his legs as a baby girl.

Mamita, who yearned for her youth again, must have remembered what it was like to be young and dumb and fun-loving. She had snuck back for us—when Mimí's back was turned—little nonsense presents. I got a paddle with a little ball attached on an elastic string, which I whacked and whammed as if it were my reading book, and Mundín got a big packet of bright pink modeling clay.

At first, neither of us knew what the packet was. My cousin's eyes flashed like bright coins. "Bubble gum!" he cried out. But my grandmother explained that no, this was a new kind of modeling clay that was easy to work with. She demonstrated. Pulling off a handful, she molded a ball, bunched little ears side by side, dotted two eyes with a bobby pin she took out of her hair and finished it off with a tiny ball of a tail. She held her hand out to me.

"Ah," I cried, for in her palm was the likeness of a tiny rabbit. But Mundín was not impressed. Bunny or not, he still could not blow bubbles with it.

All morning, I tagged behind Mundín, begging him to trade me that packet of clay. But he was not in the least bit tempted by my reading book, though he did linger a moment over the pictures of the girl in her underwear before handing the book back. My paddle ball was no good to him either. He was liable to ruin his batting swing by striking at a little jacks ball. "A girl's ball," he called it.

At that, I drew myself up with wounded pride and strode off to "our" side of the property. Mundín followed me through a path in the hedges and then lingered by my side as I sat on a patio lawn chair pretending great interest in my book. He paced by me several times, tossing his big ball of clay from hand to hand like a baseball. "What nice clay," he observed. "Very nice clay." I kept my eyes on my book.

A strange thing began to happen. I actually became interested in those dark, dense paragraphs of print. The story was not half bad: Once upon a time a sultan was killing all the girls in his kingdom, decapitating them, running swords through them, hanging them. But then, the girl pictured in bra and slip, the girl with a name that looked like a misprint—Sche-hera-zade, I sounded it out—this girl and her sister were captured by the sultan. They figured out a way to trick him. Just as he was about to cut off their heads, the sister asked him if they couldn't just hear one more of Scheherazade's wonderful stories before they died. The sultan agreed and gave Schehera-zade until dawn. But when the sun rose, Scheherazade hadn't yet finished her fascinating story. "I guess it's time to die," she interrupted herself. "Too bad. The ending is really good."

"By Allah," the sultan swore. "You're not dying until I hear the rest of the story."

A shadow fell across the page I was reading. I glanced up, keeping my place in the text with an index finger. I would have given my cousin a dirty look and gone on with my reading if it hadn't been for the magnificent creature he had created. He must have rolled all of the clay into one long pink coil and looped it once, twice around his shoulders like a circus per-former's boa. Raising his chin, he passed within inches of me, through the hedges to his side of the yard. I knew he was ready to negotiate. I set my book face down on the chair and followed after him.

But beyond the hedge, Mundín had run into a captive audi-ence. Fifi and Carmencita watched while Mundín unwrapped the snake from around his neck and poked one end at his little sister. Carmencita screamed and fled indoors. In a minute, we could hear Mundín's mother calling out in a punishment voice, "Edmundo Alejandro de la Torre Rodríguez!"

Now, Fifi, who could not be long without her other half, headed towards the house. "I'm telling," she announced. Mundín blocked her path. He tried to bribe her with a handful of his clay.

"No fair!" I hurried towards him, pushing little Fifi aside. He wouldn't even trade with me, his best buddy, and here he was giving it away to a little sister for nothing.

"Okay, okay." He motioned for me to lower my voice. He held the snake out to me. "Trade you."

My heart soared. Here was my desire, within reach. I made a desperate offer. "I'll give you whatever you want."

Mundín considered for a moment. A sly little smile spread across his lips. It was like a liquid spilling and staining something it mustn't. He lowered his voice. "Show me you're a girl."

Stalling, I looked around. My eyes fell on Fifi, who was following the transaction closely. "Here?"

He jerked his head, indicating the old coal shed at the back of the property where Mamita's gardener, Florentino, kept his tools. Since this part of our property adjoined the *palacio* of the dictator's daughter and son-in-law, my grandfather had been reluctant to erect a high wall lest it be considered a snub. Tía Mimí's hedge of bright red ginger shielded us somewhat from the sight of the eyesore palace and of the dictator strolling of a Sunday afternoon with his three-year-old grandson in a minuscule general's uniform. We children were forbidden to wander this coal shed area ever since the time Mundín and I had set off a firecracker just as the miniature general paraded by with his nursemaids. Papito had to spend the night down at the SIM headquarters explaining that his seven-year-old grandson had meant no harm. Perhaps because it was out of bounds, the coal shed was Mundín's and my favorite place to scout for Indians. Behind a sack of fertilizer, we once discovered a magazine with pictures of naked women with sly looks on their faces, as if they had just been caught stealing nail polish or tying people up to water towers.

I followed Mundín into the shed, turning every so often and glowering at Fifi, who trailed behind us. At the door I gave her a little push to go away.

"Let her in," Mundín argued, "or she'll go tell."

"I'll tell," Fifi agreed.

It was dark and damp inside. A faint light fell through the dirty wire-mesh windows. The air smelled of the black soil brought down from the mountains to make Tía Mimí's giant ferns grow tall. In a corner, hoses lay coiled like a family of dormant snakes.

Fifi and I lined up against a far wall. Mundín faced us, his hands nervously working the snake into a rounder and rounder ball. "Go on," he said. "Take them down."

Immediately, Fifi pulled down her pants and panties in one wad to her hips, revealing what she thought was in question, her bellybutton.

But I was older and knew better. In religious instruction classes, Sor Juana had told how God clothed Adam and Eve in the Garden of Eden after they had sinned. "Your body is a temple of the Holy Ghost." At home, the aunts had drawn the older girls aside and warned us that soon we would be señoritas who must guard our bodies like hidden treasure and not let anyone take advantage. It was around this time that strong pressure was put on me to stop playing with Mundín and to join the other young-lady cousins in their grownup beautician games and boy gossip inside the house.

"Go on," Mundín ordered impatiently. Fifi had caught on and lowered her pants and panties to her ankles. I gave my cousin a defiant look as I lifted up my cowboy skirt, tucked it under my chin, and yanked my panties down. I steeled myself against his intrusive glances. But all Mundín did was shrug his shoulders with disappointment. "You're just like dolls," he observed, and divided his ball of clay equally between Fifi and me.

I was dressed in seconds and lighting into him. "You promised me the clay!" I cried. "You let her come along, but you didn't say she'd be part of the deal."

"Edmundo Alejandro de la Torre Rodríguez!" We heard Mundín's mother calling from the back patio of the house. Mundín tried hushing my angry yelling. He reached over to take back Fifi's half, but she too started bawling. "Mundo Alejandro!" The voice had grown louder and was definitely heading in our direction. Now it was Mundín's face that was naked with worry. "Come on, please," he pleaded with me. "Please. I'll let you have my Human Body doll, okay?"

I tortured him with a long slow moment of consideration, then nodded. He fled out of the shed in search of his toy.

Fifi sniffled as she patted her half into a small clay ball. She looked over at the half in my hands and asked, "How much you got?"

I was beyond fury at this little creature, who had spoiled my chances at amassing a fortune of pink clay. I glared at her. She was still standing in a puddle of fabric at her ankles. She had a smear of breakfast egg on her chin and the blurry eyes of someone who has just stopped crying. I reached over and pulled her pants back up. She swayed with the force of my lifting. "How much you got?" she persisted. In her eyes was a gleam of material interest I hadn't noticed before.

I held up my half to hers. "Same as you, silly."

When the door creaked open, we were sure it was Mundín coming back with The Human Body. But two adult-sized bodies loomed before us: the gardener's lean, boney figure, his dusky face topped by a busted sombrero, and beside him, Mundín's mother, a short, broad-shouldered woman, peering into the darkness of the shed.

"I thought I heard them here, Doña," Florentino, the gardener, was saying. "I've told them to stay out. They could hurt themselves. But they won't listen to me!" Liar, I thought. Mundín and I had shown him the magazine we'd found, and he'd sworn us to secrecy and said he would dispose of "that trash" himself. But it was always an uneasy look he gave us whenever he was summoned by an adult in the family.

My aunt stepped towards us; her broad shoulders gave her an official appearance, as if she were wearing epaulettes, and representing all our parents. "Fifi?" she called in a shocked voice at the sight of one of the family darlings. Then, with more conviction, she pronounced my name. She was the favorite of our aunts; I'd never seen her this annoyed. "What in heaven's name are you girls doing here?"

Instantly, Fifi began to cry, so that right away, my aunt's suspicions were confirmed: I had dragged my little sister against her will to this dirty place. My aunt's scolding was now addressed solely to me. "What are you—"

Just then, the door swung open, and my cousin popped in, the doll held aloft as if it were a trophy he'd won. It was painful to watch the transformation on my cousin's face—from his usual cocky leer to a scared, crumpled, helpless look.

"Edmundo Alejandro!" Tía Carmen reached out and gave his arm a shake. The Human Body dropped from his hands, snapped open, and the innards scattered all over the dirt floor. My aunt teetered on the pieces as she dragged Mundín by the arm towards the door. "What are you doing here, young man?" she yelled.

"We were hiding," I piped up in his defense, having had moments to collect my thoughts. Mundín's eyes blinked with surprise and hope that there might still be a way out of our fix. "The *guardia*—" I began. I knew that in our family the least mention of the *guardia* got instant, unmitigated attention. I must have sensed the timing was right, for my grandparents had just returned from their trip, and the dictator's raids would begin.

My aunt dropped my cousin's arm. "¿*Guardia*?" she asked in a little voice. "The *guardia* were here?"

I nodded. "That's why we hid."

My aunt looked over at Florentino. The gardener was on his knees, picking up the little pieces of The Human Body. He looked up at me, his eyes boring a hole in my face as if he were trying to figure out what I was up to. Maybe he remembered the magazine, for he cast his lot on our side. "Those *guardias*," he said, then cursed them, "they've tramped through the ginger hedge so many times, Señorita Mimí has given up on it."

Smiling feebly, Mundín stood silent just when I needed him to bring in the cavalry and rescue my besieged story. His mother knew him well and sensed we were up to no good, but the *guardia* on the property meant no diddling with minor infractions: it was everybody to their houses, bureau tops cleaned off, portable objects battened down. My aunt ushered us out of that coal shed towards the big house.

We walked back in a quick single-file, my cousin leading, his mother right behind him so she "could keep a close eye" on him, then Fifí, then me, and finally, Florentino bringing up the rear. In each of his big worn hands, he carried the transparent halves of the cracked-open Human Body. We couldn't spare the time now, my aunt said, to find all the little pieces in the dark. Later, when Florentino brought what he had retrieved to the big house in the hollow of his hat, most of the organs had been chewed out of shape by the dogs or bent by my aunt's stepping on them. We couldn't tell the blue kidneys from bits of lung or the heart from a pink lobe of brain, and though Mundín and I tried using the diagram, there was no puzzling the whole back inside the little man.

Still Lives

▼▲▼▲▼▲▼▲▼▲▼▲▼▲▼▲▼▲▼▲▼▲▼▲▼▲▼▲▼▲▼▲▼▲▼III▼▲▼▲▼

Sandi

Doña Charito took the lot of us native children in hand
Saturday mornings nine to twelve to put Art into
us like Jesus into the heathen. She was an Islander
only by her marriage to Don José. She herself was cultured and
from some place over in Germany and had been to the grand
museums of Europe to look Art in the face. She had touched
with the hand she held up to us the cool limbs of the marble
boys, and those short blunt fingers had been shot through with
artistic talent. There was no arguing with Doña Charito over
the color of the vermilion coral in the umber depths of the
aquamarine oceans. She grappled the brush from your hand
and showed you how, all the while barking instructions in her
guttural Spanish, which made you feel that you were mispro-
nouncing your native tongue because you did not speak it with
her heavy German accent.

She had met Don José in Madrid during a tour of the Prado.
The young man was abroad on a medical school scholarship,
although he had no intention of becoming a doctor. Every year,

the government awarded European scholarships, each one earmarked for a certain needed profession, and if you won one and were poor, you accepted for the chance to eat three meals a day, one of them hot. Between meals, Don José sketched rather than dissected the cadavers and caught up on his sleep on a bench below a Gauguin and alongside several Van Goghs in the Prado. His lodging stipend Don José spent on art supplies.

Three years of sleeping with sunflowers and starbursts and Tahitian maidens had done what a decade of Academy training could not do. Don José came into his own: "a high rococo-primitivist church-sculpture style," our Island art critic later proclaimed it. Great brown angels with halos of hibiscus blossoms descended from heaven, pulled down by their enormous gourd breasts and ripe honeydew bottoms. Don José also came upon Doña Charito one late afternoon in the Prado as she was copying the garment folds on a Grünewald martyr. He was impressed with her big white slab of a body like an unfinished sculpture. She with his quick sketch of her as Madonna ascending in folds upon modest folds of garments. They married and returned to his island home where there wasn't anything to do—Doña Charito griped in her gutturals—but get one's work done.

On the outskirts of the capital they built a storybook cottage, two stories, fretted with eaves and little porches and window boxes, an incongruous Alpine look in the tropics. There they lived for over twenty years out of the swing of Island social life. They would have been totally ignored, in fact, had it not been for their strange house, which parents took their children to see on Sunday afternoon drives in the countryside. "There's the Hansel and Gretel house." If the curtains were drawn back and a figure peered out of one of the innumerable little windows like an eyeball trying to find a fitting socket, the children wailed, "The witch, the witch, there she is!"

You can imagine my amazement, then, when one Saturday morning of my eighth year, I was deposited on the doorstep of that house in the company, fortunately, of thirteen of my cousins for our first art lesson. It was really my doing, or rather my drawings, that had brought us to this brink. Up to this point, I had been an anonymous de la Torre child, second daughter to a second daughter of my grandparents, Don Edmundo Antonio de la Torre and Doña Yolanda Laura María Rochet de la Torre. I was born to die one of the innumerable, handsome de la Torre girls, singled out only when some aunt or other would take hold of my face in her hand and look intently at it, exclaiming that my eyes were those of my great-aunt Graciela, that my mouth was Mamita's exactly! So, you see, even these minor distinctions felt like petty theft. Whatever I, Sandra Isabel García de la Torre, was, personally, was as a dolly on wheels to roll that illustrious de la Torre name from social gathering to social gathering. But then, one Epiphany, boxes of crayons and tablets of paper were distributed among the children, and it was discovered that some small, anonymous hand was capable of capturing likenesses, dotting vision into eyes and curling hair upon a head so you ached to touch it.

"Who drew that baby? Whose cat is that?" they marveled. The artist was discovered at the bottom of the yard drawing the nursemaid Milagros's boy with a brown and a gold and a purple crayon. "Gifted" descended upon my hitherto unremarkable shoulders like a coat of many colors.

A few days after my gift was discovered, Milagros cast me

a worried look at dinner. She made a pretext of cutting up my meat, and as she cut, she whispered in bite-sized phrases: "Please . . . Señorita . . . Sandi . . . you must . . . come to . . . my house." After the meal, I snuck out to the forbidden part of the property where the servants' families lived in their little shanty shacks. Her boy lay moaning on a cot. Holy candles flickered on a shelf. Milagros had soaked the child in holy water after taking him to high mass at the Cathedral, but still he was feverish and wailed, as if he were mourning his own death before going.

"Please, please, Señorita Sandi, you must release him," Milagros pleaded, taking my drawing off the wall where she'd hung it beside a crucifix.

I stared at the little brown crayon face in my hand, then crumpled it up. The baby tossed. I put the scrap in her little cooking-stove, and then Milagros and I watched it catch and curl into yellow flames that looked like orange pencil-shavings.

"Ashes to ashes, dust to dust," she murmured and thumped her breasts. The smoke made Baby cough. He looked up at me with glazed spirit eyes. By breakfast the next morning, Milagros gave me the nod. Her baby was cured.

I had less luck with my cats. I drew them on the front wall of our white house and was put to scrubbing the stucco for hours, then fed punishment supper—a small waterbread, the cleavage unbuttered, and a tall glass of warm milk, green from the vegetables pureed and blended in it. Afterwards, I was sent to bed early to contemplate my bad character. That night, the pantry and supply closet were overrun with rats. That settled it. The family decided they had to get me trained in art.

Phone calls were made. Did anyone know of someone who gave art lessons? Doña Charito's name came up. The German lady, who lived in the two-story chalet at the edge of town. Don José's wife, that poor woman. No one had seen or heard of him for a while now. Several years back, he had been commissioned to sculpt the statues for the new National Cathedral, but the dedication had taken place in an empty church. There were rumors. Don José had gone crazy and been unable to finish this colossal project. His wife was having to take in students in order to pay the bills.

As I understand it, at first Doña Charito was insulted at the de la Torre request: she was an *artiste*; she took on apprentices, not children. But paid in advance in American dollars, she made an exception in our case, our case in the plural because the great female democracy of our blue blood dictated that all the de la Torre girls be given equal decorative skills. So, whichever of the girl cousins could control their bladders for several hours and would not try to drink the turpentine were enrolled in Saturday art lessons.

We were fourteen all told that first Saturday when we approached that house, nervously plucking at the gravel in the driveway, trying to tear off the door knob to see if it wasn't a chocolate almond. But we ended up with nothing but the taste of real things on our tongues. Then, Milagros discovered a rope dangling down, she gave it a tug, and a little cowbell jingled above our heads. We all gave it a try.

The bell had rung over a dozen times, and I was going up on my toes for a second turn when the door flew open with such force, the bell jangled all by itself. Before us stood a mountain of a woman who looked even more imposing because of the brightly-colored Hawaiian shift she wore. Exotic crimson flowers and birds poked their pistils and stamens and bills every which way up and down her torso. Her face was a pile of white cloud afire with red hair. She looked like something a child who had not taken art lessons might draw.

"Roodness, roodness." She growled the words out. "You!" She pointed at me. "You are the culpable one!"

I nodded and curtsied. We all curtsied. But it was more like genuflecting in her presence. Quickly, Milagros introduced us, handed Doña Charito a note, and fled back to one of the three black cars idling in the driveway like great, nervous, snorting horses. With a pelting of pebbles, they disappeared down the drive, and we children were left alone with Doña Charito to learn "the roodiments of art."

She opened the note in her hand, sighing with great impatience at its folds. We waited quietly while she read, and our intake of breath when she at last lifted her head made her gag with laughter. There were spaces between all her teeth; nothing dared block that woman's way even when she was smiling. "Ya, ya," she said in a soothing voice. "I am good-hearted for all this." She waved a hand over our heads, indicating the world, it seemed like to me.

"Now which of you is the little talent?" She pronounced a name. She repeated it several times before I raised my hand warily. "Ha! I might have guessed so." She smiled, or rather her mouth hooked up slightly at the corners. It was more as if she were casting for a smile than that she had caught one.

"Enter, enter," she said, suddenly out of sorts, "after remov-

ing the shoes, of course." Of course, we removed and entered.
I hoped it was the crust of mud on my shoes which made her
glare at me as I passed by her.

Our visit began with a tour of the house, which was more
like a museum than a house. Doña Charito's collected works
hung on the walls: mostly pitchers and bowls of fruit, and
violins or guitars, I couldn't tell the difference, for we hadn't
had music lessons yet. There were two or three stampeding
stallions, manes flaring, next to stormy seashores in her bedroom. But that was that, no tarantulas, no mangos, no lizards,
no spirits, no flesh-and-blood people.

When we had finally gone through the whole house, the older
cousins, who were more experienced in lying, said how much
they'd enjoyed the paintings. The rest of us nodded.

"Goot! Goot!" Again, she laughed. I ached for the lesson to
begin so I could draw and color in those ivory teeth with the
purple muscle of the tongue showing between like some fat
beast caged inside her mouth. But instead, she shepherded us
out to an open patio at the center of the house. We were invited to sit down, but there were only two chairs, and none of
us dared presume a seat.

A very old woman, whose face was so wrinkled it looked as
if it'd been used as a scratch pad, came around with a tray of
warm, sour lemonade, no ice, and all the sugar at the bottom,
and no spoons to stir it with. We drank and winced and waited
for the lesson to begin. But Doña Charito had disappeared into
her kitchen, where we could hear her barking orders to the old
woman—about how best to prepare us, I was sure. We girls
eyed each other, suddenly aware we were frail flesh, fourteen

mouthfuls crowding Doña Charito's patio and drinking up her lemonade.

Finally, Doña Charito marched us into her studio. It was a big, light room in a wing of the house, all the windows thrown open to air out the heavy oil and turpentine smells. Cane chairs had been arranged in rows, drawing boards on each seat, a crate between every two chairs with a big jar of clear water and several ripped-up pieces of old toweling on top. (This must have been the "some supplies included" of the agreement.)

"Find yourself an accommodation," Doña Charito ordered. There was a scramble for chairs in the back rows, but I was not one of the lucky ones. I had hung back at the entrance, cagily I thought, waiting to see what would happen to the others before I followed. I ended up the one in the front seat right under Doña Charito's cavernous cobalt-blue nostrils.

The lesson began with physical exercise. "*Mens sana in corpore sano*," Doña Charito proclaimed. "Amen," we girls chanted, for the sound of Latin cued us for liturgical response. Doña Charito scowled.

"One, two. One, two. One, two," she commanded. We executed jumping jacks. We touched toes. We flexed our fingers "for the circulation" and worked ourselves into quite a state of calisthenic frenzy.

At last, the actual art lesson began. Doña Charito demonstrated with her brush. "The first step, one must check the bristles for the correct alignment." Doña Charito dipped her brush into a jar of water and made all manner of finicky, tidying up, tapping noises on the brim, like a nursemaid spooning mouthfuls for a difficult baby.

Obediently, we did likewise.

She went on in her garbled Spanish we could barely understand. "The second step is the proper manner of holding the implement. Not in this way, neither in this fashion . . ." She inspected, chair by chair. She mocked us all.

It seemed with so much protocol, I would never get to draw the brilliant and lush and wild world brimming over inside me. I tried to keep my mind on the demonstration, but something began to paw the inside of my drawing arm. It clawed at the doors of my will, and I had to let it out. I took my soaking brush in hand, stroked my gold cake, and a cat streaked out on my paper in one lightning stroke, whiskers, tail, meow and all!

I breathed a little easier, having gained a cat-sized space inside myself. Doña Charito's back was to me. The hummingbird on her Hawaiian shift plunged its swordlike beak between the mounds of her bottom. There would be time.

I jiggled my brush in the water jar. The liquid turned the color of my first urine in the morning. I stroked my purple cake, and a bruise-colored cat and then a brown stick cat darted out.

I was so much to myself as I worked that I did not hear her warning shout or the slapping of her Island thongs on the linoleum as she swooped down upon me. Her crimson nails clawed my sheet off its board and crumpled it into a ball. "You, you defy me!" she cried out. Her face had turned the muddy red of my water jar. She lifted me by the forearm, hurried me across the room through a door into a dark parlor, and plunked me down on a stiff cane-back chair.

Her green eyes glared at me like a cat's. They were speckled with brown as if something alive had gotten caught and fossil-ized in the irises. "You are not to move until I have given you leave. Is that comprehensible?" I bowed my head in submis-sion. From the corner of my eye, I saw my frightened cousins obediently practicing their first brush strokes. Doña Charito filled the doorway a moment with her large body, then she pulled the door to with a great slam.

I sat as still as one of her still lives that hung on the walls around me. I felt her presence in the dark, hushed, airless room. Her brush was poised above my head. She could paint over my hair, blank out my features, make my face no more than a plate for apples, grapes, plums, pears, lemons. I dared not move.

But soon, I began to grow restless. I could see these art les-sons were not going to be any fun. It seemed like everything I enjoyed in the world was turning out to be wrong. I had recently begun catechism classes in preparation for my first communion. The Catholic sisters at Our Lady Of Perpetual Sorrows Convent School were teaching me to sort the world like laundry into what was wrong and right, what was venial, what, if you died in the middle of enjoying, would send you straight to hell. Before I could ever get to my life, conscience was arranging it all like a still life or tableau. But that morning in Doña Charito's house, I was not ready yet to pose as one of the model children of the world.

I lifted myself out of that uncomfortable chair and made my way out into the foyer, where our shoes had been lined up in a tidy row as if they were about to be shot for having mud on their soles. Just as I had found the pair that was mine, I heard a man's voice, shouting and crying curses from the back of the house. Normally, I would have run in the opposite direction, but the curses he was yelling were ones I was muttering under my breath against Doña Charito. I was drawn to investigate.

The patio was deserted. The sky hung low, a cloudy canvas with swirls of dark purple and stormy greys. I crossed a high hibiscus hedge through an unlatched gate and came upon a muddy backyard, strewn with logs and stumps like a carpenter's yard. Ahead stood an unpainted shed with one high window and one door clamped shut with a great padlock. The man's shouts had come from inside, but what drew me now was another sound, a tap-tap-tapping like us girl cousins dancing for company. I wanted to find out something secret about Doña Charito. At my age, that is what I knew of revenge. What someone kept in a bedside drawer. What color was someone's underwear. What did someone look like squatting awkwardly on a small chamber pot. Then, when that someone fell upon me with violent discipline, I could undo with a gaze: I know you, I know you.

The one window was a head above my head. I rolled a small stump over beneath the glass, climbed on top, and peered inside. At first, I could see only my own face reflected back. I cupped my hands around my eyes and felt the glass hum with hammering as if it were alive.

Slowly, I made out the objects inside the shed. Giant, half-formed creatures were coming out of logs like the ones strewn in the yard behind me. Some logs had hoofs or claws, tails or horns; some had the beginnings of a face, a mouth or an eye; some had hands with fingernails. A sheep's fleece curled from the bare nutty back of a pale stump, but the poor thing couldn't baa without nostrils or a mouth. I put my hand on my own face to make sure I was intact.

In the middle of the floor, a woman's figure reclined on two sawhorses, one at her feet, another at her neck, like my grandmother hanging from the rafters in her sling when she'd broken her back. Sharp points came out of her head, the rays of the Virgin's halo, though they could just as well have been the horns of a demon woman. Her hair coiled in complex curls over her shoulders like snakes. Her head was fully formed, but her face was still a blank.

Tap-tap-tap, the sound came from underneath her. Shavings of wood and sawdust were falling on the floor, where just this moment she was being given feet. Before my very eyes, the pale blond stumps distinguished themselves into heel and toe; the high arches made S's of the bottoms of her feet. She could have stood upon those soles and walked all the way to Bethlehem.

When his brown head emerged from between her legs, I believed him at first to be one of his own creations. He was the same shiny mahogany color as his half-formed creatures. Around his neck was a halter, trailing a chain to an iron ring by the door. —And that was all he wore! He was a tiny man, my size standing on a log, perfectly proportioned, except for one thing. I had seen the stud bulls on my grandfather's ranch during breeding season and witnessed their spectacles among the cows. Once, a saucy nursemaid had informed me that, in embroidered linens with the lights off and the fans going, my fine de la Torre mother had gotten me no differently. The little man grew big like those bulls on the ranch as he worked on the Virgin's feet. When he was done with that end, he climbed on top, straddling her, his rattling chain settling behind him like a great tail. He touched the blank of the face, tenderly it seemed, planted his chisel at the forehead and was about to come down on her. I cried out to warn the woman beneath him.

But it was his elf face which shot up. He looked about the room, bull's-eyed on my face against the window, then lunged in my direction. His chain grew taut. But before he could reach the window, open it up, and yank me inside, I threw myself off my perch and landed hard on the ground. I was too terrified to feel pain, but I heard the little bone in my arm crack as I hit the ground.

His face appeared at the window. He studied me, and an inane grin spread across his lips like a stain. Tap-tap-tap, his hand beat on the glass as if to hold my attention so he could study me a little longer, tap-tap-tap. There was no need for that; my eyes were riveted to his face, and my mouth opened in a voice-less scream. At last, sound came to my terror. I screamed and screamed even after his face had disappeared from the window.

Soon the Art Lesson came running from the house, Doña Charito leading, cousins on stockinged feet, the old woman in tow, towards the muddy heap in the yard. I did not think there would ever come the day when I would be so pleased to see her.

"What has transpired?" she cried, but her voice betrayed genuine concern. "Why were you not supervisioning her?" she said, accusing the old woman, then turning to me, she accused me: "What have you committed upon yourself?" She shot a worried glance down to the bottom of the yard. Tap-tap-tap came the sounds from inside the shed.

I lifted up my throbbing arm, an offering of broken bone. She could have my face smeared with tears, my body soiled with mud like a creature's, the small wet sobs coming out of my mouth. "I broke it," I wailed. But I knew it was best not to confess what I had seen inside her garden shed.

One could not say her face softened, for softness was not in her repertoire of expressions. She knelt beside me and reached for my arm. But even her lightest touch made me wince with pain. "Brrroke?" She gazed down at me. I now saw that the speckles in her eyes were splinters of bones, shards of things she had broken over the years.

Meanwhile, without supervision, my little cousins had begun balancing on logs, patting mudcakes, enjoying the holiday of smearing their dresses and darkening their white socks. A pair of explorer cousins marched towards the shed with sticks. Doña Charito stood up and sounded the alarm. "Attention! Back in the studio this instant, every one!" They scurried back. The rain began to fall, big sloppy drops as if someone were shaking out a paint brush.

She lifted me in her arms. I clung to her as if I were her own child. I laid my head above where her heart should be and thought I could hear, as if inside a conch shell, the dark Atlantic, the waves thrashing in high winds, the vast plains of central Europe. She knew the world was a wild place. She carried a great big brush. She made pinwheels of the whirling stars that had driven many a man mad. She could save me from the crazyman in the shed. I hung on.

But that was the last I ever saw of Doña Charito. The cars came screeching to a stop in the driveway; my mother hurried into the house; I began to cry to convince her of the serious-ness of my condition. And as the shock wore off, I did feel a piercing pain in my arm as if someone were driving a chisel through the bone. At the hospital everyone's suspicions were confirmed: my arm was fractured in three places.

I wore a cast for months, and when it was sawed off at last, the arm was discovered to have healed crookedly. There was no help for it but to break the bone again and reset it. This was considered a major enough operation that I was given gifts and a little overnight case to take to the hospital with a lock, the combination of which was the month, day, and year of my birth. A mass was said at the Cathedral for my quick recovery, and I was allowed to have dishes of ice cream between meals to make me brave and—it was explained to my envious cousins—"to give her added calcium." I was sure that I was about to die and that's why everyone was being so kind to me.

I did not die. And the bone did finally heal, almost perfectly. But for a year on and off, I carried my arm in a sling. The cast was signed by several dozen cousins and aunts and uncles, so I seemed a composite creation of the de la Torre family: Gisela de la Torre, Mundín de la Torre, Carmencita de la Torre, Lucinda María de la Torre. There were notes and rhymes. Some of the messages were smart-aleck remarks and skull-and-bones by cousins who resented me for getting out of lessons inflicted on them because of me. For though my own art career had come to a crashing halt, my girl cousins had to spend their Saturday mornings drawing circles, then on to ovals, before finally these ovals were allowed to ripen into apples. Months later, they graduated to utensils—a pitcher, a basket, a knife.

The final project was a still life with all these objects in it as well as a small hunk of plastic ham. Bitterly, they complained: they hated art; they did not want to take lessons. But American dollars, they were informed, did not grow on Island trees. Art lessons it would be for the next year.

By Christmas, the lessons were over. My cast was off. But I was a changed child. Months of pampering and the ridicule of my cousins had turned me inward. But now when the world filled me, I could no longer draw it out. I was sullen and dependent on my mother's sole attention, tender-hearted, and whiney: the classic temperament of the artist but without anything to show for my bad character. I could no longer draw. My hand had lost its art.

I did have one moment of triumph during that year of art lessons. Christmas Eve, along with the rest of the de la Torre children, I was taken to the National Cathedral for the nativity pageant where the new creche was to be unveiled. We marched up the aisle to the altar, which was decked with poinsettias and candles and curtained off with red and green draperies.

At the stroke of midnight, the bells began to peal. The side doors of the Cathedral burst open and out came a procession of priests and nuns and acolytes, clacking their censers, sending up the fragrance of myrrh and frankincense the three kings had brought over with them from the Orient. Two of the altar boys drew back the curtains—

Before me were the giants I'd seen in Don José's workshed! But these were sacred figures in rich velvet capes and glittery robes and shepherds' cloaks beautifully stitched to look ragged with patches by the Carmelite nuns. Kings and sheep and whinnying horses and serving maids and beggar boys gathered together in the frosty imagined night. God was going through all the trouble of self-creation to show us how. The wind was up. Rain splattered on the Cathedral roof. Far away, a dog barked.

When the altar gate was thrown open, the congregation surged forward to touch the infant Jesus for good luck in the coming year. But my eyes were drawn to the face of the Virgin beside him. I put my hand to my own face to make sure it was mine. My cheek had the curve of her cheek; my brows arched like her brows; my eyes had been as wide as hers, staring up at the little man as he knocked on the window of his work-shed. I reached out my crooked arm and touched the hem of her royal blue robe and her matching cloth slippers. Then I too broke into glad tidings and joy to the world with the crowds of believers around me.

An American Surprise

▼▲▼▲▼▲▼▲▼▲▼▲▼▲▼▲▼▲▼▲▼▲▼▲▼▲▼▲▼▲▼▲▼III▼▲▼▲▼

Carla

All morning my sisters and I had waited around the house, so when our father finally walked in the door, we raced to him, crying, "Papi! Papi!" Mami held a finger to her lips. "The baby," she reminded us, but Papi forgot himself and picked each one of us up with a shout and gave us a twirl. The chauffeur waited patiently at the door, a bag in each hand. "In the study, Mario," Papi directed. Then he rubbed his hands together and said, "Do I have a wonderful surprise for my girls!"

"What is it?" we all cried, and I took a guess because last night at prayers Mami had promised that one day I would see such a thing. "Snow?"

"Now, girls, remember," Mami said, and though I thought she meant Baby Fifi again, she added, "let Papi relax first." Then Mami whispered something to Papi in English, and he nodded his head. "After dinner then," he said. "We'll see who leaves her plate clean." But when our faces fell, he rallied us: "¡Ay, ay, ay! What a surprise!"

Sandi and Yoyo exchanged triumphant looks and skipped off, hand in hand, to tell our cousins next door that Papi was back with a wonderful surprise from New York City, where it was winter and the snow fell from heaven to earth like the Bible's little pieces of manna bread.

But I was not about to wander off, for supposing, just supposing, Papi finished his drink and decided to open his bags right then. As the only one there, I'd get first pick of whatever the surprise was. If only he would give me a tiny clue!

But my father was no good for clues. He was sprawled beside my mother, his arms spread out across the back of the couch as if he were about to embrace everything that was his. They were talking in those preoccupied voices that grownups use when something has gone wrong.

"Prices have skyrocketed," he was saying. My mother ran her hand through his hair and said, "My poor dear," and off they went to their bedroom for a nap before dinner.

The house grew quiet and lonesome. I lingered by the coffee table, taking sips from what was left in the glasses until the ice cubes rattled down to my mouth, tattletales, and I had to squeeze my eyes shut with the burn of Papi's highball. From down the hall came the sound of tinkling silverware and the scrape of a chair being settled in its place. Then Gladys, the new pantry maid, began to sing:

> *Yo tiro la cuchara,*
> *Yo tiro el tenedor*
> *Yo tiro to' lo' plato'*
> *Y me voy pa' Nueva Yor'.*

I loved to hear Gladys's high, sweet voice imitating her favorite singers on the radio. Someday, she was going to be a famous actress, Gladys said. But my mother said Gladys was only a country girl who didn't know any better than to sing popular tunes in the house and wear her kinky hair in rollers all week long, then comb it out for Sunday mass in hairdos copied from American magazines my mother had thrown out.

Gladys's singing stopped abruptly when I entered the dining room. "*Ay*, Carla, what a scare you gave me, girl!" She laughed. She was setting the table for dinner, taking spoons from a bouquet of silverware in her left hand, executing fancy dance steps before stopping at each placement and reminding herself, "Spoon on the right, wife to the knife." In the absence of sisters or best-friend cousins, Gladys was fun to be around.

She stood back from the table and cocked her head critically, then tucked a chair in, gave a knife a little nudge like someone straightening a straight picture on the wall. She nodded towards the back of the house. I followed her through the pantry, where everything was in readiness for dinner: the empty platters were out, waiting to be filled; the serving spoons were lined up like a family, tall ones first, then littler and littler ones.

In the passageway that connected the maids' room with the rest of the house, Gladys stopped and held open the door. "So! Your father is back from New York!"

I bowed my head with pleasure and entered past Gladys. The maids' room was dark and hot. Most of the windows had been shut against the fierce, midafternoon Caribbean sun. A hazy, muted light fell from a high, half-opened window. On a cane stool, a humming fan turned this way and that.

Slowly, as my eyes adjusted to the dimmer light of the room, I made out the plastic statuettes and holy pictures of saints which cluttered the bureau top. An old mayonnaise jar with a slit in the bottle cap glinted with the coppery dregs of a few pennies. As the fan blew upon it, the flame of the votary candle swayed and flickered. Two of the three cots were occupied. On one, the old cook, Chucha, lay, fast asleep, her fat black face looking pleased at the occasional cool breeze. On another sat Nivea in her slip, head bowed, murmuring over a rosary as if she were finding fault with the beads that dangled between her knees.

As the door clicked shut, Chucha opened one eye, then closed it. I hoped she had fallen back to sleep, since the old cook liked to scold. In fact, old Chucha was growing so difficult that Mami had decided to build a room just for her. "You know your mother doesn't like you back here," Chucha started in. I looked to Gladys to defend me.

"No harm, Cook," Gladys said cheerfully. She led me to her cot and patted a spot beside her. "Doña Laura won't mind today, seeing as Don Carlos just got in."

"Tell me the hen doesn't peck when the rooster crows," said Chucha with heavy sarcasm. She let out a grumpy sigh and turned herself over to face the wall. Softly, the fan tickled the pink bottoms of her feet. "I was changing Doña Laura's diapers before you were born!" she quarreled. "I should know how the dog bites, how the bee stings!"

Gladys rolled her eyes at me as if to say, "Don't mind Cook." Then she said in an appeasing voice, "You certainly have put your time in."

"Thirty-two years." Chucha let out a dry laugh.

"I wonder where I'll be in thirty-two years," Gladys mused. A glazed look came across her face; she smiled. "New York," she said dreamily and began to sing the refrain from the popular New York merengue that was on the radio night and day.

"Dream on," Chucha said. And now she was laughing. The fat under her uniform jiggled. Her body rocked back and forth. "Your head is in the clouds, girl. Watch out for the thunderbolt!"

"*Ay,* Cook." Gladys reached over and gently patted the old woman's feet. She seemed as unfazed by Chucha's merriment as her bad temper. "Every night I pray," she said, nodding towards the makeshift altar. Gladys had once explained to me how each saint on her bureau had a specialty. Santa Clara was good for eyesight. San Martín was a jackpot, good for money. Our Blessed Mother was good for anything. Now she picked out a postcard my mother had thrown out a few days before. It was a photo of a robed woman with a sharp star for a halo and a torch in her upraised hand. Behind her was a fairytale city twinkling with Christmas lights. "This one is a powerful American Virgin." Gladys handed me the card. "She'll get me to New York, you'll see."

"Speaking of New York," Nivea began. She hurried her sign of the cross and kissed the crucifix on her rosary. Nivea, the latest of our laundry maids, was "black-black": my mother always said it twice to darken the color to full, matching strength. She'd been nicknamed Nivea after an American face cream her mother used to rub on her, hoping the milky white applications would lighten her baby's black skin. The whites of the eyes she now trained on me were the only place where the cream magic seemed to have worked. "Show us what your father brought you."

"Lucky, lucky," Nivea continued before I could explain. "These girls are so lucky. What a father! He doesn't go on a trip that he doesn't bring back a treasure for them." She enumerated for Gladys, who had been working for us only a month, all the treasures *el doctor* had brought his girls. "You know those dancing dolls from the last time?"

I nodded. One thing you never did was correct Nivea and risk being called a young miss-know-it-all. But the dancing dolls were from two trips back. From the very last trip, the gift had been tie shoes that were good for our feet, a very bad choice, but that's what came of my mother's being in charge of what the surprise would be. Before he left on each trip, my father always asked, "Mami, what do the girls need?" Sometimes, as with this trip, Mami replied, "Not a thing. They're all set for school." And then, oh then, the surprises were bound to be wonderful, because as Papi explained to Mami, "I didn't have the faintest idea what to get them. So I went to Schwarz, and the salesgirl suggested . . ." And off would come the wrappers from three suggested dancing dolls or three suggested pairs of roller skates or this very night, three wonderful surprises!

Gladys took the postcard back and smiled at it. "What did your father bring you?" she asked.

"Not yet." I let out a sigh, disappointed that I couldn't oblige their curiosity, for even Chucha had given half a roll over to hear what the surprise had been. "We have to eat our supper first."

"Speaking of supper," Nivea said, reminding the two others,

"our work is never done." Then she added, "Night and day, and what surprise do we get!" She grumbled on as she braided her kinky black hair into dozens of tiny braids. Her complaints were different from Chucha's. They were bitter and snuck up on you even during the nicest conversations. Chucha's were a daily litany, sometimes cried out at the dog, sometimes scolded at the rice kettle she had to scrub, sometimes mumbled under her breath at Doña Laura, whose diapers she had changed and whose actions, therefore, she had a right to criticize.

Supper that night was spaghetti and meatballs, thank goodness, so it wasn't difficult to clean one's plate. I spooled the strands on my fork and rolled my two meatballs around until I got tired of that, and ate them both. Mami was in a good mood, letting the baby go off with the nursemaid, Milagros. Usually Mami insisted the baby stay, bawling in her high chair, so the family could have one official meal together like "civilized people." Tonight the family were spared the torments of civilization, and of vegetables, for Mami allowed us to serve ourselves, which I did, just enough peas to go around my neck in a necklace, had they been strung together. My sisters and I ate quietly, listening with wonder to our father's stories about taxis and bad snowstorms (How could a snowstorm be bad?!) and the Christmas decorations on the streets. We felt the blessedness of the weeks ahead: this very night, a wonderful surprise, and in less than twenty days, according to the little calendar with doors we opened with Mami every night at prayers, Christmas. And more surprises then! We were lucky girls, Nivea was right, oh so lucky.

Finally, Papi turned to Gladys, who was pushing the rollaway cart around the table, clearing off the plates. "Eh—"

"Gladys," Mami reminded him; after all, she was the new girl and Papi had not had much occasion to use her name.

"Gladys," Papi asked. "Would you bring me my briefcase?"

"In the study," Mami directed. "On the desk next to the smoking table."

Away Gladys hurried, her slippers frantically clacking, delighted to be sent on such an important errand; then she was back, his leather briefcase cradled like the baby in her arms.

"Good girl!" Papi gave Gladys a bright, approving smile and snapped open the locks. The lid flew up like a jack-in-the-box. Inside were three packages, wrapped up in white tissue paper, and clustered together in a tender, intimate way like eggs in a nest. Papi handed one to each of us and then lifted a tiny box from the side pocket of the case and smiled at my mother.

"You dear." Mami patted his hand. She opened the box, pulled out a doll-size perfume bottle, undid the stopper and smelled. "This is the one all right! You know, I never did find the old bottle. But you remembered, even without the name!" She leaned over and kissed Papi's cheek.

There was the sound of ripping paper and Papi cheering us on: "*¡Ay, ay, ay!*" Gladys lingered by her cart, organizing the dirty dishes, slowly, into neat stacks before rolling them away to the kitchen where Nivea and Chucha would wash them. But once we'd torn open the boxes, my sisters and I gave each other baffled looks. Mami leaned over and lifted a small cast-iron statue from Yoyo's box: an old man sat in a boat looking down at a menacing whale, its jaws hinged open. Sandi set hers on the table and tried to look pleased: it also was an iron statue of a little girl with her jump rope frozen midair. I didn't even bother to unpack mine. I stared down at a girl in a blue-and-white nightgown who stared up at a puffy canopy of clouds. What could the Schwarz salesgirl have been thinking of this time?

"What on earth are they, Papi?" Mami asked, picking up Sandi's little jump-roper and looking into the dotted eyes.

"Guess . . ." Papi smiled coyly, then added, "They're all the craze now. The girl at Schwarz said she'd sold half a dozen already that day."

Mami turned the statue over and read out loud from the underside: "Made in the U.S.A." Then she noted a keyhole for a tiny key. "Why"—she looked up at Papi—"it's a bank, isn't it?"

My father beamed. He took the jump-rope girl and set her down on the table before him. She stood poised on her stand; an arc of wire rose over her head and looped through two needle-holes in her fists. The polka dots on her dress and the yellow in her hair had been painted on the iron. "Watch this," he said, picking a penny from the pile of change he had rattled on the table. The coin fit in a groove on a fencepost beside the girl. Papi pulled a lever at the base of the stand, the lever popped back in, the coin dropped with a tinkle and tap, and then all of us—my sisters and Mami and Gladys and I—blinked, for the girl took a skip and the jump rope turned a turn.

A sigh of wonder passed around the room.

"Mechanical banks." Papi grinned and picked another penny from the pile. "So that my girls start saving their money to take care of us, Mami"—he gave her a wink—"when we're old and grey."

"Do mine," Yoyo begged, and Papi placed a penny in the old

man's slotted hands so that the coin looked like the wheel of a boat. When he pulled the lever, the sailor turned and the coin rolled into the whale's mouth.

My sisters and I burst out laughing. "Jonah's Bank," Mami said, reading the name on the side of the boat, and then with a look of mischief in her eye, she said, "*Ay*, Lolo, I wonder what the sisters would say to that?"

Papi's eyebrows rose up. "Wait till you see this one." He laughed, lifting my bank out of its box. "Actually, these Jonah and Mary banks are supposed to encourage the children to save for their offerings at church. Surely the sisters can't object to that?" He stood a penny in a slot on the canopy of cloud and pulled the lever at the base. The coin disappeared; the young woman, her halo painted on her hair, rose up towards the clouds, her arms lifted at the joints of the shoulders. As the lever popped back in, she descended to the ground.

"Blessed Mother!" Gladys whispered. Then everyone, including my mother, laughed because we had forgotten Gladys was still in the room, and there she was, neck craned forward, her eyes as round and coppery as those very pennies that had worked such wonders.

Papi held up a coin to her. "Here, Gladys, give her a spin." But Gladys backed off and looked shyly at her slippers. "Go on," my mother encouraged her, and this time she came forward, wiping her hands on her apron, and took the coin from my father, who directed her to stand it on the cloud. Again the coin rattled down, and Mary ascended for a moment, then fell back to earth until the next penny saved. Gladys's face was radiant. She made a slow, dazed sign of the cross.

"They're like children," my father said tenderly when Gladys left the room. "Did you see her face? It's as if she had seen the real thing."

After dinner as my parents gossiped over their expressos and cigarettes, my sisters and I shared a disappointed look. I tried giving my Mary a shake to see if I couldn't get the pennies out and buy myself a box of Chiclets.

"No, no, no, Carlita! They stay in there saved." My father patted his pocket. "Papi keeps the keys."

The banks turned out not to be such a disappointment after all. They were far better than tie shoes, that was certain. At school they created a stir among the other children. The most popular girls in my class elbowed each other in line to stand next to me. They invited me to help myself to my favorite red Lifesaver when it was the next one unwound from its wrapper in the roll, and even when it wasn't the next one, several were collapsed to get to it. Sister read Doña Laura's note explaining that this was an offertory bank, and everyone got to work a penny in the cloud and watch the little figure rise. Then Sister, whose job it was to make a lesson out of everything fun, told our class how Our Blessed Virgin did not die but got to take her body to heaven, she was so good. The class gazed dreamily at the bank, half-expecting it to shoot up to the ceiling in a puff of smoke.

I took my bank back home heavy with coins. My father unlocked the bottom and out came a few less than a hundred pennies, and he kindly made up the difference and gave me a big silver dollar that looked more like jewelry than money. Then business slowed. Once in a while, my mother's canasta friends, who declared they hated pennies in their purses, disposed of them gladly in the whale's mouth or the canopy of cloud. Of course, the jump-rope girl was the favorite, lucky Sandi. But Gladys protested that the best one of all was the Mary bank, and she used up all the pennies in her mayonnaise jar to work the miracle. The pity was it didn't take quarters.

Eventually, the banks found their way to the toy shelf along with all our other neglected toys. Christmas was coming! My mother complained that she would die of exhaustion—there was so much to be done. Our pageant costumes had to be sewn. Next door Tía Isa needed help getting the garden and house ready for the big Christmas-night bash to be held there this year on account of this was her first divorced Christmas, and she should be kept busy. Then the grape tree had to be cut down at the seashore, painted white, and hung with silver and gold balls and showered with tinsel. What a sight! Especially at night when Mami turned off all the lamps and the tree blazed with lights, blinking on, off; little vials like the stoppers of nose drops filled first with colored water and then drained out.

As the day approached, with fewer and fewer windows to open on the Advent calendar, my sisters and I were unruly with excitement, but the grownups seemed too busy to care. The house was fixed up as for a party. The giant poinsettias in the courtyard looked like flaming torches. Nuts and fruits filled the silver platters at the centerpieces of tables and sideboard. An elegant soldier took an almond in his mouth and cracked it open for you, and every time he did so, my mother sighed and said, "It's a pity there's no national ballet for the girls." Gladys was busier than ever, polishing silver, preparing canapes, following her mistress through the house with vases of calla lilies and bougainvillea. Instead of the radio merengues, Gladys now sang an endless repertoire of Christmas carols:

Glo-oh-oh-oh-oh-ohh-
Oh-oh-oh-oh-ohh-
Ria!

Best of all, Mami seemed not to mind the singing anymore and once or twice broke out into song herself in a delicate, quavery soprano:

A Santa Claus le gusta el vino,
A Santa Claus le gusta el ron . . .

And, of course, at the Christmas Eve pageant, all the children sang:

Adestes fideles
Laetes triumphantes . . .

I, costumed in a nightgown with a tinsel crown on my head, was to announce to the poor shepherds tending their flocks by night:

Do not be afraid
For behold I bring you
Tidings of great joy:
The baby Jesus is born!

But I was so flustered by the lights in my eyes and the sea of faces in the packed auditorium that I stumbled over my lines and said, "The baby doll is born!" instead of "the baby Jesus."

Mami said no one but she, who knew I wanted a baby doll from the baby Jesus, had caught the slip.

The next morning the baby doll was under the tree, a ribbon in her gold hair, and a bottle tied to her wrist. She cried out "Mama" when I laid her down and wet her diaper after she drank a bottle through a little hole in her mouth. And that was not all! The room was a treasure cave of gift-wrapped boxes. "Something for everyone," Papi said, laughing. And a lot for his darlings! Each one of us sat at the center of a pile of ripped paper and empty boxes and gaily colored toys. Even the baby had her sizable pile, though she preferred crawling about, ripping up paper, and putting the shreds in her mouth while poor Milagros scrambled after, scolding that no charge of hers was going to choke and die on the very day our Savior had been born. All the servants were there, Mario and Chucha and Nivea and Gladys, opening their gifts carefully so as not to tear the bright tissue paper. Their faces lit up: a wallet with a pretty lip of green in the billfold!

That night, although I had got to bed much later than usual, I couldn't sleep. Even when I shut my eyes tightly in an honest effort, I saw now my new doll, now my puzzle or coloring book loom larger than life in my vision, and I had to turn on my light and look at my gifts to make sure they were real. Mami came by briefly from the noisy party next door in a long, silvery gown, her pale arms bare, one arm linked to Tío Mundo's arm. She wagged her finger at me for having my light on, but she didn't seem to mind really, and she laughed a lot when my uncle shot himself dead several times with Yoyo's new revolver. Much later, Gladys stopped in on her way back from helping out next door. "It's past midnight, young lady!" But instead of turning out the light, she sat herself down on my bed, took off her slippers, and began massaging her tired feet. We could hear the uncles and aunts and Mami and Papi singing carols in the distance. "It's a gay old time next door," Gladys said. Doña Laura had danced a bolero with Don Carlos that was as good as in the movies. Don Mundo had taken off his shirt and done a workman's jig on top of the dining room table. Crazy Doña Isa had been thrown or threw herself into the swimming pool, you couldn't be sure.

Gladys's gaze wandered around the room, taking in the clutter of new toys before alighting fondly on the shelf. A hopeful look came on her face. From her pocket she brought out her new wallet, opened it and withdrew the ten pesos from the fold. "I'll buy the bank from you," she said in a hesitant voice.

The bank! Why that old thing was certainly not worth ten brand new pesos. Not since the gadget had gotten rusty from its being left out in the patio overnight. Half the time the spring didn't work at all. "Why, Gladys, no," I advised her.

Gladys' gaze faltered. She put the bill back in the fold and held the wallet out. "I'll throw in the wallet too."

For a moment, I didn't know how being good worked. Most times, Mami was around, telling me the rules: you weren't supposed to give away gifts you received. Gladys should keep her wallet. But that meant I should keep that old bank, which to give away would be a generous deed. Muddled, I looked up at the shelf.

"You can have it for nothing," I said. Gladys's mouth dropped open. The surprised look in the young maid's eyes confirmed my suspicion that I had done something I would get punished for if caught, so I added, "Don't tell, Gladys, okay?" The maid nodded eagerly as she left the room, the bank bundled in her apron and tucked under her arm.

But Mami was one to always notice the stain on one's place-mat at the table or the bruise accidentally punched on a little cousin's arm or the empty space on the bedroom toy shelf. "That reminds me," my mother said a few weeks after New Year's when the whole household had been mobilized to look for her reading glasses on top of her head. "Where's your Mary bank, Carla?" Just then, as Gladys and I exchanged a guilty look, Mami found her glasses on her head and slipped them down on her nose. She looked curiously from me to Gladys.

"My bank?" I asked, as if I'd never heard of such a thing.

"Come, come," my mother said, and again she looked at me and again she looked at Gladys.

"Ah, *that* bank," I answered, and explained that it was "around."

Mami was very patient and said nicely, "Well, let's find it, shall we?" And when we didn't, of course, find it anywhere in my room—although I gave a very credible, thoroughgoing search, looking even inside my tie shoes—Mami did not persist but let the matter drop.

That Sunday after the maids went off to early mass, my mother inspected their quarters while my father kept watch by a window. Later, I heard my parents' concerned voices behind the closed door of the study. Then the door flew open, and my father came down the hall, followed by my scowling mother, and just in time, I ducked behind the wicker chair as they went by. Then they were back again in a somber single file, my father, a grumbling Chucha, and my mother bringing up the rear. The same procession went back and forth with Nivea, then Milagros, and last of all, with Gladys, her eyes small and round. The door shut. Voices were raised in the study. I watched a powderpuff of dust turn cartwheels in a cross-breeze. In the corner, a shred of tinsel glimmered with leftover holiday cheer. Finally, the door flew open, and Gladys, sobbing into her upraised skirt, scurried down the hall.

My heart sank. Trouble was brewing in the big house. It had already landed on Gladys, and there was no use hiding, for sooner or later, it would fall on me too. I rose and lay the doll on the cushion of the chair, ignoring its cry of "Mama."

At the door of the study I paused, overcome as always by the high shelves packed with books like a library and the dark wood of the walls and jalousies. My mother was pacing up and down the room, as if neither direction would do, and smoking steadily. My father sat at the edge of his recliner, his hands drooped over the armrests, his head bowed. On the small smoking table beside the stand of pipes, I caught sight of the mechanical bank, swaddled in an apron. I took a step into the room. But no one noticed me. "It was a present," I blurted out. My mother stopped in her tracks and looked at me absently.

"I gave it to her," I confessed.

My father looked up at me, then exchanged a glance with my mother.

"Next time your father brings you a gift—" my mother began to scold, but Papi cut her off.

"We're just going to have to get better presents, Mami," he said, winking at me. "I don't see the dancing dolls being left out in the rain or given away to the maid!"

My heart soared at the thought of a better surprise than any that had come before. What could it be? I looked about the room expansively for ideas, anything, anything. My gaze fell on the bank.

My mother put out her cigarette with little, nervous jabs. "I guess I better go explain to the others." She sighed and brushed past me. The door slammed shut behind her. A rack of pipes jiggled and rattled. A whole wall of jalousies collapsed open.

Out in the driveway Mario had pulled the car up to the entrance. He went inside the house and a little later came out carrying a cardboard box and several sacks he placed in the back seat. Gladys followed, a kerchief on her head to keep her church hairdo in place, dabbing at her eyes with another kerchief. She climbed in beside her bags, and with a blinding flash from the chrome Mario polished all day long, the car disappeared down the driveway, past the guard at the gate, to the world.

"Papi," I cried, turning around. "Don't make Gladys go away, please."

My father reached out and pulled me towards his lap. His eyes were dull as if they'd been colored in brown and smudged. "We can't trust her—" he began, but then he seemed to think better of explaining it that way. "It was Gladys who asked to leave, you know. . . . She'll get a job in no time. Maybe even end up in New York." But the glum look on his face did not convince me. He gazed past me, out the window. The distant sound of a car engine died into a hum.

His glance fell on the little bank. He smiled and reached in his pocket, withdrawing pennies. "Give her a spin," he said.

I was not in the mood for play. But my father seemed sad too, and it was up to me to cheer him up. I picked up a penny from his hand, stood it in its slot and pulled the knob as far as it would go. The coin dropped with a clink to the bank below. The lever jammed and would not slide back in its groove. The little figure rose, her arms swiveled. Then she stopped, stuck, halfway up, halfway down.

The Drum

▼▲▼▲▼▲▼▲▼▲▼▲▼▲▼▲▼▲▼▲▼▲▼▲▼▲▼▲▼▲▼▲▼III▼▲▼▲▼

Yoyo

I t was a drum Mamita brought back from a trip to New York, a magnificent drum, its sides bright red, criss-crossed by gold wire held down by gold button heads, its top and bottom white. It had a broad blue strap with a pad for putting around your neck, the flat top facing up, for it was a drumroller's drum. Mamita presented me with it, slipping the strap over my head, lifting the top up. "Ah," I sighed, for in the hollow at the center, two drumsticks were stored. She took them out, tapped the top down, and handed me the drumsticks. Though her palm had given the first tap, she would not rob me of the thunder of the first wicked drumstick drumroll.

Barra-bam, barra-bam, barra-barra-barra BAM!

"Ah"—my grandmother rolled her eyes—"another Beethoven!"

"What do you say to your grandmother?" Mami asked proudly.

"Barrabarrabarrabarrabarrabarra BOOM! BOOM! BOOM! BOOM!"

"Yoyo!" my mother cried out, and I stopped drumming abruptly so that she yelled out into the suddenly silent room, "THAT'S QUITE ENOUGH!"

"Laura!" my grandmother said, scowling at her daughter. "Why are you yelling at the child?"

"Mamita," I said nicely, "thank you."

"Thank you is bare, put butter on my bread," my mother snapped.

"Thank you very much," I buttered. And then, I brought down an apocalyptic, apoplectic, joy-to-the-great-world drumroll that made Mamita throw her head back and laugh her loud, girlish laugh. My mother plugged a finger in each ear like Hans at the dike, a great flood of scolding about to come out of her mouth, which I held back by drumroll until she snatched the sticks out of my hands and said she would keep them until I was responsible enough to play my drum like an adult. I forgot all the promises I had made—before being given the drum—to improve my character and wailed. I wanted them back. I wanted them back. Mamita intervened, and the sticks were put back into the hollow of the drum, and another promise extracted from me that I would not play the drum inside the house but only out in the yard.

My grandmother pulled me towards her. She had once been, so Mami said, the most beautiful woman in the country. We called her Mamita, "little mother," because she was smaller than Mami, with the delicate face of a girl, brown doe eyes and white wavy hair in a bun that sometimes fell down her back in a braid. She looked like a girl who had had a terrible fright that had turned her hair white.

"That drum is from a magic store," she said, consoling me.

"Oh?" my mother said casually, wanting to rejoin the conversation. "Where did you get it?"

"Schwarz," Mamita said. "F.A.O. Schwarz." And she promised that one day soon, very soon, if I behaved myself and didn't drive my mother insane with my drum and drank my milk down to the bottom of the glass and brushed up and down instead of across and didn't get into things like lipsticks and perfumes and then pretended as I walked through the house reeking of Paris with a *je-ne-sais-pas* look on my face that I did not know what could have happened to the little bottle with a bow tie, she, my favorite grandmother, would take me from the Island to the United States on an airplane to see Schwarz and the snow. And at this, I could not help myself, but having tipped the lid up and kidnapped the drumsticks, I gave a modest, tippy-tap, well-behaved drumroll that made Mamita wink and Mami smile and both agree that in the last five minutes I had indeed grown up to responsible drumming.

Ba-bam, ba-bam, I tapped about the yard all day. That was just like my mother to let me have a drum and then forbid me to drum it, ba-bam, ba-bam, in any significantly inspired way. And how could I judge significance in a drum unless at least one grownup clapped her hands over her ears? And how could I judge inspiration unless there was noise in it, drumming from my ten flexed toes, from my skinny legs that would someday improve themselves, drumming from the hips I swayed when I was womanish, and up, up the rib cage, where the heart sat like a crimson drum itself among ivory drumsticks, and then the drumming rose like wings, making my shoulders shrug, my arms lift, my wrists flick, and down came the drumsticks, BOOM, BOOM, Barra-ba, BOOM!

"Yolanda Altagracia, you forget yourself," came my mother's curtsy-when-you-say-hello voice, her puree-of-peas voice. "We have a fine yard that lots of other children would give their right arms to play in."

And so it was that for a whole day, I marched in front of the hibiscus and saluted the bougainvillea and drummed until the mockingbirds were ready to fly off to the United States of America in the middle of December. All that week and the next and the next and the next, I drummed up and down, up and down, up and down the yard. Then, with the terrible luck of such toys, I lost one drumstick. And then, our crazy aunt, Tía Isa, who was unhappily married to an American and always on the point of divorcing and who, therefore, never looked where she was going, plopped herself down on my second drumstick and snapped it in two and glued it with glue that would, she promised, hold a house together. But I never believed glue could hold drumsticks together, however good it was on china cups and porcelain shepherdesses and all such grownup truck that was always finding its shattering way to the floor in my presence. And so it was that in less than a month's time, I had a drum but no drumsticks. Mamita and Mami and Tía Isa, not understanding that drumsticks are the only kind of drumsticks that will do on a drum, suggested pencils or the handles of wooden spoons used for making cake batter. I tried them all, but the sound was not the same, and the joy went out of drumming. I took to wearing the strap across my chest, the drum riding my hips like a desperado's revolver.

In those days we had a fine yard that lots of other children *would* have given their right arms to play in. Beyond the laundry room at the back of the house, the lawns rolled away, so smooth and closely mown, the ground itself seemed green rather than planted with grass. At the back of the property was a shed where the coal bins were kept for the laundry fires for boiling the white clothes, a shed known to be haunted. In those days it was an adventure to go into the coal shed and stare down the big barrels of coal bricks and breathe in coal dust; to then pluck up your courage and turn an empty barrel over, spilling the Devil out; to race all the way to the back of the house; to scramble up the back steps to the laundry room where one-eyed Pila would cock her head and say, "What? Is the Devil after you, child?"

That old laundry maid, Pila, was the strangest maid we had ever had, for it seemed everything that could go wrong with her had gone wrong. She had lost an eye, her left, let's see, or was it her right? You never knew. The two eyes took turns staring fixedly at the sky. But what's an eye? A little bit of jelly with a duplicate beside it. Who'd notice a missing eye in the face of her incredible skin. She had splashes of pinkish white all up and down her dark brown arms and legs. The face itself had been spared: it was uniformly brown, the brown skin so smooth that it looked as if it'd been ironed with a hot iron. Only around the eyes where the tip of the iron couldn't get to were there wrinkles—from smiles. She was Haitian, though obviously, only half. The light-skinned Dominican maids feared her, for Haiti was synonymous with voodoo. She was a curiosity and I, a curious child, I, with the promise of snow in my heart and the wonder of the world seizing me with such fury at times that I had to touch forbidden china cups or throttle a little cousin or pet a dog's head so strenuously that he looked as if he were coming out of the birth canal, I wanted nothing more then to get a temporary injunction from politeness and have a good long stare at her speckled arms.

As I was saying, the coal shed was haunted. And it was Pila's doing. There was a time—before Pila—when the coal shed was just a coal shed. But then Pila came, and in addition to five paper sacks of her things, she brought her story devils and story ghosts and her trances and her being mounted by spirits and her "I see a nimbus about your head, beware of water today!" All these spirits, she claimed, lived in the coal shed. And so it was that by the time of my drum, the coal shed was haunted. By the time of the drum, I should also add, Pila was gone. She had lasted a couple of months at the compound before disappearing one Sunday. The house was thrown into mathematical turmoil. The linens were counted. The clothes inventoried. The other maids and Mami put two and two together, and the sum was that now for almost two months we had been living with a thief!

"Pity for her," my mother said, "she won't get far with that skin."

Sure enough, the next day she was picked up by the police. By then, having consulted her American education, my mother decided it would be cruel to press charges. The poor woman didn't know any better. Let her and her ten shopping bags go. And she was gone, leaving behind a whole coal shed of devils and goblins, so that by the time of my missing drumsticks, to dare enter the coal shed was quite literally to be a daredevil.

The day I wandered into the coal shed looking for trouble I had the drum on my hip and two little dowels for drumsticks. Pila had been gone several weeks. In I went, pushing the door back so the hinges cried out, devils, their thumbs crushed, their pointed noses tweezed. I stood a moment in the doorway, blinded by the shaft of light that struck like a knife blade into the darkness. Slowly, I made out the barrels, eight or nine standing, a couple tipped over. I crunched coal bricks underfoot. I dared further. I stood at the end of the shaft of light, and then one toe braved the darkness. My heart was pounding. I leaned over the first upright barrel and peered in, half expecting to look down a long well into the Devil's eye. Nothing but coal bricks at the half mark. In the next barrel, coal bricks at the quarter mark, then dregs of coal bricks. The new laundry maid, Nivea, was using them up inefficiently, without a system.

The last barrel was tucked behind the others. I looked down at a full barrel. Suddenly, there was a little stirring, a whimper, a little pink mouth opened in a yawn; so pink and moist was that mouth it seemed impossible in a coal barrel. The mouth closed, another one opened, a cry came out of it, "Meow." Two or three mouths wailed in chorus, "Meow, meow." Immediately, I singled out one who had four little white paws and a white spot between its ears, fully dressed, so it looked, as opposed to the others who were careless and had lost their shoes and their caps. This one, a curiosity, was the one I intended for me.

But I did not touch her or pet her or touch or pet any of the brothers and sisters. At that time, my natural lore was comprised of a few rules, all of which I confused so that when the situation presented itself, I knew there was something to be done, but I did not quite know what exactly. If it was lightning, I was either to stand under a tree or in an open field so the tree wouldn't fall on me. If I found a nest of nightingale eggs or chicks, I was not to disturb it or the mother would abandon her roost and the chicks would die. But was it chickens or kittens? I wasn't sure. Vaguely, too, I remembered a horror story about a mother cat being vicious and scratching out the eyes of someone who had threatened her babies. I did not want to find out the hard way the *do*s and *don't*s of kittens. I needed, therefore, to question an adult who might know everything, and between lightning and chickens, I could slip in a question on kittens. But whom could I ask who would know about kittens? And whom could I ask who would be sure to know about kittens but would not suspect my secret? Mami in the house was bad on both counts; Mamita wouldn't know anything about the outdoors, which she was allergic to, she claimed, which was why she had to go on shopping trips to New York, where, she said, the outdoors wasn't really out doors, a riddle I promised myself someday to solve; Tía Isa was no good to ask either: she'd laugh her whooping laugh and scurry around and peep and meow, pretending to be a chicken and nightingale and kitten, all in one, until the whole extended family would guess what I was up to; and Pila, who knew about everything on this earth and out of it, Pila was, of course, gone.

Unsure of what to do but knowing if I stayed there debating my options, the mother cat might well come and blind me, I left the coal shack and lingered about the yard. In my exasperation, I lifted the lid of my drum and was about to take my dowels out and drum a racket louder than I had ever drummed, when I saw a man I had never seen, crossing our yard towards the orchard of wild orange trees that stretched beyond our fence. A dog accompanied him, or rather, the dog ran ahead, slowed, sniffed the ground, gave a bark, chased a butterfly, and in a dozen other ways, made the world safe for the man. The man was a dashing, handsome, storybook kind of man, dressed in jodhpurs and riding boots. He had a goatee and a mustache, which made me wonder if he weren't the Devil, and a way of addressing the dog with affection and humor, which convinced me he wasn't. He had not seen me and was passing not more than ten yards away when the dog twisted about, raised his nose, and curled one paw up. The man stopped and looked up at the sky. It was then I noticed he was carrying a gun on a shoulder strap, the barrel pointed up. The dog began to bark.

"There, there," the man said, addressing the dog. "Where are your manners?" Then he turned to me. The ends of his mustache lifted in a smile. "Good day, little miss. I hope Kashtanka did not frighten you?"

I eyed the man, his gun, the dog now poking his nose where dogs always poke their noses on a person. With a child's instinct, I knew the man was safe, for occasionally, strangers my grandfather had met on his travels came for a visit and wandered over to our property. But I was uneasy that a dog was loose and there were kittens, seven mouthfuls, nearby in the shed.

The dog sniffed my drum. "I say," the man said, "what have you got there?"

"It's a drum," I said, bringing it round from my hip to in front of me, "but I've lost the drumsticks." And I lifted the top and tilted the drum so he could look in at the two dowels. "I've got to use those, and the sound is not the same."

"It never is," the man agreed, to his great credit. He crouched down beside his dog. His riding boots creaked.

"About drumsticks," I said. And then, because I was sure I had found my man, I hurried my questions: "Can you play with a brand-new kitten or will the mother abandon it or blind you if she catches you and by when can you take a kitten from its mother to keep as a pet?"

"Well!" the man said, looking at me closely but with friendliness in his eyes. "About drumsticks, eh? Well, just as your drumsticks belong inside your drum, and dowels will not do, so a kitten belongs with its mother, and no one else will do."

"But pets," I protested, glancing at Kashtanka.

The man's hand fell fondly on his dog's head. "Pets are a different matter, to be sure. But the little creature must be old enough to survive without its mother," he concluded, rising.

Just as he was rising, Kashtanka made a dash forward. The man snatched his collar and pulled the dog back so his front paws were still treading the air. "Drumsticks, eh?" The man laughed at something over my shoulder. I turned around and saw a large black mother cat, her teats pink and sagging, slinking into the coal shed. Kashtanka barked excitedly. The cat scurried in.

"Your manners, Kashtanka!" the man said, giving the collar a jerk. The dog heeled, whining quietly to show that his feelings were hurt. "About drumsticks," the man said, winking one eye so long I wondered if, like Pila's, his wasn't real either. "While a kitten is still a suckling, it cannot, now can it, be taken from its mother to be a pet?"

I had to agree.

"To take it away would be . . ." The man considered his words. "To take it away would be a violation of its natural right to live." The man saw I did not understand him. "It would die," he said plainly. "So you must wait," he added, petting my hair so that Kashtanka gave me a jealous look, "you must wait until that kitten can make it on its own. Don't you agree?"

I looked over my shoulder at the coal shed.

The man went on. "I would say in a week, and that's one, two, three is Sunday, seven is Thursday, by Thursday I should think a kitten, even if born this very day, a kitten might be ready to belong to a fine young lady with a drum."

I drummed my fingers on my drum, one, three, five, seven is Thursday.

"That's a fine drum," the man observed, "and a good, sturdy strap."

Just then, a flock of birds flew overhead. The dog looked up and let out an excited yelp. "We're off," the man announced. And off they were, before I could count to seven, down the lawn to a creaky wicker gate, through which they entered the orchard and disappeared among the trees.

One, two, ba-bam, three is Sunday. The mother cat had gone into the coal shed to feed her kittens. Ba-bam. Mine was the best dressed one. I would name her Schwarz. Seven is less than the fingers of two hands, but seven was seven more than now, and as if to confirm my addition, I heard the thunderous report of the man's gun in the distance. There was a clatter from the coal shed and, moments later, the mother cat dashed across the yard, flushed out by the noise of the gun.

While the coast was clear, I decided to re-enter the coal shed and tell Schwarz of our plan for next Thursday. I walked in, looked over the brim of the coal barrel. Schwarz was meowing in terror. "There, there," I comforted her. But there, there would not do. I picked her up and whispered in the sweet little seashell ears, "There, there." I brought her down to my shoulder and burped her and put her in the crook of my arm and tickled her belly and poked my fingers under her arms, and she meowed that that was fun, that I should do it again. And there, there, I did.

It was Friday and it would not be Thursday for another seven days. I had every intention of putting her back. But then, call it coincidence, call it plot, the man's gun went off again in the distance, and I realized he was in the orange grove hunting. Hunting! Some of the birds he was aiming at this very moment were mothers with worms for their babies. I did not know at the time the word for saying one thing and doing another, but I did know plenty of practicing adults, and I was not going to be gypped of a well-dressed kitten by a moral imperative given to me by an exception to the rule!

Out of the shed I strode with Schwarz clapped on my shoulder. She meowed out goodbyes to her brothers and sisters as we crossed the yard. Suddenly, I stopped. Up ahead sat the fat black mother cat enjoying the warm sun on her fat black back, licking a paw as if there were cake batter on it. She had not seen me, but I knew it was a matter of moments before Schwarz's meowing reached her. In that instant the vague memory sharpened. I saw a cat slinking forward. I saw it crouch to spring. I saw it leap and land on a woman's face. I saw its claws rip out an eye. I saw that jelly spill—and I remembered suddenly with shocking clarity Pila recounting how she had lost her eye!

Slowly, my left hand patting Schwarz to encourage a hiatus in her meowing, I worked the top off my drum with my right hand. Schwarz's mother put down one paw, lifted another, and began to lick it. I picked Schwarz up, and in one deft movement, plunked her down into the hollow of my drum, grabbing up my drumsticks in exchange, slapping the lid down, shifting the drum in front of me, and then as the mother cat jerked around and caught sight of me and then of my drum, which was meowing furiously, I brought down a loud, distracting drumroll:

BARRA BARRA BARRA BOOM BOOM! (Meow!)
BARRA BOOM! (Meow! Meow!) BOOM
BOOM
BOOM
(Meow!)

I marched straight towards the house, lifting my knees high like a majorette. The baffled mother cat looked at me uncertainly and followed at a cautious distance, meowing. The drum meowed back. I drummed madly. My heart was drumming. And then, as the cat gained on me, I broke into a mad run, scrambled up the back steps, slammed shut the back door that led through the laundry room to the house. A deep sink full of soaking whites told that the new washerwoman had stepped out only for a moment. Backed against the wall, I spied out the window. The mother cat prowled in front of the door. She stopped, smelled the ground.

"Schwarz!" she meowed.

Schwarz meowed feverishly from inside the drum. The mother glanced all about her, at the door, at the sky, but she could not find where the sound was coming from.

"Schwarz! Where are you?" she meowed.

"THUNDER, THUNDER!" The gun thundered. The mother cat bolted away.

I picked the meowing kitten out of my drum. Its little human face winced with meows. I detested the accusing sound of meow. I wanted to dunk it into the sink and make its meowing stop. Instead, I lifted the screen and threw the meowing ball out the window. I heard it land with a thud, saw it moments later, wobbling out from under the shadow of the house, meowing and stumbling forward. There was no sign of the mother cat.

I must have gone to that window about a dozen times that morning and watched the wounded kitten make a broken progress across the lawn. I was tempted to go and deposit it at the door of the coal shed, but there was no leaving the house, my mother's orders. Some crazy fellow was shooting illegally in the orange grove. The police had been called. Sometime before lunch the shooting stopped. I looked out the window of the laundry room. The kitten was gone.

That night I woke with a start in the claws of a bad dream I could not remember. In those days we slept with mosquito nets strung from four poles at each corner of the bed. Everything in the dark assumed a spectral appearance through white netting: a ghostly bureau, a ghostly toybox, ghostly curtains.

That night, sitting at the foot of my bed, poking her face in so that the gauzy net was molded to her features like an awful death mask, was the black mother cat. I froze with terror. She glared at me with fluorescent eyes. She let out soft, moaning meows. I closed my eyes and opened them again. She sat there, wailing until dawn. Then I saw her rise, leap, and land with a thud on the floor and trot down the hall and down the stairs. The next morning in tears I told my mother of the cat that haunted my bedside all night. "Impossible," she said and to prove it, we went through the house, inspecting latches and windows. "Possible," Mami said when we found a window left opened in the laundry room. That new washerwoman, Nivea, was almost as bad as the old one, Mami complained.

Impossibly the next night—for the windows were locked and the house secure as an arsenal—the cat appeared again at my bedside. And night after night after that. Sometimes she meowed. Sometimes she just stared. Sometimes I cried out and woke the house up. "A phase," Mami said, worried. "A perfectly normal nightmare phase." The phase lasted. I gave the drum away to a little cousin, throwing the ghost cat into the bargain. But the cat came back, on and off, for years.

Then we moved to the United States. The cat disappeared altogether. I saw snow. I solved the riddle of an outdoors made mostly of concrete in New York. My grandmother grew so old she could not remember who she was. I went away to school. I read books. You understand I am collapsing all time now so that it fits in what's left in the hollow of my story? I began to write, the story of Pila, the story of my grandmother. I never saw Schwarz again. The man with the goatee and Kashtanka vanished from the face of creation. I grew up, a curious woman, a woman of story ghosts and story devils, a woman prone to bad dreams and bad insomnia. There are still times I wake up at three o'clock in the morning and peer into the darkness. At that hour and in that loneliness, I hear her, a black furred thing lurking in the corners of my life, her magenta mouth opening, wailing over some violation that lies at the center of my art.